KU-752-420

Contents

'You are ordered abroad as a soldier of the King . . . You have to perform a task which will need your courage, your energy, your patience . . . In this (situation) you may find temptations both in wine and women. You must entirely resist both temptations, and while treating all women with perfect courtesy, you should avoid all intimacy. Do your duty bravely.'

Horatio Herbert Kitchener

Prologue

"M r Smith," the man said. "This is Miss Cartwright. Miss Cartwright knows me as Bill, Mr Smith."

Behind its blacked-out windows the pub was dilapidated, crowded and noisy. The air was thick with tobacco smoke and the stink of alcohol. There were women as well as men in the bar, and no one had taken much notice of the rather gauntly attractive woman who had been sitting by herself in a corner, drinking gin and tonic, for half an hour before being joined by the two men. Now Margo Cartwright gave a quick, cold smile, to 'Mr Smith'.

"Like another drink?" asked the go-between.

"Why not," Margo said. "G and T."

"Mr Smith?"

"I will have a beer," Mr Smith said, speaking very carefully but immediately betraying the fact that he was not English.

"You mean draught, or bottled?"

"Whatever you are having," Mr Smith said, and sat down beside Margo Cartwright. "I have looked forward to this meeting."

"I will take that as a compliment."

"You should," he said seriously. "How long have you worked for British Intelligence?"

"Since 1934."

"Nine years." Mr Smith allowed his gaze to slide up and down what he could see of her around the table. Her clothes were shabby, but he deduced that was deliberate; this was a shabby pub. She was tall; he put her down as quite close to six feet. Thin, with small breasts, he estimated, but long,

1

slender and attractive legs. "Why, after so long, do you wish to quit?"

"They have treated me like a lump of shit," Margo said, her voice low but filled with passion.

"You worked principally in North Africa," Smith remarked. "Stirring up the Senussi against the Italians."

"That was my job, yes," she said.

"Was that not a success?"

"It was a great success, Mr Smith. But all the credit went elsewhere."

"To a man called Warrey." Smith took his tankard from Bill's hand, sipped, made a face, and continued to study the woman."

"Yes," she said. "To a man called Warrey."

"Why was this so?"

She shrugged. "My superiors thought he did the job better."

"And you do not agree with them. I think perhaps you hate this man Warrey."

"Yes," Margo said.

Again he studied her for several seconds. "And what do you think you can offer us?" he asked at last.

"A great deal of information about how British Intelligence works. Quite a few names. Several stations."

"You would be betraying your country. Betraying your erstwhile colleagues."

"Erstwhile," Margo said.

Mr Smith drank some more of his beer and seemed to find it improving. "I am told you are now a simple soldier, serving in the ATS. That you have even been demoted."

"I have been relieved of my intelligence duties, yes. And I am now a sergeant in the ATS."

"Why was this? Were you not a commissioned officer, before?"

"I was never properly commissioned. I was given an officer's rank, because occasionally I was required to command enlisted men. When I was transferred to the ATS it was as an officer."

"And have now been reduced in rank. Tell me why?"

Another shrug. "I think I spoke my mind once too often. I fell out with General Montgomery."

"A famous man."

"So they say."

"And you do not agree. You do not suppose, that as you are no longer an intelligence officer, any information you may have to give us will be out of date?"

"I only left Intelligence last November. After the battle of El Alamein. My unit did a great deal of work to make that victory possible, but all the credit went to Warrey. Nothing will have changed. It would never occur to them that I might turn against them."

"I see. If we were to employ you, on a basis of giving information, you would have to come to Germany."

Margo's head came up.

"Well," Mr Smith said, "you see, as you are no longer working *in* Intelligence, you are of no value to us as a double agent. It is only information, on people and places, that would be of use to us. You understand this?"

"Yes," Margo said, thoughtfully. "But then they will know I am a traitor."

"Not necessarily. We will arrange for you to die. There will be an unfortunate accident, and the body, your body, will be unidentifiable, save for certain personal items."

Margo swallowed. "You mean . . . someone will be murdered in my place?"

"There is a war on, Miss Cartwright. People get murdered, or certainly killed, every day. After your 'death' we will transport you to Germany. Your identity will be kept secret, and you will work with the *Abwehr* in an advisory capacity. Is this satisfactory to you?"

Margo finished her drink. This was more than she had bargained for. She had been prepared to sell herself, to sell the secrets she knew, for both money and a desire for revenge upon all those brass hats, and their underlings, who had treated her so badly. Especially on John Warrey, whom she had brought into the business, had once even recommended for a medal, and who had gone from strength to strength. While she . . . Warrey was now a full colonel. And she was a sergeant in the ATS, in charge of a motor pool.

But she had not anticipated that she would be causing the death of another English soldier, and a woman. Or that she would have to leave England. On the other hand, once she gave the Germans names, she would be sending those agents to their deaths. Especially, she hoped, John Warrey, whenever next he was sent into the field.

"Yes," she said. "That is satisfactory to me."

The Task

'The British soldier can stand up to anything except the British War Office.'

George Bernard Shaw

The Assignment

The adjutant stood to attention just within the door. "Colonel Warrey, sir."

"Ah, Warrey." The general got up and came round his desk to shake hands. "Come in, man. Come in."

John Warrey entered the room, somewhat cautiously; experience had taught him that when one is summoned to the War Office for a private meeting with a general, it is seldom simply to be asked about one's health. Not that there was anything the matter with his health, now. Well displayed in his khaki uniform, he stood six feet one inch tall, and there was no fat in his hundred and eighty pounds of bone and muscle. Only his features, coldly handsome, and his eyes, ice blue, might suggest the wealth of dangerous endeavour that had gone into the past few years. Those, and the various scars that dotted his body. But several weeks rest and recuperation following the end of the North African campaign had left those no more than blemishes, even if the skin on his back still showed signs of the horrendous burns he had suffered from that plane crash in the desert.

He saluted, then removed his cap and shook hands. "Sit down," the general invited.

John sat before the desk, placed the cap on his lap.

"All fit?"

"I think so, sir."

The general sat down himself, opened the folder on his blotter. "You've had a busy war, Colonel."

"From time to time, sir."

"Hm." The general turned a page of the file. "Trained at

Blissett Hall. Passed out with honours. Intelligence work out of Cairo before hostilities commenced with Italy. Liaison officer between British forces and the Senussi. Raised and led Senussi force in guerilla warfare against the Italian and German lines of communication."

"That is not correct, sir," John said.

The general raised his head.

"I did not raise the Senussi, sir. They were already in arms against the Italians. It was my privilege to lead them into battle."

"Oh, quite." The general resumed reading. "Taken prisoner twice, escaped twice. DSO and MC. Yes, indeed, the sort of record one enjoys reading. And on top of it all you speak fluent Italian and German."

"It was necessary to do so, sir, in order to operate behind Italian lines."

"Absolutely. You come highly recommended. General Brand?"

"An old friend of my family, sir."

"Who first picked you for intelligence work, I understand. And also General Montgomery."

"I served under him in North Africa, sir."

"Quite. He is not a man who praises lightly, but he recommends you highly for the duty we require."

"Thank you, sir."

The general leaned back in his chair, "You understand that everything that is said in this room is of the utmost secrecy, not to be discussed with anyone. Not even your wife." He glanced at the folder. "You are married?"

"Yes, sir."

"Happily, I trust."

"I think so, sir."

The general raised his eyebrows.

"Well, we haven't spent much time together," John explained. "I think a total of five weeks in a year. Up to this morning."

"She's serving?"

"In the ATS, sir."

"And does she know anything of your duties?"

"She knows I am in Intelligence, sir, and that I spent some time in Cairo. She does not know that I am employed in the field. She thinks my air crash was a civilian matter."

"Keep it that way. Now, let me put you in the picture. Our next destination is Sicily."

"I had assumed it would be France, sir."

"Not on, Warrey, at this time. Too costly. Perhaps next year."

"The Russians won't like that."

"Then they'll have to lump it. No, no. But we have a very large army in North Africa, and it must go somewhere. Sicily is the logical next step."

"I would have supposed," John said, "that if we are going to attack anywhere in the Med, Greece would be a better bet."

"You're starting to sound like Winston," the general remarked. "There are aspects of the situation about which you may not be aware. As you can imagine, Mussolini's stock is not very high since the North African debacle. I mean with his own people."

"I can imagine," John agreed. Having mixed with the Italians in Libya, both before and after they had been defeated, he was well aware that not all of them had been diehard supporters of Il Duce, even when they had appeared to be winning. When he thought of poor old Umberto, a personal friend, now dead . . . but then, so many of the friends he had made in Africa, principally amongst the Senussi, were now dead.

"Well, you see," the general went on, "our information coming out of Italy is that one more massive defeat and those who oppose him may well be able to act. This is something we need to take the utmost advantage of, Warrey. Imagine, if Italy were to come over to our side. Wouldn't that be a stupendous coup?"

"One about which the Germans might have something to say."

"They'll have a headache. But the whole thing must be

9

organised with the greatest care. Everything must be set to go off at the same time, as it were. Now, the invasion of Sicily is set for 10 July. We are using every possible means to ensure that the Italian troops there offer as little resistance as possible, and we are also working with those in the Italian government resolved to bring an end to the Fascist dictatorship. The aim is that the news of our invasion will coincide with the announcement of the overthrow of Mussolini, and that the government that replaces him will immediately sue for peace. This will be granted them, on certain conditions."

"You mean we are going to abandon that nonsensical idea of unconditional surrender?" John asked.

The general frowned at him. "That nonsensical idea, as you call it, Colonel, was dreamed up by the President of the United States. It is not our province to criticise it. The Italians will have to surrender, unconditionally. But what follows after that, how they will be treated, will depend on how co-operative they are. Our aim, as I have said, is to have them fighting on our side. And they are going to be told this. A large number of their people are already anxious to take part in the war, on the right side. If all Italy were to rise together, at the same time, we might nab the entire German army in the peninsular."

"Might," John muttered. He was very fond of the Italians, as a people, but he knew they lacked the ruthless determination of their German masters.

"It's all a matter of timing," the general said. "That's the vital thing. Timing, and leadership. Northern Italy is the key. Not only is it the industrial heartland of Italy, but it also covers the rest of the peninsula. If we could control Tuscany, the German armies in the south would be cut off."

"You mean we are going to attempt an invasion of the mainland at Pisa or Genoa?"

"That would be quite impossible, militarily. Losses would be unacceptable. However, we know there is a sizeable local element who are already on our side. These people are carrying on a guerilla campaign against the Germans. What we require is someone who will bring the various guerilla bands together, and lead them in the proper direction. At the present time they are mostly concerned with avenging local atrocities. We want them to start fighting a proper war. You did this very successfully with the Senussi, did you not?"

"Conditions were a little different in North Africa, sir. The Senussi did not actually live cheek by jowl with either the Italians or the Germans. They lived in the desert, where they could be contacted by our people, and when they made forays into enemy held territory, they could retreat into the desert again."

"But you did enter enemy territory yourself, when required to do so?"

"I did, sir. Which is why I was twice taken prisoner."

"But you escaped, eh? As you say, things will be different, but not necessarily more dangerous. The partisans will help you and protect you."

"And obey me?"

"They will obey the right man. That is why we have chosen you, Colonel."

"I see. May I ask how I am to get to Tuscany? By parachute?"

The general shook his head. "You'd never make it. The Germans have too tight a control of the air. You'll go via Lisbon and Switzerland. You will travel as a Swiss businessman. From Switzerland you will cross into North Italy. There will be support all the way."

"I'm glad of that," John said. "But if I am caught I will still be shot."

"That is a possibility, certainly. So, on this mission, it would be best if you were not caught. Now, there is one more thing I should tell you; quite a few of these Italians who are prepared to support us, in the north, are reputed to be Communists."

"Oh, great," John said. "What happens if I get there and find some ruddy commissar running the show, and he tells me to bugger off?"

"I am sure you will handle the matter in your well-known

fashion, Colonel Warrey." The general checked the file. "It says here that you once shot dead seven Italian soldiers."

"It was a reflex action."

"Seven reflexes?"

"They had just executed a young woman of whom I was extremely fond."

"Quite. That, ah, shoot-out, not only earned you the Military Cross but also the undying respect of the Senussi. The young woman in question was a Senussi, wasn't she?"

"Yes," John said.

"Well, then, I should point out that your first step on this mission should be to gain the undying respect of the Italian partisans. I hope we understand each other?"

"Yes, sir."

"Good. Major Cox will complete the briefing."

"Does he know of the operation?"

"He does."

"Right." John stood up, replaced his cap, saluted. "There is just one more thing, Colonel Warrey."

"I thought there might be."

"It would be most satisfactory for all of us if you were to volunteer for this mission." He waited.

"I volunteer, sir," John said.

John closed the door behind him. Major Cox was waiting. "If you'd come with me, sir."

John followed him along the corridor and down several flights of steps. Military headquarters, he reflected, at whatever level, never did rise to lifts. But that was the least problem on which he had to reflect. He had just been given a virtual death sentence. No matter that he had been given such a mission before; as he had reminded the general, the situation in North Africa had been entirely different. There had been the Senussi, who in the context of the war were friends, and the Italians and the Germans, who in the same context were enemies. There was no possibility of mistaking one for the other, and there had been no possibility of betrayal, either.

Northern Italy, which he knew was a seething hodge-podge of pro-Fascists and anti-Fascists, to which now apparently had to be added Communists – who were presumably anti-Fascists, at least in the short term – the whole overlaid by centuries of local rivalries and all firmly now beneath the heel of the Nazi jackboot, was a totally different matter.

He wondered, not for the first time, how he had got himself into this situation, earned himself this reputation as a killing machine? He had been an inoffensive young trainee architect as recently as 1939 – four years ago! – when as a well-known amateur yachtsman he had volunteered to navigate one of the famous photographer Margo Cartwright's expeditions across the Sahara. He had been totally unaware that Margo was an agent for British Intelligence, and that through her he would be sucked into that cauldron himself. As for his reputation, he had never killed anyone until that unforgettable day when he had found himself holding a tommy-gun and staring past Soroya's dead body at the man who had just shot her. He had gone berserk. Not something to be proud of, even if it had earned him a medal.

The trouble was that shooting, and thus killing, his way out of trouble had become something of a habit. Presumably it became a habit for all men at war. Was it a habit that would ever wear off? Now he had been virtually instructed to mow down any opposition he might encounter in Italy. Supposing that opposition didn't mow him down first.

The truly odd thing about the life he lived was that, as he had told the general, Aileen hadn't a clue what it actually involved, had no idea that he had ever killed anyone and apart from that air crash did not dream he had ever come close to being killed himself. What a way to run a marriage!

"In here, Colonel Warrey," Major Cox invited, opening a door for him. John stepped into the small office, and the man sitting behind the desk rose and stood to attention. "At ease," Cox said. "You have some things for us."

"Sir." The man opened a folder on his desk. "One Swiss passport." He held it out.

"Joachim Hasselblatt?" John queried.

"Don't you like it?" Cox was anxious.

"Bit of a mouthful."

"Various supporting documents," said the man behind the desk. "Swiss driving licence, an unpaid bill, cheque book . . . the usual things."

"Shouldn't I have an Italian identity?" John asked.

"You will receive one in Switzerland. However, it might be a good idea to hang on to these. In the event that you were captured, they might help."

"In the event," John said.

"Now," Cox said. "Communications. We are informed that the partisan group you are joining have radio. We do not know the precise range or the wavelength they use, but we have an agent in Switzerland who will monitor a watch on this wavelength . . ." He gave John a slip of paper. "Memorise that and destroy it. We will try to get you a transmitter of your own as soon as possible. But until then, use the man on the ground. It is important for you to time your major movements with ours. Your call sign will be Duce."

"Say again?"

"We thought that was rather good."

"Duce," John said.

"And your contact will be Home Affairs. Understood?"

"As far as it is possible to understand anything. Weaponry?"

"Again, you will receive those in Switzerland. It is considered safer for you to travel from England as what you are, a Swiss businessman returning home. As such you would not be armed, and please make sure that you are not."

"Right. And just what have I been doing in England?"

"Trying to obtain treatment for your wife. She will be returning with you, the treatment having proved unsuccessful."

"Would you mind repeating that?" John asked. "Slowly."

Cox looked embarrassed. "Your wife is suffering from a crippling bone disease, and you had hoped the British surgeons might be able to help her. As they cannot, you are taking her

14

home. Her life expectancy is now not great. She travels in a wheelchair as she cannot walk. This is absolutely the safest possible cover. You will, of course, show her every attention and every sympathy, plus a great deal of love. You are very much in love with your wife."

"Thank you very much for telling me," John said. "This wife, where is she at the moment?"

"In a safe place. She will meet you at the airport this evening, to catch the flight to Lisbon. Her name is Annaliese Hasselblatt, and she will have all the necessary documentation to prove it."

"And what is the truth of the matter?"

"Mrs Hasselblatt is an Italian. She is strongly anti-Fascist. Mussolini had her father executed, and her husband was killed in a gunfight with the Fascists. You may trust her absolutely. She knows of your mission, and will accompany you into Italy as part of that mission. She is in touch with the partisans there. She will act as your go-between as well as your second-in-command."

"You mean she isn't really crippled."

"No, sir, she is not really crippled. But she will act the part whenever necessary. You must bear in mind at all times that there are German agents everywhere, in Lisbon, in Switzerland, and most of all on all trains crossing the Vichy border into Switzerland."

"Now, sir," the orderly said, "if you would be good enough to remove your uniform, we have a civilian suit for you to try on. There is also a suitcase packed with your belongings which you will need to inspect and familiarise yourself with."

"I'm sure you think of everything," John said. "Tell me, Major, is my wife good-looking?"

"I have no idea, sir," Cox said. "I have never seen the lady. But she is being employed for her knowledge and her ability rather than her . . . ah—"

"Sexuality," John suggested. "There are some things one just has to find out for oneself."

"I've been posted to Scotland," Aileen said. "I find that very odd. I've only been at Farnham for three months. Scotland! I won't be able to get down for months." She drank some wine. "What's yours?"

Aileen was a neat young woman with trim features and a trim figure. In the days when they had courted, before the war, her crowning glory had been her hair, long and black; since joining up it had necessarily been cut, and what was left was now worn in a tight bun over which her sidecap could fit comfortably. She had always taken most things in her stride, even his proposal of marriage. No doubt she had expected it; they had grown up together and been an adult item without ever either of them stirring the other with consuming passion. Marriage, when he had returned from his first tour of duty in Egypt, had seemed an inevitability. Besides, he had desperately wanted to forget Soroya. As if anyone could ever forget Soroya.

"I'm still stuck in an office here in London," he said.

"How boring. But I don't suppose mine will be any the less, save I'll be getting chilblains." She reached across the table to squeeze his hand. "Do you think we'll ever be able to settle down like an ordinary married couple?"

"Of course. When the war is over."

He wondered how many extra 'wives' he would have accumulated by then? Something else of which Aileen was unaware. But he had been unfaithful to her only once, in exceptional circumstances, and he had no intention of ever being so again. One thing had to be certain: he could never afford to fall in love with any of them again. He had fallen in love with Soroya, and had not yet recovered from the shock of her death. But maybe his Italian would be as ugly as sin.

"What annoys me," Aileen said, "is the way they just snap their fingers and expect you to jump. I'm on the three o'clock train to Glasgow."

"Shit," he commented. But that figured; she had to be long gone before he left himself.

"You know what I think," Aileen said. "I think we should

stop fooling about and let me become pregnant. They'd have to let me go then, wouldn't they?"

"I imagine they would," John agreed. "A dishonourable discharge, or something. But as you're not pregnant . . . you're not, are you?"

"Not so far as I know, worst luck."

"And you're leaving on the three o'clock train." He looked at his watch; it was past one. "I don't see we can do much about it right now. I tell you what; we'll throw away all the french letters when we meet up again."

"Hooray for that." Then she frowned. "When are we going to meet up again, Johnnie?"

"When you come down from Scotland, I suppose" – which would not be until after his mission was completed.

"You're quite senior now. Couldn't you get some leave and come up to be with me? Just a weekend."

"I'll see what I can do. But there are big things in the wind. You know, where we are going to invade, and when. There's a lot of info that needs correlating. So—"

She blew him a kiss. "I have to rush."

John returned to their hotel, and went to bed, alone. He needed to think, to plan. But there was little planning he could do until he discovered exactly what was the situation on the ground. And thoughts, plans, were overlaid by the concept of the woman he had accumulated – whom he had not yet seen. He had had to work with several women in his brief career. Margo Cartwright, of course. He wondered where she was now? She had got on the wrong side of Montgomery and had her career very suddenly terminated. Samantha Carson! That had been an abrasive relationship, compounded by his being with Samantha's sister when she had drowned. Soroya! But he did not wish to be reminded of Soroya. Arsinoe the Egyptian. A total bundle of joy. But none of them had ever pretended to be his wife!

He got up at six o'clock, put on his new, Swiss cut, civilian suit, paid his bill, hefted his suitcase and went to the bus

17

stop. He rode to the appointed destination, got down, and five minutes later was picked up by a taxi. "Nice night for it, sir," said the driver. He wore civilian clothes and this was a black cab, but he was definitely a soldier.

"Not too nice, I hope," John said. It was a long flight to Lisbon, and German interceptions had been known to happen.

He was dropped at the terminal building, and the taxi immediately disappeared again. John carried his bag to the check-in desk. "My wife arrived yet?"

"Indeed, Mr Hasselblatt. She checked in about fifteen minutes ago. She's in the lounge."

John pocketed his ticket, entered the lounge, looked around himself. There weren't many passengers; these flights were strictly intended for government or service personnel travelling on business of national importance. But there were always a few seats for civilians, if one knew the right people. Annaliese Hasselblatt was easy to identify, because of the wheelchair. Otherwise it would have been impossible. He had been given no description of her. But even had he possessed a photograph, it wouldn't have done him much good, as the woman was entirely concealed beneath a heavy coat, a headscarf, and dark glasses. Not to mention several rugs tucked around her knees and thighs and over her feet.

"Darling." He bent over the chair and kissed her cheek.

Her head jerked, but one gloved hand came up to hold his. "I thought you weren't going to make it," she said.

Her voice was low, and attractive. She smelt delightful. Her complexion was perfection. And she had a strong mouth and chin, and a straight nose. There was also a trace of yellow hair escaping from the scarf. He thought she might grow on him, and reminded himself again that she was a working partner, not a sleeping one. "Traffic," he explained, and sat beside her. "So—"

"They are calling the flight."

An attendant hurried up. "Shall we go first, Mrs Hasselblatt. Ah, Mr Hasselblatt. Would you . . . . ?"

18

"You go ahead," John said. "I'm sure you fellows know more about it than I do." He bent beside the woman. "Can you walk at all?" he whispered.

"A few steps. I will be able to get on the plane."

He followed the attendant and the wheelchair out into the darkening evening. The chair was rolled up to the steps, and then he held his wife's arm and helped her up and into the cabin. They were seated side by side in the very front of the aircraft, waiting while the other passengers boarded. "How do you like to be called?" John asked.

"By my husband, Liese."

"I'm John. About what we have to do—"

"It is better we do not talk about it until we are quite alone," Liese said.

John reckoned being her commanding officer was going to be difficult.

They spoke little on the flight; the attendants were very solicitous about the crippled woman, were always offering her, and by extension, her husband, things to drink or extra rugs for warmth. John even managed to doze from time to time, always awakening with a start as their shoulders touched. It was not the first time he had set off into the unknown in the company of a strange woman and he needed to remember that nearly all of the previous occasions had turned out badly.

They landed in the small hours of the morning, to the accompaniment of flashing camera bulbs and excited media. "They always expect to see Churchill, on an English flight," explained the young man who met them, speaking English with an accent. "Your train leaves this afternoon, so I have booked you into an hotel for a rest and a wash. I hope this is satisfactory."

"Most satisfactory," Annaliese said. "I would like a bath."

The young man looked at John, somewhat uncertainly, and then at Annaliese's concealed and presumably crippled legs.

"We'll manage," John said.

"Then I'll pick you up at three. I'm afraid it will be necessary to change several times."

"We understand," John said.

The wheelchair was packed into the back of the taxi with their luggage, and Annaliese gave a little sigh of relief as she sank into the cushions. "I hate that chair," she confided, speaking English so that hopefully the driver would not understand her.

"How long have you been in it?"

"A week. Getting used to it. I can hardly wait to dump it. I am told you are a famous man."

"You don't want to believe everything you hear," John said.

"You will be even more famous when we are finished with this mission."

"Supposing we're alive."

"That is a pessimistic point of view," Annaliese said, and stared out of the window.

More solicitude from the hotel staff, but at last Annaliese was wheeled into the bedroom. "Champagne," she said. "I would like champagne."

"Why not?" As presumably the British Government was paying. He rang for room service, watched Annaliese uncoiling herself from the chair. She was taller than he had estimated. "So tell me," he said. "Are you really married?"

"I was, once," she said, beginning to undress.

John sat down to consider the situation. She was an extraordinarily handsome woman, taller than he had estimated, with long, strong legs and high breasts, square shoulders and a flat belly. Her eyes were a lustrous blue. Her yellow hair was long too, as she unpinned it and let it float down her back. "Do you approve?" she asked.

"Very much so."

"I train," she explained. "Every day. Do you train, every day?"

"Not *every* day."

She snorted. "Were *you* married?"

"Still am."

She raised her eyebrows. "Is that going to be a problem for you?"

"No."

"You have done this before?"

"A few times." He was certainly not going to let her get on top of him, at least mentally. "I am looking forward to our mission. Now, I will have a bath. There is something you must know."

"It's okay. I haven't spotted the third nipple."

She glared at him, disapprovingly. "I wish you to understand that there must be no sex between us."

"Then don't you think you are going about it the wrong way?"

"It is necessary that you become used to seeing my body as we have to share a room and a bed. But sex, no."

John scratched his head. "I accept your ruling my dear, and entirely agree with it. But . . . is there a reason?"

"I do not like men," she said.

There was a knock on the door.

"Then I'd remove myself from the line of fire, if I were you," he suggested.

She vanished and he opened the door to admit room service, with an ice bucket and a bottle of champagne. He tipped the waiter and closed the door again, turned, to gaze at Annaliese, standing in the bathroom doorway, naked, a small automatic pistol in her hand. "Opening the door like that, unarmed, was very careless of you," she admonished.

"I was unarmed because I was not armed," John said. "And neither should you be. They want us to get into Switzerland as inconspicuously as possible."

"They told me the same thing," she said contemptuously. "But I always carry a gun. Do you know what the Nazis will do to you, to us, if they capture us?"

"Yes," he said. "I've been captured by them, already." He could not resist asking. "Have you?"

"Yes," she said, and retreated into the bathroom.

21

He poured champagne, carried the glasses in. She was still running the water. "When you said you didn't like men," he remarked, "were you meaning specifically me?"

"I will make an exception for you," she said. "We are partners."

"You mean, I am your commanding officer."

"That too," she conceded, condescendingly.

"Then here's to a successful mission." He raised his glass. She drank. "It may well be."

"I don't like the use of the word may," he said. "It had better be. Successful, I mean."

"I was talking of you, and me," she explained.

The Gestapo

"These are photographs of the guests at the ambassador's ball in Madrid," the officer said. "Take your time." Margo sat at the desk and used a magnifying glass to study each photograph in turn. She had been looking at so many photographs over the past month she felt she was getting eye strain. That apart, her new life had been easier than she had expected. She had her own apartment here in Munich, ample funds, which had enabled her to replace the wardrobe she had been forced to abandon in England, was entertained very generously by the local Nazis and had even been given a cutting from an English newspaper containing the report of the death of ATS Sergeant Margo Cartwright, whose vehicle had crashed and caught fire in a blaze so fierce that both Sergeant Cartwright and her driver had been unrecognisably burned; she had been identified only by one of her shoes, which had been found beside the wreckage. "And my driver?" she had asked.

"No one you knew," she had been assured.

So, she had been a party to a double murder. But she had fought with the Senussi in North Africa and seen, and shared, death enough. And then she had been on the right side. Or was this the right side? She wished she could be sure.

The future loomed. But it still promised security. Not even the most diehard Nazi could pretend Germany could still win the war, in military or political terms. But they were all still certain they could draw it, on two counts. Firstly, they still held that fortress Europe was impregnable, and from what she had seen, it was. And secondly, they were still certain that at some time in the not too distant future the Allies had to wake up to the fact that in allying themselves with Soviet Russia they were predicating the utter destruction of Europe, and that thus co-existence with the Fascist regimes of Germany and Italy against the Communists had to be the lesser evil. Margo didn't know enough about international politics to argue against that; she could only hope and pray they were right.

So, photographs, and a sudden pitter-patter of the heart: she was about to condemn a man to death. "This one," she said.

Captain Krueger leaned over her shoulder. "Which?"

"The man on the right."

Krueger checked his list. "Harold Broughton, English timber merchant."

"William Hastings, Military Intelligence," Margo said.

Krueger took the magnifying glass and studied the photo. "Very good. I will have him checked out."

"What will happen to him?"

"That is not your concern. There is another batch. These are the passengers arriving at Lisbon airport over the past three days."

Margo sighed, and started all over again, carefully examining each print before turning it over. And then suddenly her heart gave a tremendous leap. "That one." She jabbed it with her finger.

Krueger turned to his list. "Joachim Hasselblatt, Swiss businessman, returning from a visit to London with his crippled wife. It is her in the chair."

"That is Colonel John Warrey, Military Intelligence." Again Krueger used the magnifying glass. "Your old friend? You are certain of this, Fräulein?"

"I am certain of it," Margo said. "And if the woman in the chair is really crippled, I'll eat my hat."

"You think she is really his wife?"

"No," Margo said.

"But this Warrey is married?"

"Yes. But Military Intelligence does not use husband and wife teams."

"Ah. Very good. This has been a most productive session, Fräulein. I congratulate you."

"What will happen to *him*? This really does concern me."

"We will keep him and his 'wife' under surveillance. It is necessary to find out where they are going, before we can deduce what they are doing. It is also necessary to identify the woman, because that may *tell* us where they are going. You do not know her?"

Margo studied the photograph again. The woman was so wrapped up as to be almost indistinguishable, but she did not doubt that if she was Warrey's sidekick she would be good-looking. When she remembered the couple of occasions on which they had come close to something memorable . . . it had never happened.

"I have never seen her before."

"No matter. We have other identification agents. One of them should know who she is, although it would be good to have a better photograph. Warrey is the man we want, the man we will have. When the moment is right."

"Can they not be arrested immediately?"

"In Lisbon? No, no. That would cause a diplomatic rumpus, and while we would certainly smooth it over, as the arrest would be publicised his superiors in London would learn of it, write him off, and start again. It would be better for him just to disappear, when we have discovered what he is up to. Thank you, Fräulein Cartwright. But tell me, why do you hate this man so? Is it because of an unhappy love affair?"

"That's my business," Margo said.

"Or perhaps he spurned your advances."

"You are being insulting."

Krueger was not offended. "Or is it that you hate all men, Fräulein?"

"Don't be ridiculous," Margo snapped. But she was flushing.

Krueger smiled. "In Germany, we lock homosexuals up." His smile widened. "With each other, to be sure."

"I am not homosexual," Margo said in a low voice.

"Good. I would not like you to be locked up. Well, if

you are not homosexual, you will have dinner with me, tonight."

It was not an invitation.

"It is the border in five minutes, Herr Hasselblatt," said the guard. "You have your papers?"

"Of course," John said, and the door of the compartment closed. He gazed at Annaliese, seated opposite him, staring out of the train window. As they had been travelling since dawn she looked somewhat crushed, and very warm; it had been necessary for her to play the cripple the whole way, and she was shrouded in her cloak and blankets. The hours in Lisbon, the night they had shared in an hotel in Madrid before catching this train, seemed a very long way away.

He looked forward to discovering more about her. This was an essential part of their relationship anyway, whether she could be trusted in a tight situation, how she would react to violence, how genuine was her reputed hatred of the Mussolini regime . . . in all those directions he had only the character given her by Major Cox. Just as it had been necessary to expose their mutual sexuality and eliminate it as a possible distraction when they really got down to work. However attractive she was, he had no strong feelings on the matter – Aileen was too constantly on his mind – and even if he had, he would have conceded that any woman was entitled, even on a mission such as this, to determine who she slept with. All he wanted to know was why. As she was a widow, he could not believe she was a lesbian. In any event, nothing about her suggested homosexuality. Perhaps she was just not turned on by him, which was a bit of a body blow; he had always counted himself attractive to women in the past. But he should be pleased that she was not some raving nympho, because of Aileen, even if now was the time to stop remembering his wife. He was on a mission, and domestic matters belonged in a distant world, where, even if they were sharing a war, they had never jointly, or in her case, singly, become personally involved.

That was what he had to believe he was going home to. After

having set north Italy alight – with the aid of this attractively unusual woman who was now gazing at him with that peculiar intentness of hers. "That was a deep thought," she remarked. "I have them, from time to time. You heard the man?" She nodded. "I will be glad to get out of this train." It was slowing, and a moment later came to a halt beside a platform, on which soldiers of various nationalities outnumbered passengers. Booted feet tramped in the corridor, and their door was opened. But the young Swiss soldier was only interested in getting his job done. He glanced at the passports, looked at the crippled woman, then saluted. "Welcome home," he remarked, and went on.

They reached Geneva a few minutes later, but as their destination was Montreux, they remained on the train as it took its way round the northern side of the lake, through Lausanne. It was dark by the time they reached Montreux, but the Chateau de Chillon still stood out starkly beneath the starlit sky. "That place gives me the creeps," Annaliese commented.

"Do you know Switzerland well?" John asked.

"I have lived here," Annaliese said.

The train halted, and the guard came in to erect the chair. John lifted his wife into it, and she was wheeled along the corridor; two more men were waiting to lift the chair down to the platform.

"Welcome home, Mr Hasselblatt, Mrs Hasselblatt," said the man waiting for them. "Your car is outside."

"That is good," John said. "My wife is very tired."

"I understand. I am Wilhelm Littler, your attorney."

"Pleased to make your acquaintance," John said, and shook hands. As he did so, there was a sudden flurry of movement in front of them, and a man stepped forward and using a small hand-held camera, took a photograph of Annaliese. The flash blinded them all for a moment, and the man used his opportunity to hurry away.

"What the hell—?" John complained.

"Stop him," Annaliese commanded. The train guards looked

27

at each other, and Littler, after a moment's hesitation, set off after the photographer. "Bastard," Annaliese commented.

A porter was waiting with their luggage, and the train was hissing and clanking, while everyone, both on the platform and looking out of the windows, was staring at them.

"I think we need to get off the platform," John said, and pushed the chair to the exit.

Littler rejoined them, panting. "He jumped over the wall at the end," he said.

"Call the police," Annaliese suggested.

"I'm afraid it is not a crime to take a photograph of someone, Mrs Hasselblatt," Littler said. "And we would attract even more attention."

Everyone on the platform was still staring at them, and whispering to each other.

"Let's get out of here," John said.

A few minutes later they were being driven away.

"Conard is absolutely reliable," Littler said. "You may speak freely. What about this photograph?"

"Not good," John said.

"How bad?"

"There are questions that need answering. Firstly, how did the photographer know we were arriving on that train and at that hour?"

"You think you were followed from Madrid?"

"Could even be from Lisbon, or London. But it certainly seems that someone has been keeping an eye on us, and nobody is supposed to know anything about us at all, except our controls and you. I think we need to find out about that, Littler."

"I will attend to it. But it will take time. If they have been following you—"

"They know we are British agents," Annaliese said.

"But they only photographed you—" Littler looked at John.

"That is the second question," John said. "To which the answer is obvious."

"What?" Annaliese asked.

"That they had already identified me," John said.

"Ha," she commented.

"Do you wish to abort the mission?" Littler asked.

"No way," John said. "But we need to be careful, and quick."

"My instructions are that you will be taken across the border in two days' time. That is Wednesday 7 July. It is not possible to change the arrangement, to bring the day forward. To attempt to contact the partisans with a different schedule would be to risk everything."

"And we've a safe place to spend those three days?"

"Certainly. As of this moment, Mr and Mrs Hasselblatt disappear, and you will assume your Italian identities. These are waiting for you at your destination."

"And I can get rid of that beastly chair," Annaliese said.

They drove for several hours, south-east, in and out of valleys overlooked by huge peaks. It was three in the morning before they pulled into an isolated farmhouse. By then Annaliese had gone to sleep. But she opened her eyes when the car stopped.

"You may carry me," she told John. "One last time."

"My pleasure." He lifted her into the low-ceilinged, warmly furnished interior; this was a large room, combining kitchen, dining table and a sitting area around the blazing fire; even in July, because of the height it was distinctly cool.

Waiting to greet them was a stout, red-faced man and his equally comfortable wife. "Hans and Matilda will take care of you until it is time to leave," Littler said. "They are absolutely reliable."

It occurred to John that there were too many people whom Littler apparently regarded as absolutely reliable. But he kept the opinion to himself, set Annaliese on her feet, went with Littler to the door. "I suppose there's no chance we've been followed?"

"None at all. We kept a very careful watch in the mirrors."

"So the Germans go to all the trouble to track us from

Portugal, and then have a photographer on the spot to get a shot of Annaliese, and make no attempt to find out where we went after leaving the station?"

"Well, you see, we don't know that photographer was working for the Germans."

"Make a suggestion."

"Well . . . he could have been freelance, and thought he had a celebrity. Your wife is very good-looking. He might have mistaken her for a movie star."

"In the dark and in a wheelchair?" John asked.

"Well . . . it is of no matter now. You will be perfectly safe here, and the day after tomorrow Colonel Renaldo will come. He is the one we contacted to expect you."

"Colonel Renaldo," John said thoughtfully. "Is this a pukka rank, or one he gave himself?"

"Pukka?" Littler was puzzled.

"Sorry. Army slang. I mean is his rank official, or just a title?"

"I should think it is a title. Now come, I have some things to show you." He led John out of the farmhouse and to one of the outbuildings. The door of this he unlocked with a key taken from his pocket. "There is no light here." He explained, and produced a torch. "You can inspect the goods in the morning. I just wanted you to know they are here."

He shone the beam over the row of rifles and revolvers, hand grenades and tommy-guns, the boxes of ammunition.

"Do Hans and Matilda know this stuff is here?" John asked.

"Of course. Our people have assembled this store bit by bit over the past few weeks. These weapons are for Renaldo and his people." He grinned. "Otherwise he would not come. But there is also military clothing for your wife and yourself. I hope it fits."

"So we won't be shot as spies," John suggested. As if they wouldn't be shot on sight, anyway.

"However, for free movement inside Italy, here are your identity passes."

They were in the names of Signor Alberto Siralunga and Signora Anna Siralunga. "Why does London always have to choose such mouthfuls?" John wondered. "They also supplied the photographs. Do you approve?" "Very passportish. Tell me, are you my radio contact?" "No, no. I have nothing to do with that." "I see. But there was to be a transmitter for my use. I don't see one here. I suppose you don't know about that, either?" "I'm afraid not. So, here is the key." Littler seemed relieved to hand it over.

"How far is it to the border?" John asked.

"Due south, twenty miles. But it may be safer for you to stay in Switzerland until you are closer to Renaldo's base. That is over a hundred miles away to the east. I'm afraid you will have to go on foot. But Renaldo will guide you. He is—"

"Absolutely reliable," John remarked. "I'll take your word for it." They walked back to the car together. "Do I see you again?"

"Hopefully not." Littler held out his hand. "I have carried out my instructions."

"Whenever I get around to making a report, I shall mention that." John shook hands. "Good luck."

"And to you, Colonel Warrey."

John watched the car fade into the darkness, returned inside. Annaliese was seated at the table, drinking soup, while Matilda hovered solicitously. "This is rather good. Try some."

Matilda hurried forward with a steaming bowl, and John's stomach reminded him that it was some hours since he had last eaten. "Is all well?" Annaliese asked, as he sat beside her and slurped.

"No," he said. "But then, I'm a pessimist. Which is why I'm still alive."

The telephone jangled, and Krueger stretched out an arm to find the receiver. "Yes?"

He listened, and Margo rolled on her back and stared at the

31

ceiling. She had not been a virgin, but it had been so long since the last time, she had felt virginal. And he, as might have been expected, was a crisp, conventional but commanding lover, had known what he had and where to put it. She had loathed every minute of it.

Presumably such total submission was a necessary part of her defection, of her security and even, hopefully, of her progress. She was surprised it hadn't happened earlier.

Krueger was sitting up, and speaking animatedly. "That is very good," he was saying. "You know what to do. I wish the matter decided today." He hung up and turned to her. "Our people obtained a good snap of Frau Hasselblatt, last night when they reached Montreux."

"You mean they are in Switzerland?"

"Well, obviously, using a name like Hasselblatt, that is where they were going. The important thing is that the snap was developed immediately, and checked by our experts. They have just identified it. Annaliese Coparro. She is a well-known anti-Fascist. Her father was executed by Mussolini for an attempted coup, some years ago. Her husband was killed in a gun battle with the Fascists just before the war. She was arrested, but managed to make her escape with the help of the local partisans. There is a warrant out for her arrest in Italy."

"And now she is in Switzerland. With Warrey."

"Now we know their destination. They are heading for north Italy. There has been some Communist-inspired agitation there recently. Obviously your friend Warrey has been sent to take advantage of it, if he can."

"What are you going to do?"

"I think it is time to, as I said, make them disappear."

"Do we know where they are?"

"No. But we can easily find out. I have given orders that this should be done immediately."

"I would like to be there," Margo said.

"You are a sadistic little bitch," Krueger said. "You will have to forego that pleasure. You can give me pleasure instead."

"My God, Wilhelm, do you know the time?" You have been out all night." Gertrude Littler was a small, plump woman in her early twenties, with curly yellow hair and a disordered nightgown. Now she drew the curtains to allow daylight to flood the room. "I have been so worried," she said.

"I had a job to do," Littler explained. "I did tell you I would be late." He locked the apartment door, poured himself a glass of milk.

"Not this late." Gertrude thrust both hands into her hair to scratch her scalp. "This job—"

"Does not concern you," Littler said. "It is better you do not know." He looked at his watch. "Nine o'clock. Look, make me a quick breakfast while I take a shower, then I must go to the office."

"With no sleep?"

"I'll keep awake. And we'll have an early night, eh? Hurry now." He slapped her bottom.

Gertrude went into the kitchenette, and Littler went into the bathroom, but checked as there was a knock on the front door. "You get it," Gertrude called. "I'm not dressed."

Littler strode through the lounge, opened the door. "Yes?" he demanded, irritably, and then gaped at the automatic pistol, fitted with a silencer, that was thrust into his waist by the man standing there. Behind him were two more men. All wore slouch hats and belted raincoats. But it was not raining. "What—?"

"Quiet," said the man with the gun. "Back up."

Littler backed into the room, and the three men followed, the last closing and locking the door.

"Wilhelm? What is it?" Gertrude appeared in the kitchen doorway, checked at the sight of the men, and opened her mouth.

"Scream, and I will blow your husband apart," the first man said.

Gertrude closed her mouth, gazed at her husband.

"You cannot do this," Littler protested.

"We are doing it," the first man said, and nodded to one of

his companions, who was carrying an attache case. This he now placed on the table and opened it.

"The police—"

"Will know nothing of it, for some time," the commander said. "You. Frau Littler, sit in that chair."

Gertrude swallowed, and sat in the straight chair indicated. The man by the table took out a length of thick cord, pulled her arms behind her back, tied her wrists together, and then secured them to the crossbar below the seat. Then he knelt in front of her. Gertrude panted and went very red in the face, breasts heaving against the thin material of the nightgown. The man secured first one ankle and then the other to the two uprights, so that she was helpless. Then he produced a roll of tape and cut off a length to place across her mouth, effectively gagging her.

"If you harm my wife—" Littler said.

"Whether we harm your wife or not is up to you," the commander said. "Sit." He jabbed Littler in the ribs with the gun muzzle, and Littler sat down on the settee with a thump. The commander sat beside him. "You collected two people, a man and a woman, at the station tonight," he said. "Where did you take them?"

"I have no idea what you are talking about," Littler said.

Gertrude gave a little moan, and strained on her bonds. One of the men stood behind the chair, holding it, so that she could not tip over.

"Mr Littler," the commander said, "we have very little time. Tell us where Colonel Warrey and Signora Coparro are to be found, and no harm will come to you and your wife. See? I know their names. I know all about them. Save where they are at this moment. And this I must know."

"I cannot tell you," Littler said, his voice harsh with strain.

The commander nodded, and his second henchman stood in front of Gertrude, dug his fingers into the bodice of her nightgown, and ripped it open down to her waist. Then he freed her left breast of the material as he might have unwrapped a loaf of bread.

"This will be very painful for your wife," the commander said. "It would be better to co-operate."

Gertrude was staring at him with enormous eyes, and she began to scream, which came through the tape as a very thin little wail.

"She will make more noise than that," the commander said. Another nod, and the man standing in front of Gertrude took a box of matches from his pocket. He struck one of these, allowed the flame to flare, and then held it to the exposed nipple. Gertrude gave an immense heave and almost lifted the chair from the floor, but it was held down by the man behind her.

"For God's sake," Littler shouted.

"Sssh," the commander recommended. "Does not her flesh smell nice as it burns?"

"You—"

The commander again jabbed him with his gun barrel. "All you have to do is tell me where you took Warrey and Coparro."

Littler sighed, and licked his lips. Gertrude's tormentor struck another match and exposed her right nipple. "I took them to a farmhouse in the mountains. I can show you where it is on a map."

"Then do so." The commander nodded, and the second match was dropped to the floor and extinguished by the man's foot. Then he took a map from the attache case. The commander indicated it, and Littler got up. Trembling, he spread the map and indicated the road he had taken.

"The farmhouse is there." He prodded the stiff paper.

The commander took a pencil from his pocket and marked the spot with an X. "Why did you take them to this place?"

"There are to wait there until they are contacted by Italian partisans, who will escort them across the border."

"When will this happen?"

"Tomorrow night."

"You would not lie to me, would you, Herr Littler? Otherwise we might come back."

"I am not lying," Littler said. "Please."

"So tell me, in this matter you are acting for the British Government?"

"Yes," Littler said. "I am a ground agent for the British. I take and receive messages, nothing more. In this instance I was told to meet these people and deliver them to that farmhouse. Nothing more."

The commander studied him for several seconds. "We shall see," he said. He raised the pistol, pressed the muzzle into Littler's neck, and squeezed the trigger. There was only a muted sound. Blood flew, and Littler slumped to the floor.

Gertrude uttered another strangled sound as she watched her husband die. The commander stepped up to her, and shot her as well, through the neck. She slumped in the chair in a welter of blood. The commander folded the map and put it into the attache case. "Tomorrow night," he said.

"If this man was telling the truth, Herr Hauptmann."

"He was telling the truth," the commander said. "As he said, he was only a messenger boy. He was terrified. I think we may well be able to take these Italian partisans as well. That will be very good."

John unlocked the storeroom door and let Annaliese look at the weaponry. "Now this I like," she said, examining several of the guns. "But we will need a small army to move it all."

"According to friend Littler, that is what we are going to have, tonight," John said.

"But you are not happy," she suggested.

"As I said, I'm a pessimist. Let's walk." He gave her her new identity card, pocketed his own, locked the storeroom door.

It was a beautiful, sunny, July day. It was quite impossible to believe there was a war on, that only a few hundred miles to the east there were massive battles being fought, or that only a few hundred miles to the south an enormous invasion was being prepared. Presumably all his old friends in the Desert Rats, like Blanchard the tank commander, would be involved in that. He wished he could be with them.

On the other hand, if this mission was a success, he would be playing just as vital a part in the coming battles as any brigade of tanks. If it was going to be a success.

He was quite used to the somewhat slap-happy methods so often employed by Military Intelligence, the way his superiors changed their minds and often gave the impression that their right hands did not know what their left hands were doing. Presumably they regarded this as a good thing for security reasons, but it could be very irritating for the men in the field. As for security on this operation . . .

Annaliese strode at his side, skirt fluttering in the breeze. Her golden hair was loose, and also scattering. The hillside was a pasture for several cows, who regarded them incuriously.

"What is bothering you, especially?"

"It would be simpler to tell you what isn't bothering me," he said. "This is supposed to be a top secret exercise. Yet the Germans seem to have known exactly where we were and what we were doing from the moment we left London."

"And have done nothing about it," she pointed out.

"I have a suspicion they are doing plenty about it," John said. "They're just not telling us. But they are going to, soon enough."

"They don't know where we are. Just that we got off the train in Montreux."

"That narrows it down a bit. And then, this fellow Renaldo, who calls himself a colonel . . . I wish I knew a bit more about him."

"I know him," she said.

"Come again?"

Annaliese sat down on the hillside, drawing deep breaths. They were several hundred feet above the valley now, looking back down at the farmhouse, the wisp of smoke rising from its chimney, the cattle scattered on the slopes beneath them; it was a real chocolate box cover scene. John thought this could be one of the most relaxing days of his recent life. He had slept heavily, as had the woman. That had been a combination of exhaustion and tension. But today the atmosphere had been conducive to relaxation, for the last time before the real business began.

"I think I know him," she said. "I remember the name."

"Tell me about him."

"I do not know enough. Except that he is an anti-Fascist."

"Is he a Communist?"

"I do not think so. He was not when last we met."

"You have actually met him?"

"He helped me escape, after my husband was killed."

"So you have a nodding acquaintance, shall I say."

She glanced at him. "It is good, for a husband to be jealous of his wife," she remarked. And pointed. "There is your friend coming back."

John sat up, shading his eyes. It was definitely Littler's car, or one very like it, bouncing along the track from the road. "That's odd," he said. "He told me we wouldn't meet again. He seemed rather pleased to be rid of us."

"There must have been a change of plan," Annaliese said. "We should go down there and see what has happened." She made to stand up, and John held her wrist and jerked her back down again. "Oof," she complained. "You have driven my spine through my brain."

"Lie down," he snapped.

"Here?" But she did not look displeased. "Don't you wish to speak with your friend?"

John forced her on to her stomach and lay down himself, watching the car pulling to a halt in front of the farmhouse. The door opened, and Hans came out. They were too far away to hear the sound of a shot, but the farmer suddenly collapsed to his knees and then his face.

"Holy Mother!" Annaliese muttered.

Four men got out of the car, and ran into the house. A few minutes later two of them came back, to seize Hans' legs and drag him through the door.

"Matilda?" Annaliese whispered.

"I would say she's already dead," John replied.

One of the men was having a conversation with the driver

of the car, then the vehicle drove away, bouncing into the distance behind a plume of dust. The man went inside and closed the door.

"Why have they murdered those people?" Annaliese asked.

"Because they are after us," John said.

"And now?"

"Now they are obviously going to wait for us to return."

"What are we going to do?"

John tried to concentrate his thoughts, with desperate urgency – so much for a last period of relaxation. The fact that German agents – as he had to assume these men were – had both come to the farmhouse and had been driving Littler's car meant that either Littler was a traitor or he had been taken prisoner and tortured into revealing their whereabouts – in which case he was probably dead now as well. A lot would depend on how much else he had told them. But he had not known all that much more, save that they were on their way to Italy, escorted by this mysterious Colonel Renaldo.

"I would say we sit it out," he decided.

"Here? There is no shelter, no food, no water—"

"A few hours dieting isn't going to harm us," he pointed out. "And up here there has to be a stream somewhere close. As for shelter, the weather looks very settled to me."

"You do not know the Alps," she complained. "Look there."

"Don't point," he snapped, catching her arm. "If they find out where we are, we're done. I don't suppose you have your little pistol with you?"

"You told me not to carry it. It's in the bedroom."

"Well, I don't suppose it'd do much good against the kind of firepower they'll have. What were you going to show me? That little cloud peeping round the hill over there?"

"There will be another cloud behind it," she said. "A bigger cloud."

She was right.

"Let's find that water," he said. "Stay on your belly until we're out of sight."

"It is ruining my dress," she complained, wriggling behind him.

"A bullet would make an even bigger mess."

They crawled upwards and to one side until they rounded the brow of the hill and were out of sight of the farmhouse.

"Now we will not know if they go away," Annaliese remarked.

"They're not going to go away," John said. "Not without us. *Voilà!*"

A hundred yards away a stream poured over the lip of the next hill in a miniature waterfall.

"Can I get up now?" Annaliese asked.

"I should think so."

She hurried towards the water, which gathered in a little pool at the foot of the fall and then hurried down the hillside. She lay on her stomach to lap at it, her hair drooping past her face, the ends trailing in the water. John lay beside her and also drank. He was surprised at how thirsty he was, and the woman. Sheer fright, he supposed.

She rose to her knees, shook her head. "I was so looking forward to another delicious lunch. Those poor people—"

He wondered if she was more concerned about Hans and Matilda, or about the food she was missing?

"We must find some shelter," she said.

He rose to his knees as well; the sun had disappeared behind the suddenly now very large, and very black clouds.

"Those trees," she suggested. Pointing at a small copse a few hundred yards away.

"I don't think that would be a very good idea," John said.

Even as he spoke there was a vivid flash of lightning followed almost immediately by a crash of thunder.

"We will get hit," Annaliese shouted.

"The trees are a better bet for being hit. If you're wearing metal false teeth, take them out," he recommended.

She stuck out her tongue at him, then gave a little shriek as there was another tremendous crash. Then the rain started.

John put his arm round the woman and held her close, and

they crouched together on the bank of the stream while the rain slashed into them, and the lightning flashed and the thunder roared. The copse was indeed struck very quickly, but the storm itself lasted little more than half an hour before the clouds passed on and were replaced by bright sunlight.

"My God!" Annaliese moaned. "I am soaked to the skin." John reckoned that was an understatement; there was water everywhere, and whenever they moved, they squelched. But the sun was warm. "So strip off," he suggested. "Spread out your clothes."

He set an example, and after a few minutes observation she also undressed, while wagging her finger at him. "No sex."

"I never felt less like it."

She peered at him. "You *are* feeling like it."

"I meant I'm still not in a proper state to consider it."

She made a moue. "It is not that I do not like you," she said. "But after they shot my husband, I was raped by the Fascisti. Twelve of them one after the other. They even sodomised me. Since that day I have no wish for it. You understand this?"

"I do. I am very sorry."

"That I was raped, or that I no longer wish sex?"

He grinned. "Both, I think."

They sat in silence for some time. Despite what he had said, for some reason he was far more aware of her, out here, than he had been in the hotel room. He supposed it had to do with the fact that they were in the open air, and that they were in a position of extreme peril. But he was her commanding officer, and had to act the part. Besides, he could genuinely understand her feelings.

"You know what we could do?" she asked. "When it is dark, we could sneak back down to the farmhouse and get to the shed. You still have the key?"

"It's in my pocket."

"Well, then—"

"I would bet my last penny that our friends have already broken into the shed,. And will be mounting guard over it. And we don't have any weapons until we can get inside."

41

"Are you not proficient at unarmed combat? There will only be one guard."

"That kind of odds only works in the movies," he pointed out.

"Then what do you intend to do?"

"Sit it out," John said. "And hope that Renaldo is on time, and that he comes mob-handed."

Their clothes dried by evening, but the air remained chilly. They returned round the hillside to a vantage point from which they could look down on the farmhouse, which glowed with light.

"I bet they are drinking that lovely soup," Annaliese growled. "I am so hungry."

"The soup will be there tomorrow," John told her. But he was worried. If Renaldo didn't come, they were in a difficult situation. The only contact they had in Switzerland had been Littler, who was either dead or working for the Gestapo; in either event, Montreux was a long way away on foot.

They had been absolutely trapped, That they were alive at all was pure fortune, that they had elected to take a walk just before the Gestapo had turned up. But how in the name of God had their movements been so pin-pointed? A traitor at the MOD? That was possible. But his orders and their departure from England had all happened so quickly it didn't seem possible for a traitor to have got the information to Germany in time. And then, that photographer at the railway station, concentrating upon a snap of Annaliese. As he had said at the time, that could only be because the Germans already had a photograph of him. But how?

He snapped his fingers. There had been that photographer in Lisbon, taking shots of the passengers coming off the plane. It hadn't seemed important, because the man had been taking generally. But if *his* face had been enlarged . . . it would still have had to be identified. All the Germans, certainly the members of the Gestapo, who had been close to him when he had been captured in North Africa were either dead or in prison. The same went for the Italian Military Police. There was no one in the German Secret Service who had a clue what he looked like. Yet someone had identified him landing in Lisbon. How that had happened he really needed to find out. Supposing he ever had the opportunity.

"I am so cold," Annaliese muttered.

It was quite dark by now, and the temperature was dropping. It seemed certain that the Gestapo were staying the night, and the storm had long gone, so John led the woman back round the hillside and up to the copse. Here there was some bracken and a layer of fallen leaves, and he bedded them down in these, holding her in his arms.

"Are we going to die, Johnnie?" she asked.

"Not if I can help it," John told her, rubbing her back and inhaling her scent.

"I suppose there are worse ways to go," she said, "than lying in a man's arms."

"But no sex," he suggested.

"I am too cold."

"Sex usually warms you up," he teased.

"Perhaps tomorrow," she said.

He wondered if their relationship was progressing, or if she was so miserable she would agree to anything. And what was he going to do if she did?

He felt pretty miserable himself, and coherent thought was made difficult by the emptiness of his stomach. Tomorrow he would have to make a decision, whether to try to get into Italy on their own, and risk being arrested and shot, or whether to abort the exercise and seek the shelter of the nearest British consulate.

He had never aborted a mission in his life.

He awoke just before dawn, somewhat surprised to have slept. The woman was still snoring gently. He laid her head on the ground and got up. Every bone and muscle in his body was aching, and they each seemed to be shivering separately. He went to the edge of the trees, looked down the hillside, just coming into view as the first light spread across the hills; the sun was still hidden behind the mountains.

He turned back to the copse, and heard the click of a rifle bolt.

Italy

John's first reaction was to throw himself down and try to find some shelter, but a moment's reflection told him that would be committing suicide: there were several men around him, having approached unseen and unheard through the semi-darkness of the hillside.

"Up," said the first man, in Italian.

John gave a little sigh of relief, and raised his arms.

"What is happening down there?" the man asked.

"Would you be Colonel Renaldo?" John asked.

"*Si.* That is me. Who are you?"

"Colonel John Warrey, British Secret Service."

"Warrey!" Renaldo gave a shout of laughter. "I have been expecting you. You can prove who you are?"

"I'm afraid not, right this minute."

"Ah. You see—"

"But you know the lady, I think."

Renaldo turned to look at Annaliese, who was being escorted towards them by two of his men, hair scattered, clothes crushed and untidy, looking distinctly ruffled at having been woken up so abruptly. "Signora Coparro," he said. "I was told to expect you, too."

"And I am glad to see you, Renaldo," Annaliese said.

"What has happened at the farmhouse?" Renaldo asked, while his men clustered round. They were, John was happy to note, very well armed with tommy-guns and automatic pistols. "Why were you sleeping out here?"

"We were betrayed," Annaliese said. "And the Gestapo have taken it over. We were lucky we were taking a walk when this happened. Now they are waiting for us to come back. Listen, do you have any food?"

"Food? You wish food?"

"We are starving," Annaliese said.

"Then you must eat." He signalled one of his men, who was wearing a heavy pack. From this he produced two loaves of stale and very hard bread, and an equally stale and hard sausage. But it tasted like a meal at the Ritz, especially when topped with rough red wine. "You were to bring us arms," Renaldo said.

"There are arms in one of the outbuildings," John said. "But the Gestapo have them."

"Then we take them back, eh?"

"You don't think it might be a better idea for us just to take off and cross the border?"

"We settle with the Gestapo first," Renaldo said. "Every German killed is a good German, eh? Your people say this."

"And the Germans say the same thing about my people," John agreed.

"So tell me how many there are in the farmhouse?"

"I think four."

"And I have twenty men with me. Plus you two."

"We have no weapons," Annaliese said. "Give us weapons."

"Of course." Again Renaldo signalled his men, and several guns were held out.

"I will take the pistol," Annaliese said, selecting a Browning automatic.

"I'll take a tommy," John said.

He was not at all sure they were doing the right thing, looked at in the cold light of day. Equally he was not sure whether he should exert his seniority in rank, right this minute. On the other hand, he did wish to avenge Hans and Matilda, and probably Littler as well. And he reckoned the best way, perhaps the only way, to assert his command over these people was as quickly as possible to show them he was every bit as proficient a killer as they. He suspected he might be even more so.

"Now, here is what we will do," Renaldo said.

"Correction," John said. They all looked at him. "I will tell you what we will do."

"He is a colonel," Annaliese pointed out, loyally. "A real colonel."

"You have fought before?" Renaldo inquired. "Like this?"

"Once or twice," John said modestly.

"He is a famous fighting man," Annaliese said. "He has killed Germans in North Africa. And Fascisti."

Renaldo looked at his men, and decided to go along with the Englishman, at least for the moment. "Tell us what we must do."

John didn't really have a plan. He knew the Gestapo would be well armed and that they were experienced people; they would have at least one man on lookout duty all the time, to give them warning of the return of their intended – and hopefully unaware – victims. And there was very little cover around the farmhouse. It would have to be a frontal assault, but obviously he wanted as few casualties as possible amongst his new friends.

"You have grenades?" he asked.

"*Si, si*, we have grenades."

"Then we must get close enough to throw them. Is that a hunting rifle?"

"*Si*." Renaldo held it out. It was a Mauser, and had a telescopic sight.

"I will take this as well as the tommy-gun," John decided. "And five men with grenades. You take the remainder of your men round the back of the building. How long will you need?"

"One hour."

They checked their watches "Right. Keep out of sight, and do not fire until I do. Understood?"

"I will be with you, Johnnie," Annaliese said. He thought she might be becoming quite fond of him.

Renaldo led his men away, crawling across the hillside to gain their position. John led his small group straight over the hill until they looked down on the farmhouse. The distance was still half a mile, and the remainder of the descent was totally exposed, save for the cows, standing around, peering at the invaders in their world, and occasionally lowing – they had not been milked for twenty-hour hours.

"Spread out," John said. "But keep down."

The men moved to either side, on their stomachs, wriggling through the grass and amidst the loose stones. Annaliese lay beside John, who was sighting the hunting rifle on the windows of the farmhouse. "Can you hit anything at this distance?" she asked.

"I think so."

"It would have to be a very good shot."

"I am a very good shot."

She made no reply to that. Instead she said, "If we attack the farmhouse with grenades, and destroy it, will we not also destroy both Hans and Matilda?"

"They are already dead," John told her.

He moved the telescope slowly from window to window. He could see movement within the building, but he needed something more definite than that. Patience was the name of the game. He remembered lying above the road leading south from Benghazi, watching the Germans and the Italians retreating, waiting for the right moment to strike. Then he had been surrounded by Arabs, men, and women, with whom he had fought for the previous two years, people whose worth he knew, and who in turn had trusted him absolutely, and who had been prepared to die for him – quite a few had. To these partisans he was an unknown quality, as they were to him. But he could at least hope that the Italians were a little more civilised in their treatment of prisoners than the Senussi. Not that he supposed there would be any prisoners from this business.

Annaliese squeezed his arm. The farmhouse door was opening. John stared through the telescopic sight, watched a man emerge. He was in his shirt sleeves and wore braces; his shirt was blue and he was smoking a cigarette. John closed his hand on the trigger. The high-velocity bullet struck the man in the centre of his chest with bone-shattering force, hurling him against the doorjamb, where he collapsed in a welter of blood.

"Holy Mother!" Annaliese said. "What a shot."

"Advance fifty yards," John shouted, and his men got up and ran down the slope, firing as they did so, before again going to ground. He did not immediately move, because he knew the first reaction of the Germans would be to try to retrieve the body, which might not be dead, but which was in any event necessary if they were going to close the door.

Sure enough, a few moments later a torso appeared, the man obviously on his knees, tugging at his comrade. John fired again, and again with deadly accuracy. Shot through the head, the second man fell on top of the first. Annaliese clapped her hands.

"Come on!" John leapt to his feet and ran down the slope, the woman behind him.

By now the remaining two Gestapo agents had regained their nerves; glass shattered as the windows were knocked out to give them a clear field of fire. But now there was shooting from behind the farmhouse, as well. John waved his men forward again and, with the Germans distracted, they reached the road, within some twenty yards of the house before going to ground again in the parapet. John looked left and right; there were no casualties and Annaliese was still at his side.

Cautiously he raised his head, and a bullet whined close by. He pushed his tommy-gun over the lip of the parapet and sprayed the front of the house, then stood up and hurled his first grenade. The men to either side followed his example, one giving a choking gasp and falling forward before he could get rid of the bomb. He actually fell on it, and there was an explosion which disintegrated his body. Annaliese gave a little shriek as she was splashed with his blood.

But three of the grenades had landed, two against the side of the house, shattering more glass, and the third in the still blocked doorway. This blew the door off its hinges and scattered more flesh and blood from the bodies already there. John led the rush at the doorway behind his chattering tommy-gun, stepped over the dead men and burst into the farmhouse. There was only one man left alive, and he had been firing through one of the rear windows. He turned, tommy-gun thrust forward, and received a burst from John that tumbled him over backwards, arms and legs flung wide.

Men crowded into the house behind John. Renaldo and his people came down the slope from the rear. "That was well done," Renaldo said. "You are a proper soldier, Colonel."

"I'm afraid one of your people bought it," John said.

Renaldo went outside to look at the dead man, kneel beside him, and cross himself. Presumably that was all the funeral the man would get.

The farmhouse was beginning to burn, from the various explosions. They needed to hurry. Annaliese opened the bedroom door, and hastily shut it again; Hans and Matilda lay on the bed, both were dead, and inside the house it had been a warm twenty-four hours.

"I'll get our gear," John said. "Renaldo, the new arms are in the shed." He gave him the key, just in case the Germans hadn't broken the door.

Holding his breath, he went into the bedroom, hastily closed their suitcases; fortunately they hadn't actually unpacked. He carried the bags outside, to where Annaliese knelt on the ground, being sick. He knelt beside her, wiped her mouth with his handkerchief.

"Are we going to bury them?" she asked.

"No. We are going to get the hell out of here before any Swiss policeman shows up. That smoke is soon going to be visible a good way away." He went to where Renaldo still knelt beside the body of his dead comrade. "Was he very close?"

"They are all very close," Renaldo said. "When you have fought together, killed together, seen your comrades killed together, you are very close. Is it not like this in the British Army?"

"Yes," John said. "How far is it to the border?"

"To the nearest point, about sixty kilometres. But to Lake Garda, which is where we operate, it is two hundred and sixty."

"Then we had better get going," John said, and pointed at the building, which was now well alight. "Some time soon someone must come out here, and he will report what has happened to the police."

"I have been thinking about this," Renaldo said. "It was my plan to take you to my headquarters over Swiss territory, until we are due north of the lake. That is to avoid the German patrols out of Milan and Turin, and the Fascisti. But if we are to be wanted by the Swiss police—"

"I don't think *we* will be wanted by the Swiss police," John said. "Only the Germans know we have been here, and I don't think they are going to broadcast it. So we probably will be safer north of the border for as long as possible."

Renaldo appeared to consider. "You understand this is rough country. We must pass by the Jungfrau. You have heard of the Jungfrau?"

"I know it's better than twelve thousand feet," John said. "We don't have to climb it, do we?"

"No, no. We will use the valleys. But these valleys are still high up, eh?"

"So is this one," John pointed out. "And we were going to take that route anyway, weren't we, if there had been no trouble?"

"That is true. And the woman?"

"You don't think she can make it?"

"She has suffered much," Renaldo said.

"You know about that?"

"I was there."

"You must tell me about it, some time," John said. "How long will this journey take?"

"Eight, ten days," Renaldo said. "We have a lot to carry, and there will be times when we cannot move. And much of our movement will have to be at night."

John nodded. "Then we'd better get started." He returned to Annaliese. "We'd better change into these army fatigues. You can do it behind the shed. Then we'll empty our gear into one of those kitbags, and dump our suitcases on that fire. We don't want to leave any trace that we were ever here."

She clutched his hand. "We're going to Italy, now?"

"We're working on it."

Ten days, he thought. Trust London to have supposed he could just snap his fingers and be translated from Montreux to Lake Garda. For those ten days he would be totally out of touch with anything that might be happening in the war, including the invasion of Sicily.

And Mussolini?

He had never been very keen on mountaineering.

Kurt Krueger stamped into the office and threw his cap into a corner. Both Margo and the woman secretary who was working with her looked up in alarm.

"There has been a disaster," Krueger announced.

They waited. Even Margo had learned that with Krueger it was not wise ever to be facetious, although the temptation to say, "Another one?" was enormous. But she was thinking of Russia.

"Four of our people are dead," Krueger said.

"But . . . how?"

"Shot to death, you silly cow," Krueger said. "By Warrey."

"Warrey? How could he kill four men all by himself?"

"Well, it seems he had some assistance. But he is undoubtedly responsible. The man appears to be a devil."

"Tell us what happened," Margo begged.

"I told you, we traced them to Montreux, and through the local British agent to a lonely farmhouse in the hills south-east of the town. We sent in four of our best agents to arrest him and the woman. They disappeared from our knowledge for three days. Then a Swiss police patrol found the farmhouse burned out. In it were six dead men and one woman. All shot or blown up by hand grenades, several burned out of all recognition.

What is left of the farmhouse is a shambles of bullet marks. There seems to have been a pitched battle. The Swiss police are highly agitated about it."

"You said six men," Margo pointed out.

"Four were our people. They had sufficient identification to reveal that they were Germans, so our consul was called in. He realised what must have happened and summoned our local head agent, and he has identified the men, privately, of course."

"Then who were the others?" Her heart pounded. Could one of them possibly be Warrey? Shot down in a gun battle in a neutral country? She didn't know whether to be pleased or sorry about that.

"One of the other men, and the woman, have been identified as the owners of the farmhouse. They were obviously in British pay. The other man is a mystery. He had no identification. But he was blown up by what seems to have been his own grenade, outside of the farmhouse, so we may presume he was one of Warrey's people."

"Did he have people? Could it not have been Warrey himself?"

"We do not think so. This man was very young, early twenties. Warrey is much older than that, is he not?"

"Yes," Margo said thoughtfully. John would be in his middle thirties, she supposed. "Then there is no sign of Warrey or the woman Coparro?"

"Not a trace. The Swiss detectives have established that there were quite a few people surrounding the farmhouse, from the footprints. These footprints indicated that the assault force moved into the mountains, but the ground is very hard and the trail was soon lost."

"Do the Swiss police know the truth of the matter?"

"At the moment, no. But they know our people were involved, and they are making diplomatic representations. These will not amount to much; the Swiss cannot afford to offend us. It is Warrey that matters. He has got clear away. Into Italy."

"So he has gone into Italy," Margo said. "We were sure that was his destination, anyway, the moment we identified the woman Coparro. What can he do there?"

"A great deal," Krueger said. "There was another piece of news this morning: the Allies have invaded Sicily."

"Oh, my God!" Margo clasped both hands to her neck.

"Oh, I shouldn't think they are going to get very far," Krueger said. "Sicily is very strongly defended. It is the coincidence of these two events that is sinister. Warrey is sent to North Italy as the Allies land in Sicily. He is obviously intended to raise an anti-Fascist force in the north. And there are quite a few anti-Fascists around already, I can tell you. Besides, he has killed four of our men, after God alone knows how many in North Africa. He must be stopped."

"I think you are overrating him," Margo said.

Krueger glared at her, then reached across the desk, twined his fingers in her shirt front, and dragged her to her feet. She gave a little squeal of apprehension, while the secretary hastily removed herself to the far side of the room. "I will decide when I am overrating anybody," Krueger said. "Remember this." He threw her away from him so violently she all but overbalanced as she hit her chair.

It was several seconds before she could think straight. But getting angry was a waste of time; she had made this bed, and she had to lie on it for the foreseeable future. "What are you going to do?"

"We are going to find him, and hang him," Krueger said. "And his lady friend. To do this, we will need to take hostages. But this has not worked very well in the past. Too many of these people like to regard themselves as martyrs. We will have to beat Warrey's whereabouts out of them. So, in the first instance, you are being seconded to SS headquarters in Milan."

"Milan?" Her voice rose an octave. "Me?"

"Yes, you, you silly bitch," Krueger said. "You know Warrey. You know what he looks like. You should be able to identify him, even disguised. You know his habits, how he works. You will sit in on all interrogations of the partisans we pick up, and you will determine how much of what they tell us is the truth. This is a top priority assignment. Warrey must be taken, and soon. Do you understand this?"

Margo licked her lips. "Yes, Herr Captain."

How odd, she thought, that she, who had once been captured and interrogated by the Italian secret police, an experience she would never forget, should now be working with an even more sinister force, the Gestapo. But again she had to remember that it had been her decision to bring this about; she could not change her mind now. And was not John Warrey also *her* prime objective?

"When do I leave, for Milan?" she asked.

"This afternoon," Krueger told her.

"I do not think my feet will ever be the same again," Annaliese complained, slowly drawing off her boots to look at them.

"We should've brought your wheelchair," John quipped, sitting beside her.

One of Renaldo's men was lighting a fire for their evening meal, and the scene on the hillside was positively sylvan, as they had bivouaced in a clump of trees. Only the pile of weapons jarred; it jarred in other ways as well – he doubted his back and shoulders were going to recover in a hurry from carrying several tommy-guns and their cans of ammunition slung around his neck.

They had now been walking for five days, making surprisingly good time. They kept to the foothills, and although, with the weather clear, they had indeed seen the Jungfrau looming in front of them – John even thought, early on, that he had caught a glimpse of the Matterhorn, away to the south on the Italian border – they had not been forced into any real mountaineering.

They had by-passed several hamlets, cosily lit at night, while they had shivered out in the open. But their progress had only been seriously impeded once, when a Swiss army airplane had flown low along the valleys. They didn't doubt it was looking for them, but they saw it long before it came too close, and were able to shelter beneath the trees.

"Tell me your plans," Renaldo said, that evening. "It is to disrupt the Germans, eh? Blow up their railway lines. But you know, they are our railway lines, as well."

"Not right this minute, if they are controlled by the Germans," John pointed out.

Renaldo considered this. "We would need a lot more dynamite than we have now," he said. "Is it possible to obtain this?"

"It may be," John said. "But I have not come specifically to blow up railway lines. That is incidental. How many partisans would you estimate are in the mountains?"

"Many," Renaldo said.

"Could you be a little more specific?"

"I cannot put a number on it," Renaldo said. "There are many bands. Maybe twenty or thirty. Each with perhaps fifty people. But these include women and children."

"Can these women fight?"

Renaldo grinned. "They would like to fight. But women . . ." he glanced at Annaliese, who appeared to be asleep. "They are not reliable."

"You think not?" John recalled women like Soroya or Uluma, who had been more reliable in battle than many men. He did not suppose Italian woman would be very different to the Senussi, when the chips were down. "Are there enough weapons for all?"

"No," Renaldo said. "With these weapons you have brought me, my people will be the best armed in North Italy." Another grin. "Apart from the Germans."

"Still, fifteen hundred men, and women, if we could arm them all, would be a sizeable force."

"And children," Renaldo put in.

"Are they all anti-Fascist?"

"I do not think so. Except for the Communists."

"Eh? I was given to understand—"

"They are all anti-*German*," Renaldo explained. "And so

they are against the Italians who fight with the Germans. But they are not necessarily anti-Fascist. Fascism has done a lot of good for our country. Il Duce, until he took up with Hitler, was a great man. He did great things. He gave us work, and he drained the Pontine Marshes to clear the malaria." Another grin. "He even made the trains to run on time. In Italy, that is a great achievement. We are not a punctual people."

"You sound as if you admire him."

"Like I said, he was a great man."

"And now?"

Renaldo shrugged. "He should not have gone into this war, on the side of the Germans. That was not wise."

John was wondering if he had not been forced to bite off more than he could chew, if these people were so totally ambivalent, politically. "My business is to organise a partisan fighting force that can face up to the Germans," he said. "Distract them from fighting the Allies."

Renaldo gazed at him for several seconds. Then he snorted. "That is not possible."

"Because of German strength?"

"They are strong," Renaldo agreed. "But our people—I said there might be thirty bands. They call themselves partisans, but that is just a word, eh? Some of them are brigands, and they have always been brigands. Their fathers and their grandfathers before them have always been brigands. That they are now fighting the Germans is only because the people they have always robbed have nothing left to steal. Then there are the Communists. They oppose the Fascists and the Nazis. They have been doing this for a long time. But they also oppose you British and the Americans. They pretend to be on your side at the moment because they are told to behave so from Moscow. But in their hearts they would just as soon fight you."

"And then there are the partisans like yourself," John suggested. "True patriots."

Talk about ass-licking, he thought. But without Renaldo he was a dead duck.

Renaldo grinned. "I am a brigand, Colonel. My father was a brigand, and so was my grandfather.

"What are you going to do?" Annaliese asked, snuggling against him in her blanket; they were both too cold to take off any clothing.

"You mean you were awake all the time?"

"I am your support. I need to be awake, all the time."

"So tell me, what are you, a brigand, a Communist, or a patriot?"

"I am an anti-Fascist. I wish to see Italy restored to what it was before Mussolini."

"May I ask a personal question?"

"Certainly. I do not have to answer it."

"How old are you?"

"I am twenty-eight."

"Then you were only ten years old when Mussolini took office. You can't remember too much about what Italy was like before then."

"I can remember. And my mother told me of it."

"Your mother being—?"

"Dead," Annaliese said.

John decided against asking how she had died. Or why. "According to Renaldo, in those days the trains didn't run on time," he reminded her.

The train clanked to a halt in Milan Central, and Margo, waiting in the corridor, stepped down. The sun was shining, and it did not appear that Milan had ever been bombed. People sauntered to and fro, smiling and chattering, but there were a lot of soldiers to be seen, most of them Germans.

"Fräulein Cartwright?" The officer clicked his heels and bent over her hand. He wore the black uniform of the SS, and was very smart. He was also very handsome, with surprisingly dark hair and brown eyes. Even more disturbingly, he was very young. My God, Margo thought, he is younger than I. Which wasn't all that difficult, she supposed, as she was on the wrong side of thirty-five. He wore the insignia of a major. "My car is waiting." An orderly picked up her bag and the officer escorted her through the throng to the station forecourt. "My name is Johann Wiedelier."

"My pleasure," Margo said, getting into the back of the open touring car.

"I am to be, how shall we say, your control," Wiedelier explained.

"I'm happy with that. It's a matter of sitting in on interrogations, right?"

"Not entirely. We really need to apprehend this man Warrey, and quickly. So you may have to go out into the field. But you have served in the field before, I am told."

"Yes," Margo said. "But I thought I was done with that."

Wiedelier glanced at her. "You are not afraid of this?"

"I . . . no, I am not afraid."

"I am glad of that, because, you see, if you are afraid, your value decreases."

It was her turn to glance at him. Was he threatening her?

He smiled. "But you will be well protected, at all times. I shall be with you, as well as an escort of my men."

"Thank you. May I ask what is the news from Sicily?"

He frowned. "How do you know about Sicily? Officially, there is no news."

"But I know there is."

"That is careless of someone."

"I had assumed I was someone who could be trusted."

"Everyone assumes that," Wiedelier commented. "However . . . the news is not good. The Allies are ashore and seem able to maintain themselves. I have no doubt we shall hold them. Especially if this attempt to raise northern Italy in their behalf can be nipped in the bud. Here is where you will stay."

It looked quite a good hotel. Wiedelier actually held the door for her, and escorted her into the lobby, where an obsequious manager in a morning suit greeted the SS officer effusively.

"You have a room for us," Wiedelier suggested.

"Of course, Herr Major. If the signorina would just sign—"

"I will sign," Wiedelier said, and did so.

A bellboy picked up Margo's suitcase and led them to the lift. "We do not wish anyone to know that you were ever here," Wiedelier explained.

The bellboy carefully studied the controls, never moving his eyes.

Margo was escorted along the corridor and the bedroom door was opened for her. The room was not nearly as good as that she had occupied at Shepheard's in Cairo, when she had been working for British Intelligence in Egypt, but it seemed comfortable enough. The bellboy placed her bag on the rack and withdrew; he did not seem to expect a tip, and Wiedelier did not offer him one.

"No doubt you will wish to change," Wiedelier said. "Then . . ." he turned back his cuff with a gloved forefinger to look at his watch. "We can lunch. Is that satisfactory?"

"Most satisfactory. But I should point out that I already have a . . . lover. Captain Krueger."

"As you say, Fräulein. Krueger is a captain. I am a major. And I am not going to have sex with you. I am your Control. I will wait." He took off his cap and gloves, and laid them together with his swagger stick on the table.

"Ah . . . I would like to take a bath."

"Use the shower," he recommended. "It is quicker."

He obviously didn't intend to move. Well, she thought, if it gives him a kick . . . She undressed, facing him. His expression never changed, although a little colour crept into his pale cheeks.

"Have you ever been married?" he asked.

"No."

"Why is this? You are an attractive woman."

"Marriage is a dead end," she told him, and went into the bathroom. When she re-emerged, towelling herself, he had not moved.

"You have a tight ass," he remarked. "I like tight asses. Who knows, I may wish to have sex with you after all. One day. Now get dressed. It is time for lunch."

"There it is," Renaldo said proudly.

John sank to his haunches to look down from the hills onto the broad sheet of water beneath him, still a good distance away.

"Lake Garda is famous in history," Renaldo told him. "A thousand years ago a queen of Italy, Adelaide – she was actually French – was imprisoned in the castle overlooking the lake. She appealed for help to the then King of Germany, Otto the Saxon. He came and rescued her, and married her, invading Italy to do so." He grinned. "I think we have hated the Germans ever since that time."

A thousand years, John thought. But then, the English and the French had hated each other for almost as long, and were now allies.

"And then," Renaldo went on, "just on the other side of the lake is the River Adige, and the town of Rivoli. At Rivoli in 1797 Napoleon Bonaparte defeated the Austrians, and virtually conquered Italy, for France."

"I thought you were enemies of the French?" John asked.

"Ah, but Napoleon was actually Italian, by birth," Renaldo riposted.

"How far from here to your camp?" Annaliese asked, a trifle impatiently. She was not apparently into history.

They were all exhausted, and they had not bathed for a fortnight; John's beard was as straggly as that of any of the partisans, and he felt that if he stepped out of his clothes they would simply keep on walking without him.

"Another day or so," Renaldo said. "My camp is to the north-east of the lake."

"Holy Mother," she muttered.

The ten days had turned into twenty, as their progress had slowed. The mountains had seemed to cluster more closely together, and the valleys were shorter and less easy to traverse. John could not imagine what it might be like here in the dead of winter.

"But now we are in Italy," Renaldo said proudly.

"Is that good?" John asked, pointing at the aircraft circling overhead. It was well up, and he did not suppose its crew could see the small band of partisans, concealed as they were by the trees, but it carried German markings, and was an indication that they were now in enemy controlled territory.

"They are always there," Renaldo said contemptuously. "Sometimes they even drop bombs. But they seldom hit anything save the ground. As soon as it is gone, we will move on."

"A bath," Annaliese said. "I would give a thousand lira for a bath."

"It's coming closer," John assured her.

It was dawn, and they crept down the slopes, not that they were in any way approaching sea-level; the lake was several hundred feet up. It was behind them now, over their right shoulders. But they were approaching civilisation; below them there was a good road, and on the road they saw a line of trucks.

"Are those Italian, or German?" John asked.

Renaldo studied them through his binoculars. "German, coming out of Austria." He licked his lips. "What do you reckon?"

"That we should let them get on with it," John said.

"I think, that as they are there, and we are here, we should attack them."

"To what purpose? There are eight trucks. At even twenty-five men to a truck, that is two hundred men. They have machine-guns and rifles. We are twenty-one, with tommy-guns and pistols. It would be suicide, and we would achieve nothing."

Renaldo looked at Annaliese.

"He knows about these things," she said.

Renaldo snorted, and then jerked his head, as there came a burst of firing from below them. All the partisans stood up to have a better look. The lead German truck had struck some kind of obstacle, probably a land mine, John thought. It had slewed sideways and come off the road, plunging down the parapet to come to rest with its hood in a bush. The second had also skidded, right across the road. Those behind had necessarily halted, but they were now spewing men, who fired as they leapt from the vehicles, while machine-guns were also being uncovered.

"We must help them now," Renaldo said. He waved his arm, and his men dumped their surplus gear on the ground before moving down the slope.

John looked at Annaliese, then shrugged, and followed, the woman behind him. They each carried two tommy-guns as well as their pistols, and John had a string of grenades. They could indeed be Senussi, he thought, in their anxiety for a fight, their refusal to accept any orders in the presence of the enemy, save attack.

For the moment their advance was unnoticed, as the Germans were concentrating their fire on the lower slopes, where the other partisans were embedded. Renaldo's men had almost reached the road before they were spotted, and then a hail of bullets were sent in their direction. Renaldo's people returned fire, while going to ground amidst the trees and bushes, but at least one of them had been hit, from the sudden screams close at hand.

"Keep down," John told Annaliese. They lay together, firing their tommy-guns. "I need to get close enough to use the grenades," he said. "Keep me covered."

"Johnnie!" She held his hand for a moment. "Do not get killed. Please!"

"Hasn't happened yet," he assured her, then sent himself rolling down the slope. Presuming he had been hit, the Germans paid no attention to him; they were in any event suffering severe casualties, exposed as they were on the road to fire from both sides, but they were still maintaining both discipline and aggression, and John presumed the partisans were also taking losses.

He arrived on the ditch beside the road, gasped for breath as he drew the pin from the first grenade, and lobbed it over the parapet on to the second truck. The explosion was instantaneous, accompanied by shrieks of pain and dismay. Immediately he sent another grenade behind the first, and was surrounded by a vast "Oorah!" as the partisans realised they had the victory. John threw three more grenades, in the direction of the next trucks in line, before he got up to admire his handiwork. Three of the trucks were blazing, surrounded by dead bodies and wounded men; some of these also were on fire. The three at the rear had managed to turn by shunting to and fro, and were driving north as fast as they could; they too had left several casualties behind them. The remaining two were immobile, hit in their engines and with their tyres shot out, and from these men were emerging, hands raised, shouting their surrender.

"You are a demon," Renaldo said, slapping John on the shoulder.

"I'm well trained, you mean," John said.

"*My* demon." Annaliese put her arms round him and kissed him on the mouth.

"Renaldo!"

The other partisans had emerged from the trees below the road. There were about fifty of them, led by a short, swarthy fellow, with very broad shoulders and a deep torso; he wore a heavy black beard. Mixed in with his men were several women, wearing a variety of clothes from dresses through pants to previously captured German tunics, and all armed, their hair floating in the breeze. They made John think of Greek maenads. But they were the people he had come to lead.

"Shit!" Renaldo muttered.

"Problem?" John asked.

"These are Communists," Renaldo said, then went forward with arms outstretched. "Alexandro, my old friend."

The two leaders embraced, but Alexandro was more interested in John and Annaliese. Now he disengaged himself from Renaldo and came towards them. "You are not Italian," he told John.

"As a matter of fact, I'm English," John explained.

"He is the great Colonel Warrey," Renaldo said enthusiastically. "Come to lead us against the Nazis."

Alexandro snorted.

"Colonel Warrey threw the grenades that destroyed those trucks," Annaliese said, even more enthusiastically.

"And who are you?" Alexandro demanded.

"I am Annaliese Coparro. My husband was Roberto Coparro," Annaliese said proudly.

"Roberto Coparro was a capitalist swine," Alexandro said.

John caught Annaliese's hand as it was reaching for her pistol. "We're all on the same side now," he reminded her.

Alexandro gave another snort. "You have come to command, Englishman? Where are your men?"

"You are my men," John said, staring at him.

Alexandro returned the stare, and was distracted by one of his people. "What do we do with these prisoners, General?"

General, John thought. Now here was a problem.

"We do not take prisoners," Alexandro said. "Kill them."

The man grinned, and waved his arm.

"Now hold on just one moment," John said.

"It is true," Renaldo said. "How are we to take prisoners? What are we to do with them?" He had a point.

"We are certainly not going to murder them in cold blood," John said. "If we cannot keep them, then we must let them go."

"Let Germans go?" Alexandro was horrified.

"I wish one of them," one of the women said.

"Eh?" John asked. "What for?"

"Luana and her sister were raped by the Nazis," Alexandro explained. "Her sister died because of it. Ever since she has dreamed of having a German to cut up."

Shades of the Senussi. But these people were supposed to be Christians. John looked at Annaliese. "She has a right," Annaliese said.

"Do you think you have that right?"

"Yes, I do. But I am waiting for the right one."

John scratched his head.

"I will choose one," Luana said, and went towards the prisoners, who had accumulated in a group, surrounded by the partisans. Presumably they did not speak Italian, but they could tell their fate was being decided. Luana walked round them, slowly. She was quite a pretty young woman, or she would have been but for the demonic gleam in her eyes.

"If necessary, I will need your backing," John told Annaliese. "And yours, Renaldo."

"You cannot interfere," Renaldo protested. "This is a matter of honour."

"You left out the 'dis'," John said, and went forward, right hand resting on the pistol at his hip.

"I will have that one," Luana said, pointing at a very young man, hardly more than a boy. "He will scream very loud when I cut off his balls."

"Forget it," John advised her. "You—" he had spotted someone wearing the insignia of an officer. Now he spoke German.

"Are you going to let them murder us?" the officer asked.

"No," John said. "Get your men together and go, up the road to the north."

The lieutenant stared at him in amazement. "You are going to let us go?"

"That's the idea. I would get on with it, if I were you. I don't know for how long I am going to be able to hold these people in check. But if you hurry you should be able to regain your trucks."

The officer shouted orders, and his men lined up, glancing right and left in apprehensive disbelief. Several of the partisans took up positions across the road in front of the Germans, tommy-guns levelled.

"Tell your people," John said to Alexandro, "that I have given an order that these people are to be allowed through, and that I will shoot the first man, or woman, who disobeys me."

"You think you can do this?" Alexandro inquired. "I have forty-three men and women here, who will obey me to the death."

"That is probably very good," John said, "If they disobey *me*, you will be the first to die."

The two men glared at each other. Alexandro was clearly dumbfounded by such impudence. But John, as so often in the past, was filled with a white-hot determination. It had carried him to a great many successes, and it was the only way he knew how to deal with situations such as this. It was a matter of wills, and determined readiness.

As he had anticipated, Alexandro attempted to react violently to the threat, and reached for the pistol in his belt. But John was quicker, and had drawn his own weapon and presented it to Alexandro's head before the Italian could get his hands on the butt of his gun. There was an immense rustle throughout the assembled partisans, but no one moved, because no one at that moment doubted that if they did, Alexandro would have his head blown off.

Alexandro licked his lips. "You can permit this?" he asked a frightened but delighted Renaldo.

"It is his way," Renaldo said. "Anyone who gets in his way, he shoots them, dead."

"And you will support him," Alexandro grumbled.

"He is our commanding officer, sent by the Allies," Annaliese said, severely.

"The Allies," Alexandro sneered, but he took his hand away from his gun, and then grinned. "Oh, let the Nazis go. We can kill them the next time they come down. We are to celebrate, eh? Have you not heard the news? Il Duce has been arrested."

The SS

"What did you say?" Renaldo shouted.

"Mussolini has been thrown out of the Grand Council of Fascists," Alexandro said. "He has been placed under house arrest."

Renaldo looked at John. "What does this mean?"

"It means the end of Fascist rule in Italy," Annaliese declared. "This is a great day."

"Not so fast," Alexandro said. "There has been no talk of an ending of Fascist rule. Only that there has been a change at the top. Our struggle goes on."

"Absolutely," John agreed. "Our business is to beat the Germans."

"And the Fascisti," Alexandro added.

"Of course. Are you going to tell your people to stand aside?"

Alexandro hesitated a last time, then shouted at his people to let the Germans through. Luana jumped up and down and waved her arms in frustration, but she was restrained by her friends. "Where do you go, now?" Alexandro asked John.

"Colonel Warrey comes with me, to join my people," Renaldo said proudly.

"Your people," Alexandro sneered.

"You are welcome to come too," John said. "In fact, I would like word sent to all the partisan leaders in this area, that I would like to see them, to discuss our plans."

"They are fools and brigands," Alexandro said. "And some of them are Fascisti at heart."

He looked speculatively at Renaldo.

"Nevertheless, if they are fighting the Germans, I would like to speak with them. Can you get word to them?"

"I can do anything," Alexandro said. "Now let us see what we have here."

His people were already stripping the dead, seeking boots and helmets, as well as any money that could be found. Now Alexandro had them assembling the captured weapons and ammunition. Renaldo sent some of his own people back up the hill to bring down the weapons they had discarded in their attack. "Now we must move on," he told John.

"Should we not remain here awhile, and cement our friendship with these people?" John asked.

"Friendship?" Renaldo snorted. "You gained a great victory, just now, by virtue of your courage and determination. But Alexandro hates you, for humiliating him in front of his people. He will kill you, the moment he gets the opportunity."

John looked at Annaliese. "Renaldo is right," she said. "We are not safe here."

"If he wants to kill me," John said, "will he ever have a better opportunity than right now?"

The Communist band was now armed with the German weapons as well as their own; even the women were brandishing at least two rifles with strings of ammunition pouches hanging round their necks.

"He will not start anything now," Renaldo said, "because he is afraid he would have to fight my people as well. Many would be killed, and there would be bad blood. But if he could come upon you alone, at night—"

"I see," John said. "You understand I had to do what I did."

"No," Renaldo said. "When the Germans capture our people, they hang them. Why should we not do the same to them?"

"Because we are fighting this war to stop things like lynchings and wholesale executions."

Renaldo snorted. "You will never do that, Signor Colonel. It is in man's blood to lynch and shoot his enemies, those who have destroyed his homes and his loved ones. Now let us move out."

Alexandro came back to them. "You will not stay? We have found food, and good German beer. We will have a feast."

"Bring your food and beer to my place north of the lake," Renaldo said. "We will have our feast there."

"Ha ha," Alexandro said. "Perhaps we will do that. I will see you again, Signor Englishman."

"I hope so," John said.

The Communists watched Renaldo's people filing off along the road. One or two fired their guns, but these were into the air.

"Will he come?" John asked.

"Oh, he will come."

"And will he send out word to the other commanders?"

"Maybe. Maybe they will come too. Everyone will be curious, to see the great Englishman. As to what they will do then—" Renaldo shrugged.

As to what, John thought. His task, uniting these people into a single fighting force, seemed more difficult every time he considered it. But it had to be done, or at least, attempted. And actually, his path seemed quite clearly delineated. Renaldo was following him like a faithful dog because he had proved himself a superior fighting man. Alexandro had surrendered to him, at least in the short term, because he had shown himself prepared to kill to have his own way. The partisans as a group would only follow him, and obey him, and fight together under his leadership, if he continued to prove he was the man to give them victory over the Germans. Obviously he had to avoid attempting victory over the Fascists until he saw how things worked out down in Rome – and how people reacted to those events up here. He already knew that Renaldo, while prepared to fight against Mussolini as long as the Fascisti supported the Germans, was a great admirer of Il Duce.

Annaliese walked beside him, through the trees. "I am so proud to be your woman," she said.

"You are not my woman," he pointed out.

"Yet," she said, enigmatically.

The retreating Germans must have made contact with their forces, because that afternoon the valleys were ranged by fighter-bombers, roaring up and down between the mountain peaks. The partisans had to take shelter in the trees, while the Germans shot up anything that moved and occasionally dropped bombs.

"If we are lucky, one of those planes will fly into a mountain," Renaldo said.

"If we are more lucky, one of those bombs will fall on Alexandro," Annaliese suggested.

Renaldo gave her a startled glance, and John added another assessment of the situation to those he had already made. Renaldo disliked Alexandro – he did not think it could be put stronger than that – because he was a Communist. He also feared him, although that could just be because at the moment Alexandro commanded more men. But he did not wish to see him killed.

They trekked on, mostly downhill, until later that afternoon Renaldo pointed. "Garda."

John peered through the trees, again saw the glistening water, now much closer at hand. It was certainly a large lake, some twenty miles long, he estimated; its width varied from quite narrow in the north to perhaps ten miles wide towards the south. From this distance it was difficult to make out details, but he thought he could see the roofs and spires of a town on the far side, and there were some boats on the lake itself.

"There is good fish in that lake," Renaldo said.

"And where is your camp?"

"It is in the hills north-east of the water. We go there now."

They reached Renaldo's encampment at dusk, an untidy accumulation of tents and lean-tos sheltering beneath the trees, to a wildly excited welcome, from dogs as well as people.

"Oh, Renaldo!" cried an elderly woman, hugging him and kissing him on both cheeks. "It has been so long. We did not think you would come back."

Renaldo was embarrassed. "My mother," he explained, apologetically.

John also received a hug and a kiss. "Now we win the war, eh?"

"I sincerely hope so, Signora."

She turned her attention to Annaliese. "You," she said. "I remember you. Such a pretty girl."

"I am a woman now, Signora Pescaro," Annaliese pointed out.

"A beautiful woman. You are with him?" She looked at John.

"Should I not be?" Annaliese asked.

Signora Pescaro cackled happily.

"This is my wife," Renaldo said, having been doing some more hugging and kissing. "Maria Theresa."

The girl was disturbingly young; John did not place her a day over sixteen. She had somewhat plain features but a mass of curly dark hair and a plump figure.

Renaldo could see that the Englishman was critical. "My first wife was killed," he explained. "By the Nazis."

"Ah." John shook hands. "I am pleased to meet you, Signora Pescaro."

"And this is my brother, Cesare," Renaldo said, proudly. Here was a younger edition of the bandit chief, with somewhat stronger features. And at the moment, sceptical features as well. "Cesare is my second-in-command," Renaldo explained. "Now he is your third-in-command, eh?" He grinned.

Cesare did not grin. "We have expected you, Signor Warrey."

"Colonel Warrey," Renaldo corrected. "He will lead us against the Germans."

"But you lead us against the Germans, Renaldo," Cesare said.

"Colonel Warrey is a great fighting man. I have seen him kill Germans. Oh, yes. This is my other brother, Marco."

A very young boy, hardly a teenager, John estimated.

"He does not command yet," Renaldo explained. "But if the war does not end soon, he will, eh?"

Marco had the burning eyes of his brothers.

"And this is my sister-in-law, Bianca."

John was surprised. Bianca Pescaro was a truly beautiful young woman, in her early twenties, John estimated. She had long, straight black hair shrouding almost Madonna-like features, and, so far as could be judged as her dress was entirely shapeless, an excellent figure. Certainly her bare feet could not be faulted.

"My pleasure," he said, taking her hand.

"And mine, Colonel Warrey," she said, in a deep and surprisingly cultured voice. But everything about her suggested that she was a cut above the people with whom she now lived – and into whom she had married.

"Bianca's family were rich, before the Fascisti," Renaldo said.

"Maybe they'll be rich again, after the Fascisti," John promised.

The introductions went on for some time. Nearly everyone in the group was at least a distant relation of Renaldo and his mother and brothers; their father had been killed early in the war. But there was grief as well. "Arnaldo," a woman wailed. "Oh, my Arnaldo."

"He died well," Renaldo assured the widow. "Fighting the Germans."

"My Arnaldo," she shrieked again, and threw herself on the ground to weep. One of the dogs licked her face.

"They had not been married long," Renaldo told John. Maria Theresa and Bianca comforted her.

Then it was time to eat, a huge feast considering that these people were essentially fugitives. But they were fugitives in their own back yard, and as Renaldo had said, there were fish in the lake as well as game in the mountains, while John gathered they received a good deal of support from the villagers of the area – how much of this was voluntary and how much requisitioned there was no means of telling, but he felt he should find out.

"You are not where I expected," Renaldo remarked to his brother.

"We had to move camp because of the planes," Cesare told him. "Many planes."

"They were looking for us," Renaldo said. "We destroyed a German column, yesterday."

"A column?" Cesare's eyes were wide.

"Colonel Warrey led us," Renaldo said, as proudly as ever. "He destroyed the column."

"With a little bit of help from Alexandro and his people," John said, modestly.

"You have seen Alexandro?" Cesare asked.

"He helped us with the Germans," Renaldo said contemptuously, apparently deciding to overlook the fact that the Communists had been attacking the column before his men got there.

"They think you are a demi-god," Annaliese remarked, in English; she was sitting beside John, chewing on a chicken-bone, her arm repeatedly nudged by one of the dogs.

"Every little helps," he agreed.

"Especially that Bianca. I saw the way you looked at her, and she at you. She would lie down beside you in a wink."

"I don't think—"

"If she did that, Cesare would put a knife in your back," Annaliese said.

"I don't doubt it for a moment."

"And I would put a knife in her back."

"Because you think you're my woman? I thought there was to be no sex between us?"

"Things have changed," she promised him.

Shit, he thought. The idea of having sex with Annaliese – or with Bianca for that matter – was extremely attractive, especially for a man who had had no creature comfort for three weeks now, but he really had not come here to engage in a series of adulterous romances.

"Tomorrow we talk, eh?" Renaldo said, pouring the last of the wine. "But tonight, we sleep."

"I think that's a good idea," John said. "I really am exhausted."

"I will make you strong again," Annaliese said. "Come."

The partisans were bedding down for the night; there was a good deal of giggling coming from the Pescaro tents; the girls were apparently glad to have their menfolk back again. It was just dusk, the sun long gone behind the hills but the afterglow throwing up shadows in the trees. Annaliese was climbing further down the slope towards the small river than ran through the bottom of the valley; following her, John slipped once or twice, but he arrived on the bank beside her.

"I have looked forward to this for the past three weeks," Annaliese said.

He wasn't sure whether she meant the bath or what she hoped might come afterwards. She threw her clothes on the ground and slipped into the water, gave a little shriek. "Cold!"

John followed her. The water was distinctly chilly, as was her skin when he caught up with her. She laughed, and slipped through his fingers, diving beneath the surface to soak her hair. "That feels so good," she gasped when she came up. "I believe that is the longest I have ever been without a bath. I was beginning to hate myself."

"Snap," he said, and caught up with her again. They were both out of their depths now, and when they twined their legs they sank for a moment, to surface again, spluttering.

"Now I feel clean enough to fuck," she said, and climbed out.

"What changed your mind?" he asked, following. "About sex?"

"It is a woman's privilege, to change her mind," she said primly, finding a patch of ground suitable for sitting on. Or lying.

He knelt beside her. "I hope it was not the sight of me killing people."

"You kill people very well," she said. "I think you will make love as well."

"You are a monster," he said.

She gazed at him, sadly. "And you have nothing for me. You have held me naked in your arms, and you have nothing for me. Is this wife of yours so beautiful?"

"She is not as beautiful as you, Annaliese. But she is my wife. And . . . I'm just too tired."

"Too tired for sex," she remarked. And then smiled. "No matter. You will soon not be tired. Tonight we can sleep."

John did not know if the partisans knew where they had spent the night, or indeed cared. Next morning they were all very serious as they gathered round for breakfast, and to talk.

They also had a visitor, a short, squat man in a cassock and wearing a flat black hat.

"This is Father Pasquale," Renaldo said. "He looks after our souls."

The father was actually hearing confession from all of them in turn. When he was finished he sat beside John. "You are the famous Colonel Warrey," he remarked.

"Even to you?"

"I spent last night with Alexandro."

"I thought the Communists did not believe in religion?"

"Italian Communists are not as others. In Italy, all men believe in religion." He scowled at Annaliese, sitting on John's other side. "And all women, too. You have not confessed."

"I have nothing to confess, Father," Annaliese said, a trifle sulkily.

Pasquale considered this. "Everyone has something to confess," he pointed out. "Even if it is only their thoughts. And you, Englishman?"

"I am a Protestant, Father."

Pasquale made the sign of the cross. "May God have mercy on your soul. You have come here to kill Germans?" His tone suggested that might go some way to saving that soul.

"In due course. I have come here to create a partisan army, if that is possible. Renaldo says it is not."

"Renaldo has no vision."

"Now, that kind of talk I can listen to," John said. "I need to speak to all the partisan leaders. Is this possible?"

"I do not know why it should be difficult."

"You know where to find the other groups?"

"*Si, si,* I can find them. But it will take time."

"How much time?"

"Maybe two weeks, to find them all, and persuade them to come to a grand council."

"Only their leaders," John reminded him. "If we accumulated all of our people in one place the Germans would find it too easy to wipe us out. But I would like you to start right away. Until we have that meeting, we are going to keep a very low profile . . . out of sight," he explained, as they looked puzzled by the idiom. "Now . . ." He turned to Renaldo and Cesare. "This news of Mussolini's downfall, how did Alexandro receive it? Does he have a radio?"

"I do not think so," Renaldo said.

"Then how did the news come? Where is your radio?"

Cesare shook his head. "We do not have a radio, either."

Shit, John thought; another foul-up. "I was told you had a radio."

"We have a friend in Rivoli. Bianca's uncle. He has a radio. He takes messages for us. He will have heard the news and sent it into the hills."

"Right. I need to contact Bianca's uncle."

"You must go to him. He will not come to us."

John looked at Renaldo. "Is this possible?"

"Why not? With your beard and our clothing, no one could mistake you for an English officer. You have an identity card?"

John nodded.

"But you will need a guide."

"I will guide Colonel Warrey," Bianca said.

"Do you think that is a good idea?" John asked, glancing at Cesare, who did not seem in the least concerned.

"It is best she do this," he said. "As I said, the man with the radio is her uncle."

"She can guide you," Annaliese said. "I will come too. One man and two women, eh?"

"That is best," Renaldo said. "It will take you two days to go to Rivoli, and two back. By then Pasquale will have found

77

some of the partisan groups, and we will have their initial responses, eh?"

"Up, up," Wiedelier snapped.

Margo sat up and pushed hair from her forehead. Although he had never touched her – she had no doubt he was homosexual – she had become wary of his moods over the past fortnight, which had become increasingly unpredictable since Mussolini's removal from office. No one in the German army could doubt there was a crisis ahead, and neither German nor Italian troops were proving capable of stopping the steady Allied takeover of Sicily; rumours were starting to circulate that some Italian units were showing too much willingness to surrender.

But this morning, although as impatient as ever, Wiedelier was triumphant. "We have located Warrey," he announced.

"In Italy?"

"Well, of course in Italy. This was always his destination."

"You have arrested him? Killed him?"

"Not yet. But we have a rough idea of where he is. Yesterday one of our troop convoys was attacked and shot up by a band of partisans. Some of our men were taken prisoner, but then released again." He grinned. "That is not partisan habits, eh? Usually they cut their prisoners' throats, at the very least. But these men were released at the behest of an English officer, who was in command of the partisans."

"Warrey?"

"It cannot be anyone else. So get dressed. We are going over there,"

"Over where?"

"The attack took place north-west of Lake Garda. That is where we will find him, if we act quickly enough."

Margo hurried. Quite apart from the pleasure of at last destroying Johnnie Warrey, his capture and elimination would, she felt, be a feather in her cap. She wanted to get back to Germany, and inspecting photographs. Although she would not admit it even to herself, she had been frightened by the ability of the Allies to land in Sicily, and maintain themselves. Fortress Europe! Of course they would never get across the straits of Messina. Wiedelier was quite definite about that. But suppose they did? Fortress Europe's southern rampart would then have to be the Alps! And she was on the wrong side of those, at the moment.

They moved out in style and force, several command cars, surrounded by motor-cycle outriders, and several truckloads of soldiers, each truck equipped with a heavy machine-gun, in front and at the rear.

"How many trucks were in the column attacked by Warrey?" Margo asked.

Wiedelier grinned. "More than this. But we are covered." Planes circled overhead. "In any event, we are not venturing into partisan country. I have sent troops there. Our business is to see what they bring back out."

It was some fifty miles to Brescia, and then another twenty to Desenzano del Garda, the town at the southern end of the lake. Their route was all on the Tuscan plain, but the mountains always loomed to the north. They reached Desenzano for lunch. The town was filled with German soldiers, as well as a body of Italians; the civilians prudently kept indoors, aware that something was happening.

They ate at the town hall, served by obsequious waiters, and then Margo was left to herself while Wiedelier went off for a conference with the local commanders. When he came back, he was rubbing his hands. "Several partisan groups have been identified from the air," he said. "Our people are moving out now to seek and destroy them."

They stood at the window to watch the trucks roaring up the road and out of the town. Beyond, the waters of the lake were covered in whitecaps as there was a brisk northerly wind. "It is very regular," Wiedelier explained. "It blows from the north in the morning, the locals call it the sover, and then from the south in the afternoon. That they call the ora. This will commence in about an hour."

"When will your people return?" she asked.

"Two or three days. You can holiday. But be careful."

He saw that she was, and while she was allowed to stroll through the town and down to the edge of the lake to look at the water, she was always accompanied by two armed soldiers. The locals stared at her in silent curiosity. They had no idea who she was, only that she was clearly someone of importance.

But there were few locals to be seen. Mussolini had been succeeded by Marshal Badoglio, who had announced himself to be the head of a non-Fascist government. Everyone was totally confused by this, especially in the north, where the Italian Fascist administration was of necessity working very closely with the German authorities, but as Badoglio had also proclaimed a state of martial law throughout the country, it was not possible for the locals to get together and discuss the situation without risking arrest.

"Depend upon it," Wiedelier told Margo at dinner. "That bastard means to betray us. Well, we shall see about that, if we have to shoot every Italian soldier."

Margo gulped, because she did not doubt he meant what he had said.

On the third day the seek and destroy mission returned. Margo was present when its captain reported to Wiedelier. "They are hard to catch, in those mountains," he complained. "They melt away, and take pot shots, and make themselves a thorough nuisance." He grinned at Margo. "It makes one understand what the British suffered on the north-west frontier of India, all of those years."

"But you did catch up with them?" Wiedelier asked, impatiently.

"We caught up with some of them," Captain Carlstein said.

"Did you find the Englishman?"

"We found no one who admitted he was the Englishman."

"But you have prisoners?"

"I have brought in six. Including one who might be the man you are looking for. But he will not speak."

Wiedelier grinned. "I think he will speak to us. Let us go and look at these prisoners, Fräulein Cartwright."

Margo discovered that her knees were quite weak as they went down the stairs into the courtyard, where the German soldiers were still disembarking and being marshalled. Against one wall the six prisoners were huddled, watched over by four soldiers, their rifles pointing at the unhappy people. Wiedelier and Carlstein led Margo up to the guards, while she felt physically sick. There were four men, a woman and a boy. The woman was quite old, in her sixties, Margo thought. The boy was very young, hardly a teenager, but clearly the woman's son.

The four men were all heavily bearded and had several bruises; one or two were even bleeding. "They did not surrender easily," Carlstein remarked.

"Are any of them Warrey?" Wiedelier asked Margo.

"No," she said. Was she relieved?

"How can you tell beneath the beards? Do you wish them shaved?"

"That will not be necessary. I have said, none of them is Warrey."

Wiedelier considered for a few moments. Then he said, "Very well. You." He pointed at the old woman. "You know this Warrey? An Englishman?"

Signora Pescaro gazed at him for some seconds, then spat on the ground. "I shall make you regret that," Wiedelier said. "You." He addressed the boy. "Tell me about this man Warrey."

Marco attempted to follow his mother's example and spit, but his mouth was too dry. Wiedelier gave another grin. "We will question these two," he said. "Take them inside."

Margo caught her breath. "What will you do to them?"

"Whatever takes my fancy. Come."

She glanced at Carlstein, who looked apologetic. He was a

professional soldier, and as such obeyed his orders, whatever they were. But he clearly did not enjoy interrogation sessions. "I will see you later, Fräulein," he said, clicked his heels, and returned to his men.

"What about the men?" Margo asked.

"They will be shot. When we have finished with these." He beckoned to more guards. "Up," he told Marco and Signora Pescaro.

Slowly they got to their feet. The men made to move also, but were kicked back to the ground by the guards. The two prisoners went through the opened door, into the basement of the building, where several more men waited.

"Put them in the shower," Wiedelier said.

"Strip," one of the guards commanded.

Marco looked at his mother in alarm.

"It is surprising how modest these people are," Wiedelier said. "Strip them," he told his men.

One of his men laid his hand on Signora Pescaro's arm, and she jerked herself free, and began to unbutton her dress, her cheeks flaming. Marco also began to undress.

"Why must they have showers?" Margo asked.

"Because I dislike interrogating people who stink of dirt and sweat," Wiedelier said. "I like my prisoners to be clean and sweet-smelling. Am I not fastidious?"

Yes, Margo thought. You are fastidious. She watched the two prisoners throw the last of their garments on the floor. Signora Pescaro no longer looked the least embarrassed, but Marco was trembling.

"In there." The guard pointed at the open shower stall.

Marco and his mother looked at each other, then went into the stall, where immediately two powerful jets of water exploded from nozzles set in the walls. Marco gave a little scream as he was almost thrown into his mother's arms, then regained his balance. "Give them soap," Wiedelier said.

A cake of soap was thrown into the stall. Signora Pescaro failed to catch it, but after scrabbling about on his hands and knees, Marco straightened with it in his hands.

"Scrub yourselves clean," Wiedelier commanded.

The prisoners obeyed, while Margo wondered whenever, if ever, they had had such a bath before. The men standing outside the stall could direct the jets as they chose, and they were moved from their victims' hair and faces, sending them spinning round, to their breasts and stomachs and groins, causing them to twist and turn as they desperately soaped their bodies.

"An amusing sight, is it not?" Wiedelier asked.

Margo turned away. "It is humiliating."

"It is nothing, compared with what will happen to them," he pointed out.

"Enough." The water was turned off, and the two prisoners panted for breath.

"Out here," Wiedelier said. They stepped out, hands touching, fingers twining.

"Now," Wiedelier said. "Tell me about this man, Warrey."

Marco opened his mouth, and then closed it again as his mother squeezed his fingers. Wiedelier had observed the exchange. "Throw the old bitch out," he told his men.

Signora Pescaro was grasped by the arms and hustled to the door, then expelled into the courtyard, naked as she was. The door was closed. "Now," Wiedelier said. "There is just you and us, eh, little boy?"

Marco trembled, his warming flesh a gigantic blancmange. "First, what is your name?" Wiedelier asked.

Marco licked his lips. "Marco Pescaro."

"Pescaro?" Wiedelier looked at his sergeant.

"That is the name of a well-known guerilla leader, Herr Major."

"So, Marco Pescaro, are you related to this wanted criminal? Are you one of his band of traitors?"

"I am his brother," Marco shouted. "And he will avenge me."

"His brother," Wiedelier said. "You are young for a partisan. But you will be old by the time I have finished with you, if you do not co-operate with me. Tell me of the man, Warrey."

Again Marco licked his lips. "Put him on the wall," Wiedelier said.

Marco's arms were gripped and he was forced face to against the wall, his wrists being secured to iron rings. Then his legs were pulled apart, and his ankles also secured, so that he was spreadeagled against the stone, although his feet were still on the floor.

Wiedelier picked up a switch from the table; it was made of leather and had a hardened thong. He stood immediately behind Marco. "The man, Warrey. An English army officer. He has joined your brother's band of partisans, has he not?" Marco panted. "I know this, Marco Pescaro," Wiedelier said. "You revealed your knowledge of him when I first mentioned his name. I know he has come to join your people, to lead them against us. But he was not with you when my people raided your encampment. Neither was your brother. Tell me where I can find them, Marco Pescaro, and you will save yourself a lot of pain."

He thrust the switch between Marco's legs, and drew it up the valley of his buttocks, slowly. Marco gasped. "My brother is in the mountains," he said.

"Was it he attacked a German convoy, two days ago?"

"Yes," Marco said. "It was he."

"And the Englishman?"

"I do not know. I was not there. I do not know this Englishman."

"I say you do," Wiedelier said. "Are you calling me a liar?"

"No," Marco gasped. "No—" his pants ended in a strangled cry as Wiedelier slashed his naked buttocks with his switch. Then he gave another cry as Wiedelier hit him again, the other way. Then Wiedelier twined his fingers in the boy's wet hair, pulling his head back.

"The Englishman was there, Marco Pescaro. We know he was there, because our people saw him. He was there with your brother. Is he with your brother now, in the mountains?"

"Yes," Marco said. "He is with my brother in the mountains."

Wiedelier gazed at his half-turned face for a moment, then gave a jerk on his hair. "You are lying. I get very angry with little boys who lie to me."

"No," Marco gasped. "I am not lying, You asked me where he is, and I have told you."

Wiedelier released his hair, and turned to his sergeant. "Whip him," he said. "Whip him till he bleeds. Or tells us the truth."

The sergeant grinned, and picked up what looked like a bull whip.

"You cannot!" Margo grasped Wiedelier's arm. "He is only a young boy. That whip will scar him for life. It will destroy him."

"Very probably," Wiedelier agreed. "But it will also make him tell the truth. As you say, he is a young boy. He will not be used to standing pain."

"Please," Margo said.

"Don't be stupid, and weak. You want Warrey, do you not? This is the way to get him. You may commence," he told the sergeant, who had been waiting patiently, while Marco had been giving a series of little whimpers.

Now the whip cracked, and the boy gave an unearthly shriek as the thong bit into his flesh, immediately drawing blood from the little cut. The second blow landed while he was temporarily out of breath, and this time his strangled sound was even more unbearable to hear.

Margo ran out of the cellar, pushing the guard on the door to one side. Regardless of the stares of the soldiers in the courtyard, or indeed the other prisoners, she ran across the yard and up the stairs to her bedroom. She threw herself across the bed, her hands over her ears, as if she could still hear the screams of the unfortunate boy being torn apart. She had no idea how long she lay there, her stomach rolling, before she heard the door open and close. Still she did not move, until Wiedelier touched her with his switch.

The switch! She rolled over and sat up, gasping, half expecting a beating herself. "Silly girl," he remarked. "I had not really expected you to be this weak. I was told you were a very strong woman."

"I have never seen anyone tortured," she muttered.

"Not even in North Africa? You surprise me. Anyway, it is done."

"What is done?

"He has at last told the truth. He has told us everything we need to know. Warrey has come here to organise a resistance army. And two days ago he left the partisan encampment, with two companions, to go into Rivoli, where there is a traitor with a radio set. Warrey is obviously intending to use this equipment. So, get up and wash your face. We are leaving for Rivoli."

"Do you expect him still to be there?"

"I should not think he has got there yet. He has to walk. We can be there by this evening."

"You know where he is going in this town?"

"No, we do not. This boy did not know. And I do not think he is lying about that. He was speaking without thinking at the end."

Margo had got up. Now she sat down again. "At the end? What has happened to him? Is he dead?"

"Oh, no, he is alive. But a trifle cut up. It will be a long time before he will wish to sit down again, much less lie on his back."

"It is horrible, to do that to a human being."

"Well, now, imagine what we are going to do to your friend Warrey when we catch up with him."

The walk from the mountains down to the river was invigorating. At the end of July the weather was fine and warm, and there was sufficient daylight, morning and evening, to allow a long day. John was again fully fit from his trek across Switzerland, and to his surprise and relief both women seemed able to match him for strength, at least in their legs.

Nor did they actually quarrel, at least in the beginning. They saw no one, Bianca knowing the best ways through the valleys and amidst the little woods; their only concern was the aircraft which swooped overhead several times during the day, but by keeping alert they could see the planes and take cover long before they could themselves be spotted.

"I remember you, when I was a little girl," Bianca said, when they camped for the night.

Annaliese snorted, not enjoying being reminded that she was by several years the older of the pair.

"Our fathers were friends, I think," Bianca said.

"They knew each other," Annaliese corrected.

"Do you remember the day the Fascisti came?" Bianca asked.

"Yes," Annaliese said.

"I was only a small child. I do not remember much of it. I remember my mother screaming when they raped her. They did it again and again. It was a terrible time."

"My father shot at them, and was killed," Annaliese said, and then asked, curious despite herself, "Were you raped?"

"I was only four years old," Bianca pointed out.

"That is not an answer."

"My nurse hid me, and we got away. But then it was very hard. There was no money. Without my nurse I would have died. She prostituted herself to feed me. And then I met Cesare, and he took me into the mountains."

"I was married too," Annaliese said. "But they killed my husband, just as they killed my father. Now I am going to kill a lot of them. Am I not, Johnnie?"

"It's the general idea," John agreed.

"I would like to kill the Fascisti too," Bianca said, thoughtfully. "But Cesare, he says they have done much for Italy." She gave John a rather anxious glance. "You do not believe this?"

"I'm sure he's right," John agreed. "But no matter what they have done, how much good they have created, they have no right to shoot, or maim, or rape, those who oppose them. That's what this war is all about."

Next morning they resumed their walk, Annaliese having insisted on proving her pole position by sharing John's blanket, even if they never actually took off any of their clothes. Bianca did not appear to mind this public show of affection, and ostentatiously removed herself and her blanket a good distance away.

"If you can bring all these people together," she asked, "What will you do then?"

"Much will depend on what happens further south," John told her. "In Rome. But our business will be to commence an organised war against the Germans here in the north."

"And the Fascisti?"

"I'm afraid against them as well, as long as they are supporting the Germans. I hope your Cesare will understand this."

"I do not know," Bianca said thoughtfully. "We must hope so."

"It is them or us," Annaliese said fiercely. "The Germans, and any who support them. There can be no middle way."

John wished she would learn to keep her mouth shut. But he also hoped, and felt, that Bianca was basically on their side.

That afternoon they reached the Adige.

"What are we?" John asked.

Bianca smiled. "Mountain people, sheepherders, going to town to shop. The Fascisti will wish to see our identity papers, but there should not be any difficulty." Her smile widened as she looked at John. "You at the least look like a mountain man."

"What if she betrays us?" Annaliese whispered as they resumed their journey.

"She won't," John said.

"Ha," she commented.

"Because that would also mean betraying her husband and her new family," he pointed out.

Annaliese was not reassured. "If she betrays us," she said, "I will kill her."

"Just be sure," John suggested.

They had a rendezvous at an isolated farm some miles from the town. Here they were welcomed by the farmer, Benito Trasacco, his wife Carlita, and their son Carlo. Benito was a distant relative of the Pescaros and, although not an active partisan himself, was a valuable go-between, as was his son, who ran errands for the Pescaros in and out of the town.

"There is much activity down there, and south of the lake," Benito told them. "Many soldiers."

"Doing what?" John asked.

"I do not know. But they are up to something."

"Maybe we'll find out," Annaliese suggested.

Next morning they caught the bus from Trento, having left their spare gear at the farm. Carrying weapons was risky, but they had to chance being searched. As it happened, there was quite a lot of traffic in and out of the town, and passes and identity cards were only perfunctorily examined. John and the two women disembarked at the terminus and mingled with the other passengers, all standing servilely by the roadside as a parade of staff cars drove by, equally servilely standing in line to present their papers at the check point where the road entered the town. Bianca was as cool as always; Annaliese was agitated, but they got through without difficulty.

"We go now to my uncle's house," Bianca said, and led them through the narrow streets.

It was rush hour in the morning, and even the side streets were busy, but not so busy as the main street they came to a few minutes later, where traffic in every direction was being held up by what appeared to be a convoy of German troops entering the town, with the usual escort of outriders and the usual centre complement of open cars. John stood behind the two women to watch the parade, looked without serious interest at the woman seated in the first of the staff cars, and found himself gazing at Margo Cartwright.

The Partisans

'I must have women. There is nothing unbends the mind like them.'

John Gay

The Radio

Margo was looking at him. John made himself stand absolutely still, for the first time in his life cursing his height – he was taller than any of the men around him. But to take to his heels would confirm her first half recognition. He had to put his faith in his clothes and his beard. She looked away, and the car continued to move. He gave a sigh of relief. Then the car braked, so suddenly one of the motor-cycle escort nearly drove into it. Margo was standing up in the rear, and turning, speaking rapidly to the German officer beside her.

"Let's get out of here," John snapped. They had known each other for too long, and too well, for a scrubby beard to disguise him.

The two women understood that something had gone wrong, without knowing what. They followed John as he dashed down a side-street, while behind them whistles started blowing, and the watching people began to surge to and fro.

"You know this town," John told Bianca. "We need some place to hide. Fast."

"My uncle is only a block away—"

"Definitely not your uncle, right now. If they find us going there, he's done."

"Who was that woman?" Annaliese asked.

"An old friend." Margo Cartwright! Driving around in a German command car, seated next to an SS officer! That was going to take a lot of thinking about. But so were a lot of other aspects of the situation. Supposing he survived their little encounter.

"I have a cousin," Bianca said. "She will not yet have started work."

Still the whistles were shrilling, and they could hear the commands of the soldiers as they forced the people aside. They were only a block behind. Bianca gathered her skirt and ran down a succession of small streets. People stared at them, and John wondered how many would betray them?

Annaliese was panting; she had spent almost the entire previous three weeks on her feet and was feeling the effects.

"Here!" Bianca was also breathing heavily as they reached a shabby apartment building. The street door was open, and for the moment there was no one about. They hurried into the hall, and she closed the door behind them.

John sniffed. The air was rancid, the paint peeling, the floors unswept and unwashed for some considerable time. But the hallway was also empty. Bianca pointed at the stairs, and they went up, treading as lightly as they could on the creaking steps. The whistles were coming closer.

They reached the third floor landing, and Bianca pressed the bell. And again. The whistles and shouts had reached this street.

"Who is it?" a woman's voice asked. "Do you not know I am closed? Come back at two o'clock."

"It is Bianca. I need help."

The door opened a crack, and the woman peered at them. She was surprisingly young, John thought, not much older than Bianca herself, and quite pretty too, although her hair was untidy and her eyes bleary with sleep. But her face was much older than her cousin's. She wore a dressing gown and clearly nothing else, had a very full figure and good legs. "Bianca?" she asked. And looked past her. "You have brought a man? At this hour?"

"We need help. Please."

The woman was listening to the whistles and the shouts. They were now outside the house. "You have brought the Germans here?"

"They are following us. If they find us, they will shoot us. Please, Claudia."

"Fucking partisans," Claudia grumbled, but she stepped

back and allowed them in, then locked the door again. "They will come here. You know that. They always come here."

"But they would prefer not to look for us," Bianca said.

Claudia giggled. "They will want it for free. When they are on duty, they always want it for free."

"I will pay you," John said, understanding the situation.

Claudia looked him up and down. "I am expensive."

"So am I," John said.

There were feet on the stairs, shouts and screams and complaints closer to hand as doors were opened to imperious knocks and then banged shut again. John wondered if the whole building was a brothel.

"All right," Claudia said. "But I will charge double."

"Where can we go?" Bianca asked. "In the bathroom?"

"You stupid girl, that is where they will go, after. Get in the chest."

The very large chest stood against the wall. Bianca opened it, peered inside. "It is half full. There is not room for three."

"So you will have to get to know each other," Claudia said. "There is nowhere else."

"Can't we take out some of this stuff?" Annaliese asked, picking up a piece of linen.

"No, you cannot, stupid," Claudia said. "Everything must be as normal. But I will put some on top of you." She took out three layers of various sheets and pillowslips and napkins herself.

They looked at each other. "John on the bottom," Annaliese said.

John sighed and climbed into the chest, He lay on his back, and with a thick layer of Claudia's spare linen between himself and the bottom, felt quite comfortable. For the moment.

"You next," Annaliese said.

"You should go next," Bianca argued.

"You are heavier than me," Annaliese pointed out. "Your tits are bigger."

Bianca pulled a face as she looked down. "I am sorry about this, Colonel Warrey."

"We'll manage."

She lowered herself so that she was sitting on his groin, then lay back on top of him. Her hair clouded his face, surprisingly sweet-smelling, and he moved it to one side; his mouth rested against her ear. Above them Annaliese lowered herself on top of Bianca. She preferred to lie on her stomach, against the other woman. Her arm came down and her fingers sought John's. Whether this was a gesture of affection, of fear, or to make sure he didn't touch Bianca, he couldn't be sure.

Claudia arranged the linen on Annaliese's back and legs. "Remember not to move," she admonished. Then she began to lower the lid.

"How do we breathe?" John asked, already finding it difficult with the two women on top of him.

"It will not be for too long," Claudia assured him, and the lid clamped down, plunging them into utter darkness, each, he felt, with some fairly consuming thoughts to pass the time – quite apart from the risk of being suffocated.

He was acutely aware of Bianca, and despite his situation could not prevent an erection against her thigh. When he attempted to move slightly to be more comfortable. Annaliese's fingers closed on his, while his right hand was suddenly grasped by Bianca, pressing it against her breast, which meant his knuckles were pressing against Annaliese's in turn. Fortunately, neither woman dared speak; the thunderous raps had reached Claudia's door.

Her routine did not change. She allowed the Germans to knock three times before answering. "Who is it? Do you not know I do not work before two?"

"Open up, Claudia," a man said in poor Italian. "Or we will break it down."

"Men," Claudia muttered, shuffling across the floor to release the lock. "Why do you not come back later?"

Boots stamped on the floor. "We are looking for three people, a man and two women."

"I do not do women," Claudia said.

"These are not johns. They are partisans."

"And you think they will come here? Out of hours?"

"They were seen on this street," the soldier insisted.

"Well, they are not here. You are welcome to look."

Feet stamped across the room into the bathroom. "You saw them come into this house?" Claudia asked, innocently.

"No," the soldier confessed. "No one saw them come in here. But they must be somewhere in this street."

"If I see them I will let you know," Claudia volunteered.

"You better. All right. Next floor. But . . . as I am here, Claudia—"

"I do not work before two," Claudia reminded him.

"Who said anything about work? Out, out," he bawled. "Search the next floor." He was clearly an NCO.

John listened, to the sound of clothes being thrown on the floor, and of bedsprings creaking. The women grew heavier by the moment, and Bianca moved her bottom on his groin. He couldn't be sure whether she had become uncomfortable, or was affected by what was happening on the bed – or because she was still holding his hand against her breast. Annaliese was certainly moving on top of them both; he thought she might be trembling. And now the air in the trunk was getting very stale.

"Ah," the sergeant said. "Aaaah. That was so good. So very good. You are a precious thing, Claudia."

"I am not a thing," Claudia pointed out. "That will be one hundred lira."

"You are joking. In any event, I do not have one hundred lira on me. I am on duty."

"That is my charge out of hours," Claudia said.

"Listen, I will come back tonight, eh? And maybe bring a friend. That will be good for you, eh?"

"Perhaps," Claudia said. "If you also bring one hundred lira. Now go. I have to get some sleep."

"Before two o'clock, eh? Ha ha. I will come back tonight."

The door slammed, and a moment later the lid of the chest was thrown up.

"Thank God for that," Annaliese said, drawing deep breaths. "We were about to suffocate."

"Don't move," Claudia told her. "They may come back. Are you all right, Bianca?"

Bianca didn't reply for a moment, then she said, "I am all right," in a low voice, at the same time moving her bottom again. John realised that he might, inadvertently, have accumulated a problem.

"I will make coffee," Claudia said.

Fifteen minutes later the street door banged as the soldiers left. "You can get out now," Claudia said, removing the layer of cloth.

Slowly Annaliese pushed herself up, climbed out of the trunk, and collapsed on to a chair. "I shall never get into a trunk again as long as I live," she said.

"Would you help me, please," Bianca said. John didn't know which of them she was addressing, but as Annaliese showed no sign of moving, he put his hands on Bianca's shoulders and pushed, and Bianca got her hand on to the lip of the chest and sat up, then heaved herself out. Her cheeks were pink, and she did not look at either himself or Annaliese.

"Are you all right, Johnnie?" Annaliese asked. "Your dick must be squashed flat."

"In a manner of speaking." He climbed out and stretched. He did feel rather squashed, but that was in the rib area.

Claudia served them coffee in a variety of chipped cups. "When do you leave?" she asked.

At last Bianca looked at John. "There's a problem," he said.

Claudia looked at the battered clock on the mantelpiece. "It is nine o'clock," she said. "I usually sleep until twelve, then I go out and have lunch and do whatever shopping is necessary, then I come back here and have a bath, and then I am ready for work. Well, there will be no more sleep, so I will go out now. I will be back by eleven. You must be gone by then."

"We cannot safely leave until dark," Bianca objected.

"The Germans know what you look like?"

"I'm afraid they do. Two of us, anyway," John said.

"Two?" Annaliese inquired.

"If they recognised me, the odds are that they will be able to recognise you, too. They have a photograph of you, remember."

"Ha," she commented.

"If we could stay here until dark," Bianca said. "Then we could leave the town."

"That is not possible," Claudia said. "There is a curfew beginning at six. Anyone found on the street after that hour will be shot on sight. Some already have been."

"You mean you have no clients after six o'clock?" John asked.

Claudia giggled. "Well, the curfew doesn't apply to German soldiers. But that is another reason you cannot stay here. My first client comes at two."

"I think we will have to risk it," Bianca said. "It is only a few blocks to the river. If we could get to the river, we could escape. Can you swim, Colonel Warrey?"

"I can swim," John said. "But we didn't come here just to leave again. We need to get to your uncle's house and use his radio. Is he your uncle too, Claudia?"

"He does not approve of me."

"Who would?" Annaliese inquired.

"A girl has to live," Claudia pointed out, coldly. "You kill people that you may live. I give them joy. Which do you think is preferable?"

"Ladies," John said, before there could be a punch-up. "This is no time to be arguing about lifestyles. Claudia, when you go out, I wish you to go to your uncle's house and make sure it is not being watched. Then you must go in and tell him that Bianca will be coming along to see him this afternoon. There is no need to mention Signora Coparro or myself."

"Why should I do this?" Claudia asked. "You think I am some messenger girl?"

"You will do it," Bianca said. "Because Colonel Warrey has told you to do it. Colonel Warrey is the commander of all the partisan forces in North Italy."

"I am not a partisan," Claudia pointed out.

"You are now, because you have helped us. If the Germans catch us, they will hang you too. And if you do not help us now, when the war is over and we have won, we shall hang you. Whereas, if you help us, we shall heap you with honours."

Claudia gazed at her, while John reflected that Bianca was far tougher than she either looked or normally acted – but then, she was clearly far more highly-sexed as well. And he had presumed that keeping Annaliese in order was going to be his biggest problem.

"When the war is over, I would prefer to be heaped with money," Claudia said.

"Then you shall be," John said. What was a stray promise here or there?

"Very well. I will go to see Uncle Boris," Claudia agreed. "And hope he does not throw me out. And when I come back, you go, eh?"

"Immediately," John assured her. "Providing it is safe."

"Ha," she commented, and began to dress.

"I would like to take a bath," Annaliese said.

"You can take a bath," Claudia said. "But you do not use the hot water, eh?"

"Why not?"

"Because when I come back, *I* will wish to take a bath, and there is only enough hot water for one." She looked at John and Bianca. "I suppose you wish a bath also."

"It might be a good idea," John ventured.

"Well, you can only fill one tub. There is not that much water, either." She put on her dress, peered at her face in the mirrow, brushed her hair, and added some very heavy make-up. "I go now. Don't forget, Colonel Warrey, that you have to pay me for that German."

"I will pay you when you come back,." John said.

"Ha," she commented as usual, and went to the door. "Keep this locked, and do not answer it." The door closed behind her.

"I did not know you had a cousin who was a whore, Bianca," Annaliese remarked.

Bianca shrugged. "As she said, a girl has to live. When the Fascisti shot her father, she had nothing. They had already shot her mother."

What a country, John thought; these people were all flesh and blood.

"Who is going to have the first bath?" Bianca asked.

"Me," Annaliese said.

Bianca looked at John. "Oh, I'll be last," he said.

"I am older than you," Annaliese reminded Bianca. John presumed this was the first time she had been pleased about that.

"Of course," Bianca said. "It is your privilege."

Annaliese went to the bathroom door, stopped, and looked over her shoulder. "And no fucking," she said. "I am the Colonel's woman. Not you." She closed the door on herself.

"Do you wish to fuck me?" Bianca asked. "She need not know."

"I think fucking you would be one of life's great pleasures, Bianca," John said. "But I have a wife. And what about Cesare?"

"Cesare? Pouf. You are a general."

"Not quite." He had to suppose that a great many women exposed to war in their front gardens, as it were, would lose their moral values.

"And this wife of yours," Bianca said. "You are saying that you have not slept with Annaliese? I have seen you."

"Not guilty as charged, at least in the sense you mean. She keeps me warm. But right now, I have a lot on my mind."

"Me also." She lay on the bed. "I am thinking that we should abandon my uncle and the radio and get out of Rivoli while we can."

"I have to make contact with my superiors."

"What good will it do if you are dead?"

"I think it is perhaps the only way we are going to stay alive. The woman in the car is, or was, a British Secret Agent."

Bianca sat up, puzzled. "You mean she was a prisoner of the Germans?"

"She didn't look like a prisoner to me."

"Then you mean she has turned traitor?"

"It begins to look like it. That would explain quite a few things that have been puzzling me. Like how I was picked up so quickly after leaving England. Someone who could recognise me was shown a photograph of me getting off the plane in Lisbon. It can only have been her. And now she is here in Italy, still looking for me. And finding me, too."

"But why should she do this? Betray her country? Betray you?"

"She always was a crazy mixed-up woman. Always bitter and twisted. And she has a personal dislike for me."

"Aha." Bianca smiled. "You fucked her and went off."

"As a matter of fact, no. But I think there were a couple of occasions when she wanted me to fuck her, and I went off instead. Women resent that."

"Not enough to betray their country," Bianca said. "This woman must be a devil. I will cut out her heart."

"Chance would be a fine thing," John said. "Now here is something else you may care to ponder: it's reasonable that Margo can have identified my photograph. It's reasonable that thanks to her the SS had Annaliese and me followed all the way from Lisbon, and it is reasonable that they somehow found out where we were staying in Switzerland. But then we disappeared. Okay, so it's reasonable that, having identified Annaliese as an Italian partisan, they would deduce that we were coming to Italy. Tell me, how wide is North Italy, say from San Remo to Venice?"

Bianca shrugged. "Maybe four hundred kilometres."

"Right. But we are in Rivoli, and so is Margo. Out of four hundred kilometres, she is in the one place that we are also. Do you believe in coincidences?"

Bianca clasped her neck. "You are saying someone has betrayed you? Here in Italy? One of our people?"

"Give me a better answer."

"Never one of our people. The Communists. That Alexandro. There must be a reward out for you. He will do anything for money."

"Bianca, all that Alexandro knows is that I have joined up with Renaldo's band, and that I want an assembly of all the partisan leaders. He does not know that I have come to Rivoli, or was even planning to do so. No one knew that, outside of Renaldo, Cesare, Marco, Maria Theresa and their mother. And you and Annaliese."

"What you are saying is impossible," she declared, angrily.

"So tell me how you think the Germans found out where I would be?"

She glared at him. "I will cut out his heart," she said. "After I have castrated him, slowly."

"Who exactly are you thinking of?"

She flushed. It could only be one of the brothers – or all together. If that were the case, he was absolutely up the creek. Without Renaldo's knowledge and support he could do nothing. But he couldn't believe it any more than the girl. Because he didn't want to believe it. But there was the money factor. If there *was* a price on his head, a large enough price, might not the brothers have been tempted? He had come here with grandiose plans for creating a partisan army. They had been getting on very well without him in the past, in their own small fashion. Might they not have decided that he was more trouble than he was worth, especially if they could betray him, collect a substantial reward, and then resume their old ways?

But would Cesare, or any man, send his own wife to a dreadful death: they had to understand that if John Warrey were taken, his female companions would also be taken, and tortured before execution. Or had Cesare perhaps come to understand that his wife, for all her beauty and sexuality, had a savage underside caused by what she had seen and suffered in her youth, and was simply too hot to handle?

Annaliese appeared in the doorway, naked, using a some-what dirty towel. "It is there."

Bianca glanced at John, got up, and went into the bathroom.

"I hope it is not too filthy," Annaliese called.

"Go fuck yourself," Bianca riposted, and closed the door.

"I do think it might be a good idea for you two to start getting on," John suggested. "We have problems enough without dissension in the ranks. Why do you dislike her so?"

"She has designs on you. I felt her, moving about, in that chest, holding your hand against her. I heard you just now, talking away. You were talking about me, eh?"

"Believe it or not, no." He gave her the gist of his conversation with Bianca.

"But, Holy Mother, if we were betrayed—" Annaliese suddenly looked like a very small girl.

"We'll have to do some sorting out," he agreed.

"How can we do this? We are trapped."

"Only if the Germans find out where we are."

"We are at the mercy of a whore and this doctor. He may have betrayed us."

"He doesn't even know we exist, yet. No, I think he is one person we can trust. If he has radio equipment, he is breaking the law. The Germans will hang him as a spy if they find out."

"Well then, this cousin who is a whore—"

"She too is trustworthy, simply because she's involved."

"So, what are you going to do?"

"What I came here to do, and then get out, and find out who betrayed us."

Annaliese gulped.

Claudia returned closer to twelve than eleven. John and the two women were tense as she opened the door, because for all his pretended confidence, she *could* have betrayed them. By then he had also bathed and felt better for it, although the water had been already brown when he had got into it. And to his relief, Bianca and Annaliese had stopped slanging each other, although he reckoned that if looks could kill they'd both be well dead.

They faced the door, each with a weapon in their hands.

Better to go down in a hail of bullets than surrender to the SS. But Claudia was alone, her arms filled with groceries. "Those steps will kill me," she said, placing her parcels on the table.

"Unless the Germans save them the trouble," Bianca remarked. "Did you see Uncle Boris?"

"He was not pleased to see me," Claudia said. "He told me that if I was seen visiting his house his reputation would be ruined. Ha! Everyone knows I am his niece, and everyone knows I am a whore. What does it matter whether I visit him or not?"

"Did you tell him I was coming to see him?"

"Yes. That made him even more angry. He has heard all the disturbance. Now he knows you are the cause of it. He is afraid."

"You told him I was the cause of it?"

"He guessed, as soon as he knew you were in Rivoli," Claudia said, caustically. "Now it is time for you to go. The streets are clear. Well, reasonably. The Germans and the Fascisti, they are drinking their aperitifs and preparing for their lunch."

"You mean they have given up looking for us?" John couldn't believe that.

"I think they will start again after their siestas," Claudia said. "But I have heard they have doubled the checkpoints in and out of town. So you will have difficulty leaving. But that is your concern," she hastily added.

"Quite," John agreed. "Now tell me, is the woman who identified me still in Rivoli?"

"How should I know?" Claudia asked.

John supposed that was reasonable. But he guessed Margo would still be here, together with her SS officer friend, simply because they knew he was here and he hadn't yet been captured. So . . . decisions. Margo had recognised him wearing a beard. Obviously she would recognise him even more easily without his beard. But to the Germans hunting him, he was a bearded partisan. It was sheer bad luck he had run into Margo that morning; he simply had to take care not to do so again. "Have you got a razor?" he asked.

"Of course I have a razor," Claudia said. "What do you wish it for? To cut your throat?"

"I'd like to shave," John said.

"I will do it for you," Bianca volunteered.

"I am his woman. I will do it," Annaliese declared.

"It is my razor," Claudia pointed out.

In the end, all three took turns; as it was a cutthroat razor, John felt distinctly apprehensive. But there was not even a nick. "I never knew you were so good-looking," Claudia remarked. "You stay for half an hour. I charge you half."

"I haven't paid you for the German sergeant yet," John reminded her, and did so. "Now we really have to rush."

She looked disappointed, but helped them make sure there was no trace left of them in the apartment. Then they cautiously went down the stairs and out of the back door. It was lunchtime, and as Claudia had suggested, the soldiers were enjoying themselves. The only attention they attracted as Bianca led them through the side streets were wolf whistles at the two women. Then they arrived opposite a rather smart-looking house. "You wait here," she said, "and I will get him to let us in."

John squinted at the shingle. "Just what does your uncle do?"

"He is a . . . what do you say, a bone-setter."

"You mean an osteopath."

"That is it."

"Is he licensed?"

"I doubt it. But he is very popular. Many people come to Rivoli to have their backs rubbed."

"Then won't he have a client with him now?"

"Now is siesta," she pointed out. She crossed the road and rang the bell.

"Do you trust her?" Annaliese asked.

"Absolutely."

"Because you wish to get into her."

"Because she is here with us, and if we are caught, then so will she be."

The door was open, and Bianca was waving at them to come. They hurried across the now empty street and stepped into a dark hallway, a place of high polish and parquet floor. The door was closed behind them, and they looked at a white-haired but handsome middle-aged man, clearly a relative of Bianca's; it was even possible to make out the resemblance to Claudia. "You are Warrey?" Boris Fabrico asked.

"Yes." John held out his hand, and after a moment's hesitation Fabrico took it.

"You are being hunted throughout Rivoli," he said. "You know this?" John nodded. "Then you also know it is very dangerous for you to come here."

"I need to use your radio."

"That is dangerous too."

"It is necessary, if we are to beat the Germans."

"And the Fascisti," Fabrico growled. "It is upstairs." He led the way up a somewhat narrow staircase, past a couple of landings, to a fourth floor attic.

"I thought the Fascisti were finished," John remarked, following him. The two women came behind them.

"You think because Badoglio made that announcement they are finished? They are everywhere," Fabrico said. "Particularly here in the north." He opened the door and let them in. The attic had glass shutters and was very well lit. "My hideaway."

John crossed the room to stand before the large and extremely modern radio equipment. "Where is the aerial?"

"Here." Fabrico showed him the carefully positioned wire. "You see? It goes out of the window, there, beside the gutter, and thence up to the chimney. It cannot be seen from the street."

"Very ingenious. What range do you have?"

"Several hundred miles."

"Holy Hallelujah. And the Germans have never traced it?"

"Not to my knowledge."

"When is the best time to use it?"

"Now."

"In the middle of the afternoon?"

"In the middle of siesta. No one will be listening now."

"If you're sure. May I?"

"You will use code?"

"No. I have too much to say. I will speak English. It is a special wavelength."

Fabrico looked sceptical. The women crowded round to watch John at work, but he sent them all to the other side of the room, especially Fabrico, whom he could not bring himself altogether to trust. Using the wavelength delineated by Cox he called, and again, and again. "Code name Duce," he said. "Code name Duce."

At last there was a reply. "Duce. Home Affairs here. Come in."

"Thought you'd gone off, old man," John said. "I do not have much time. Update me on the situation."

"Sicily goes well, but slowly. Badoglio is interested. Action in the north would be useful, but must be co-ordinated. We are thinking of the railhead at Milan."

"Could happen," John said. "But I will need essentials."

"List them at the end of this transmission," the voice said. "But wait for further orders before you undertake anything major."

"I understand. Co-ordination will be difficult without the transmitter you promised me."

"I have it here. Can you have it picked up?"

As if it were a bottle of milk, John thought. "It can be included with my requirements," he said, and read out his list. "That is ASAP."

"We'll do what we can. You will arrange a rendezvous?"

"Have your people cross the border due north of Lake Garda. That is, to the west of the road Trent-Rivoli. My people will be waiting for you."

"Understood."

"Lastly, information. I wish present whereabouts and occupation of Margo Cartwright, late of Military Intelligence, currently serving with the ATS. This is urgent."

"Give me two hours, then call me back."

John replaced the handset, looked at Fabrico. "I need to call again in two hours."

"By then I will have a client."

"You don't bring them up here, do you?"

"After the first one, I have appointments all afternoon until eight o'clock tonight. You must leave immediately."

"Sorry, old chum; I must make that second call."

Fabrico looked at Bianca.

"If Warrey says it is important, it is important, Uncle."

"He endangers all of our lives," Fabrico said. "Very well. But if you stay for two hours, you will not be able to leave until after my last patient. And by then there will be the curfew."

"The curfew starts at six," John pointed out. "And you said you had appointments up to eight. Explain that."

Fabrico shrugged. "My appointments after six are Fascisti. Or their wives. My eight o'clock is a German officer. He comes with his wife."

John considered. He couldn't afford to endanger Fabrico, whose radio he needed, certainly until he had his own. But he had to get out of Rivoli.

"Here is what we are going to do," he said.

The Arrest

Alarm bells were still jangling when Wiedelier got to SS Headquarters. Men were still rushing about, sirens were wailing . . . Wiedelier surveyed the three people seated in the chairs before the desk. Colonel Kolvig looked a mess; he was wearing a borrowed dressing gown over his underwear, and there was a bloody gash on his forehead. He was trembling, and the marks of the cords that had bound him were still clearly visible on his wrists.

Frau Kolvig had also been stripped to her underwear. She too wore a borrowed dressing-gown, and her hair was a tangled mess. Like her husband, her plump body trembled. But she did not appear to be injured apart from the rope burns on her wrists and ankles.

Fabrico was worst of all. He had not been undressed but he too had been hit on the head, and he too had been bound and gagged.

"Speak," Wiedelier invited. They all spoke together, while the lieutenant in charge of the investigation looked apologetic. "One at a time," Wiedelier shouted. "Frau Kolvig." She had seemed the most coherent.

"It happened so suddenly," she moaned. "I was on the table, and Boris was manipulating my back, and the door burst open and these two desperadoes burst in."

"Wait a moment," Wiedelier said. "You were on the table. What was Colonel Kolvig doing?"

"I had already received treatment," Kolvig explained. "And I was sitting in a chair at the side of the room, reading a magazine and waiting for my wife to be finished."

110

"Right. And these two men burst in—"

"No, no," Frau Kolvig said. "Only one was a man. The other was a woman."

"Describe them."

"The man was big, clean-shaven, very aggressive."

"Italian?"

"I do not think he was Italian. Although he spoke the language fluently."

"And the woman?"

"Oh, she was Italian. Dark-haired, pretty, young."

"And what did they do?"

"Before we could do anything they had hit poor Reinhardt over the head . . . they had guns, pistols. Then when Boris tried to protest, they hit him too. Then they took off our clothes, my husband's and mine . . . well, I was already undressed, and they tied us up. Boris too. He was unconscious. They tied us up and gagged us, and then they left, wearing our clothes."

"And murdered your driver," Wiedelier observed.

"Well, he was expecting me," Kolvig said. "And it was dark. They must have been on him before he realised anything was wrong."

"Yes," Wiedelier said drily. "And then this man, and this woman, pretending to be you, calmly drove through our check points, without a question being asked."

"Well," Kolvig said. "A German officer—"

"Quite. You had better go to bed. All of you." Wiedelier peered at Fabrico. "Are you all right?"

"No," Fabrico said. "I have a headache, and I feel sick."

"One of our cars will take you home."

"Will you catch those thugs?"

"They have a start of several hours. If you hadn't managed to get loose . . . but I suspect they will have abandoned the car and be with their friends, by now. But we will catch them. One of these days we will catch them."

Margo was sitting up in bed when he entered her room. "What was the emergency?"

"Your friend Warrey has escaped," Wiedelier said, throwing his cap in the corner and taking off his belts.

"But how? You said all the exits from town were closed."

"He used the simplest method in the world. He tracked one of our senior officers and his wife to their appointment with an osteopath, broke in, attacked them, tied them up, made off with their clothes and the colonel's weapon, and then took the colonel's car, having murdered the driver. He is very cunning; he waited until the last appointment of the evening. As Fabrico's housekeeper had gone home, they were not discovered until they had managed to work themselves loose. This took several hours."

"But the check points—"

"No one had the gumption to ask an officer in uniform for a pass."

"Warrey did all this, by himself?"

"He had a woman accomplice."

Margo frowned. "When I saw him on the streets, he was with two women."

"Well, he either had the other one out of sight and hidden in the back of the car, or she is still in Rivoli. But as we don't know what she looks like, there is fuck-all we can do about it."

"There's a whole lot you can do about it," Margo snapped. "First, there is a photograph on file of one of the women Warrey is with. That should be enlarged and circulated."

"That is shutting the stable door after the horse has bolted," Wiedelier pointed out.

"Second," Margo said, "you need to find out how Warrey knew of this osteopath, and how he discovered that the last appointment for the night was a German officer and his wife."

"Everyone in Rivoli knows Dr Fabrico," Wiedelier said. "He treats half of the officers in the garrison. And their wives."

"And the appointment?"

"Someone must have told him when the doctor shuts up shop. Or he got lucky."

"Warrey makes his own luck. And third, you need to find out where he and his lady friends spent the day, before going to the doctor's house, and how they managed to walk the streets, after the curfew, without being arrested."

"Are you trying to tell me how to do my job?"

"I am merely trying to help."

"Trying to help," he shouted with sudden rage. "Stupid bitch!" He seized the sheet and whipped it off her body. She gave a gasp and reached for it, and received a slap across the face that left her sprawled on the bed. "Teach me my job. Eh?" Wiedelier bawled, picking up his waist belt and slashing it through the air.

"No!" Margo screamed. "No, for God's sake . . . aaagh!" she screamed as the leather slashed into her naked buttocks. She tried to rise to her knees, and was thrown flat again, and struck again and again. She recalled that this was one of Wiedelier's favourite pastimes, and buried her head in her hands, screaming and weeping, as the belt seared her flesh.

After several blows he threw down the belt, panting. "Bitch," he snarled, stripping off his uniform.

No, she thought. He cannot possibly want that, now. But he wanted more. You have a tight ass, he had told her. Now he held her on her face, surging into her, every thrust accompanied by the banging of his groin against her lacerated buttocks, bringing a moan of pain. Then he threw himself away from her and lay on his back. Margo continued to lie on her stomach, her face buried, panting and moaning. And seething inside as well as out. I will kill him, she thought. I will get out of this bed and take his pistol from his holster and shoot him, in the balls, again and again. I will castrate him, with his own pistol, and then watch him die. And then . . . die herself. There was no escaping this building, no escaping this room, with every corridor guarded by a black-uniformed sentry.

And the execution of a woman who had murdered an SS officer would undoubtedly involve prolonged agony. She had chosen this path, to get even with her superiors, to get even above all with Warrey. Now she had to live with it to the bitter end.

Warrey! He was the reason for every catastrophe that had

affected her life. And now he was again tormenting her. If there was one thing she wanted to do, even more than avenging her insult by Wiedelier, it was get even with Warrey. She rolled over and sat up, gave a gasp of pain, and lay down again, on her stomach, beside the man.

Wiedelier rumpled her hair. "You should not make me angry. To have had him *there*—"

"You have destroyed his camp, his base. Now he is just a fugitive, on the run. Sooner or later he will be betrayed."

"Sooner, or later," Wiedelier said. "We have not the time. Within a month we will be thrown out of Sicily."

She rose on her elbow. "You cannot be serious."

"It is a matter of simple arithmetic. And betrayal, to be sure. The Italians do not wish to fight against the Americans. Do you know, the local crime bosses, they call themselves the mafia, are urging their soldiers to throw down their arms at the first opportunity. They are, of course, being bribed by the Americans. It is a sickening business. And our agents in Rome tell us that Badoglio is already negotiating with the Allies. He has sent an envoy to Lisbon, to meet with Eisenhower's representative there."

"You think Italy will surrender?"

"At the very least. Italy may well change sides. It was Mussolini's will that his people align themselves alongside the Reich. His will alone. Now that he is gone . . . at least for the time being."

"He is going to come back?"

"We are working on it. It may be possible to reinstate him, at least here in the north. But not if that madman Warrey is creating mayhem and mobilising the partisans."

"Can he do that?"

"He intends to try. I did not tell you this before, but that boy, Marco Pescaro, told us after we had whipped him a bit more that Warrey has summoned a meeting of all the partisan leaders in north Italy, to co-ordinate action against our lines of communication with Germany. I do not think the mere destruction of one of his camps is going to affect that. All the important partisans got away. And if he can effect such a mobilisation, while southern Italy declares for the Allies . . . it will be a very serious business."

Margo lay down again. "You want Warrey," she said. "You shall have Warrey."

"By snapping my fingers?"

"By neutralising him. Perhaps even having him surrender."

"That is a dream."

"Listen. I am here because I know him. Not just what he looks like, but what he thinks like. Oh, yes, that was Warrey tonight. He has pulled that trick before, stealing a German officer's uniform and his car. He did it in North Africa. He is a very bold, very determined, very ruthless man. But yet, you know, he is also an English gentleman. His honour, his responsibilities, his public behaviour, are more important to him than life itself."

"So how do we make him appear dishonourable, to the partisans?"

"We remind him of his responsibilities, to his family, and thus to his personal honour."

Wiedelier sat up. "His wife?"

"I think he is very much in love with her."

"You mean, have her assassinated. Yes, we could do that, easily enough—"

"What good would having her assassinated do?" Margo demanded. "It would only inspire him to more desperate acts out of a desire for revenge."

"Then I do not understand."

"Have her kidnapped."

"Out of England? That would be very difficult."

"Your people got me out of England."

"That is true." Wiedelier stroked his chin. "And then?"

"Have her brought to Italy. Have it broadcast that she is being held, that unless Warrey surrenders she will be publicly hanged."

"Hm. It might work. But surely he will try to rescue her before he surrenders?"

"Does that matter? Either way you will get him. More important, no matter what he does, he will be distracted from his plans."

"Yes. That is good thinking, Margo. I will have to discuss the matter with my superiors, but . . . yes, it could work."

Wiedelier considered that using Aileen Warrey as a bait to catch her husband was a very long shot, both in terms of time and probable end result. There were things closer at hand, aspects of what had happened which Margo had touched on and then forgotten. She had said Warrey made his own luck. Whether he did or not, he had to have known Boris Fabrico was an osteopath, and he also had to have discovered, somehow, that his last two patients would be Kolvig and his wife. Just as he had been able to remain hidden all day, and walk the streets at night, after the curfew, unhindered. How?

Wiedelier went to see the osteopath. "Dr Fabrico is resting," the housekeeper said. "He was hit on the head when the robbery took place." The official line.

"I just require a word," Wiedelier said. "You would like us to catch the robbers, would you not, Signorina?" He was admitted to Fabrico's bedroom, where he found the osteopath looking much better than he had expected, sitting in a chair and reading a newspaper. Only the piece of plaster on his half-shaven head indicated that he had been beaten. "You are recovering well," Wiedelier remarked.

"From the blow? Bah! It was nothing. It is the mind. I am frightened all the time, frightened that those bastards may come back."

Wiedelier sat down, rested his cap and swagger stick on his lap. "I can understand," he said sympathetically. "But I do not think they will come back. They were not robbers. They were partisans, seeking to escape the town. They only wanted Kolvig's uniform, and his wife's dress."

"Can you be serious, Herr Major?"

"Yes, I am serious. We will catch them, soon enough, and hang them in that square out there. But we will catch them

116

even sooner if we receive a little help. You saw their faces clearly."

"I have given descriptions."

"Quite. Now tell me, had you ever seen either of them before?"

"No, no."

"I am asking this because their appearance at your surgery, just at the right moment, from their point of view, is too much of a coincidence to be accepted. Someone told them where to come, and when to come."

"I do not know who that could have been," Fabrico said.

"You have lived in this town a long time," Wiedelier remarked.

"Nearly all my life."

"And your family also?"

"My brother owned a vineyard outside the town. My father was like me, an osteopath."

"They are both dead?"

"My father died of cancer, here in this house. My brother . . ." Fabrico sighed. "He was an anti-Fascist. He was killed by the Fascisti. A long time ago."

"And their wives?"

"Are also dead."

"And what of their children?"

Fabrico hesitated before replying, and Wiedelier knew he was preparing to lie. "I have no children," he said. "My brother had two children, a boy and a girl. I do not know what happened to them."

Wiedelier considered him for several seconds. "Do you not have a niece named Claudia Mirandola?"

Fabrico's head jerked. "We do not speak of her."

"Why not? Is she a partisan?"

"I do not think so. She is a whore."

"Here in Rivoli?"

"It is a great embarrassment to me," Fabrico said.

"I can imagine. But you said you did not know what had become of your brother's children."

117

Fabrico sighed. "I had another brother. He died young. But before he died, he fathered this, this—"

"Prostitute," Wiedelier said, delicately. "Do you ever see her?"

Another hesitation. He does not know how much I know, Wiedelier thought. But there was obviously more here than met the eye. "She comes here, sometimes," Fabrico admitted.

"Why?"

"Asking for money. I always send her away."

"But you have her address."

Once more the brief, betraying hesitation. "No," Fabrico said. "I do not know where she lives."

"Well, we will find her," Wiedelier said.

"Why?" Fabrico asked. "What do you wish with her? I thought—" he bit his lip.

Wiedelier smiled. "That I have a whore of my own? That is true. But a man gets tired of the same ass, over and over again. Besides, I wish to speak with this niece of yours." He stood up, put on his cap. "Thank you, Dr Fabrico. You have been most co-operative. I hope you soon feel better." He closed the door behind himself.

Fabrico stood at the window to watch the SS major get into his car to be driven away. He was pouring sweat. Claudia! They had forgotten about Claudia. But all the Germans would have to do was show her the whip or the electrodes, and she would tell them everything they wished to know. Including how she had brought Warrey and the two women to this house, where they had lain concealed until it was time for them to make their break.

He paced up and down. What to do? But there was only one thing he could do. Had he the time? Wiedelier apparently did not yet know where Claudia lived. He would not take long to find out. But even a couple of hours would be sufficient. He went downstairs. Carlotta, his housekeeper, a middle-aged woman of great efficiency, peered at him from her pantry. "I am going out, Carlotta," Fabrico said, carefully adjusting his hat to hide any sign of his bruise.

"There is an appointment at eleven, Doctor. Signora Lusardo."

"Ask her to wait. Or if she cannot wait, make another appointment. I have some urgent business that needs attending to." He hurried out of the house before she could argue, paused on the street to look left and right. At ten in the morning there were quite a few people about, but none of them looked like a police spy; indeed, several he knew as his neighbours. He gave them a pleasant greeting before hurrying away, turning down a side street, keeping to the back lanes until he reached the street where Claudia lived. Here again he paused at the corner, checking. And again he saw nothing suspicious. Nor did he know any of the people on this street, so therefore none of them would know him.

He reached the shabby apartment building, went up the steps and into the hall, climbed the stairs quickly, pausing on the last landing to make sure his breathing was fully controlled. Then he knocked on the door, and again and again. It would be just his luck that she should be out. Then he heard a shuffling sound from inside. "Who is it?" Claudia demanded. "I am not open for business until two o'clock."

"It is your Uncle Boris," Fabrico said.

"Uncle?" The bolt scraped and the door swung in. "Uncle?" she asked again. "You have come for a trick?"

"No, no," Fabrico said. "I have come to speak with you."

"I hope it has nothing to do with that business the day before yesterday," Claudia said. "I helped out Bianca and her friends, that was all."

"I understand," Fabrico said. "Have you nothing to drink?

"There is some wine." Claudia turned her back on him, as he had anticipated, to go to the table. Fabrico hit her on the base of the neck, a savage chopping blow. It was not as accurate as he had intended, and did not knock her unconscious, but she was stunned, and her knees gave way. He wrapped both hands round her neck and kept her upright while he squeezed. She began to recover her senses and drummed her heels on the floor; she could not speak against the pressure of his fingers. Fabrico dragged her across the floor and fell on to the bed with her, still grasping her throat. By now her thrashing was dwindling, and she was no longer breathing. But Fabrico lay beside her, half on top of her, still squeezing for several minutes, before he was satisfied. When he released her throat her suffused face was already clearing again; he had to straighten his fingers, slowly and carefully. But she was certainly dead.

He stood up, looking down at her. He felt no remorse; hers had been a wasted life, anyway. Whereas his life was important, both to himself and the eventual overthrow of the Fascists. And the Nazis, to be sure. He went to the door, and heard the stairs creak. Someone was going either up or down. He could not risk being seen leaving the apartment, so he waited, for several minutes, until there was no sound outside. Then he cautiously opened the door, saw nothing, pushed it back to step out, and faced Wiedelier, who, with one of his men, had been standing out of sight. "Why, Dr Fabrico," Wiedelier said. "What a pleasant surprise!"

"Well, you see, you are guilty of murder. And of your own niece, too. That makes you a monster, Dr Fabrico." Wiedelier sat behind his desk, leaning back, tapping the surface with his swagger stick. The woman stood behind him. Fabrico wished she was not present. He felt he might be able to stand what they were going to do to him, without the woman. He had already been stripped of his pants and underpants, and was tied to the chair in front of the desk, his hands handcuffed behind his back; the chair was bolted to the floor. The manhandling, the humiliation, had caused an erection, which was only now dwindling from fear. And the woman continued to stare at him.

"You underestimated us," Wiedelier pointed out. "It is always fatal to underestimate an opponent. And we are opponents, are we not, Doctor? You did not suppose we already knew where your niece lived. All we needed to do was find out if you considered her dangerous. Now . . . it is my duty to hand you over to the civil authorities to be tried and hanged. Do you wish to be hanged, Doctor?"

Fabrico's head jerked. "On the other hand," Wiedelier said, "I could keep you as a military prisoner, of value to us, if you were to co-operate."

Fabrico licked his lips. "I will do anything you wish."

"That will be very wise of you." Wiedelier got up and came round the desk, seated himself on the edge, immediately in front of Fabrico. With his swagger stick he flicked the end of Fabrico's penis, and Fabrico again jerked, but more in fear than discomfort. "I am assuming that Warrey and his female companion sheltered with your niece until it was safe for her to bring them to you. I am assuming they came to you to use that radio equipment we have found. Tell me what use they made of it."

Fabrico licked his lips again. "They will kill me."

"No, no," Wiedelier said. "They will not kill you. *I* will kill you. And I will do it very slowly and painfully. I will burn your balls until you can never pee again. Then I will hand you over to the civil authorities, to be hanged. Slowly. Now really, is misplaced loyalty to your friends worth all of that? And you know, before you are hanged, you will tell me everything I wish to know, simply because the pain will be so great you will not know what you are saying."

Fabrico was panting. "Warrey contacted a British agent, I think in Switzerland."

"Where in Switzerland?"

"I do not know."

"What wavelength did he use?"

"I do not know. He made me stand on the far side of the room while he used the set. I swear it, Herr Major. I swear it."

Wiedelier studied him for some seconds, then nodded. "Very good. What did he say on the radio?"

"I do not know. He spoke English. But . . . I think he was asking for something. And he also used a name."

"What name?"

"Ah . . . Margo Cartwright. That is what it was. Margo

Cartwright." The woman gave a little gasp, and Fabrico realised who she was.

"Now they will know that you did not die in that fire, Margo," Wiedelier said. "No matter, although this of course lessens your value to us, as the British will almost certainly pull out any of their people who might be known to you."

"Except Warrey," Margo said in a low voice. "He is too heavily committed."

"Oh, indeed. And we still want him. Well, Fabrico, the rest of what happened that night we know. It was very brave of you, very loyal, to allow Warrey to hit you on the head."

"I did not know he was going to hit that hard."

"He was always a realist," Margo said.

"Now," Wiedelier said, "as far as Warrey is concerned, the whole thing went off very well. He used the radio, and then escaped, and we have entirely accepted your story, Doctor. We shall keep the whore's death secret for the time being, or at least, the identity of the murderer. When will Warrey come back to use the radio again?"

"I do not know. I do not know if he will, ever."

"Oh, he will," Wiedelier said. "But we cannot wait forever. When you receive a message for the partisans, how do you get it to them?"

Fabrico glanced from face to face. "There is a boy, the son of a shepherd, who comes into town every week. He takes the messages for me. The partisans know where to contact him, and they do that, usually once a week."

"Very good. Now, we will wait for a decent while; we must do nothing to arouse Warrey's suspicions. But in a week or so you will tell this boy that you have received an urgent message for Colonel Warrey. It is top secret and can only be delivered to him personally. And then, why . . . we shall wait for the gallant colonel to come and get it. However, in the interim, Fabrico, I am going to have you tried by a military court, in secret, for the murder of your niece. You will be found guilty, and the sentence will be death by hanging."

Fabrico gasped. "But I will help you catch this man."

"Of course you will, Fabrico. I just wish you to be absolutely sure about this. Once we have Warrey, I give you my word that your sentence will be quashed. But if there is any failure to co-operate on your part, the sentence will be carried out, immediately. So, all we need to do is wait for Colonel Warrey to walk into our trap." He grinned at Margo. "But we shall make the situation appear even safer to him by ourselves leaving Rivoli and returning to Milan. Heinrich Osterman can look after things here."

"What about my plan regarding his wife?" Margo asked.

"I have it in mind. But this is simpler, is it not? Should this plan by any chance fail, we can always go after the woman. But this plan will not fail."

Renaldo was in tears. "My mother," he moaned. "My brother. Gone. All gone."

Maria Theresa hugged him. John had an idea she was not all that unhappy to have seen the back of her mother-in-law.

"You do not know they are dead," Father Pasquale pointed out. "They were taken prisoner."

"To be taken prisoner by the SS is the same as being killed," Renaldo said. "Do you know what they will do to them?"

John was studying the abandoned encampment through binoculars; they had not risked returning to the site as there was no doubt the Germans had it under surveillance, and now they were gathered over a mile away. The camp had been thoroughly destroyed, but most of the partisans had managed to escape further into the mountains, and quite a few had even retained their weapons. At least, he thought, now we know how the SS found out I was going to be in Rivoli – and no treachery had been involved, although he too did not like to think what had been done to Signora Pescaro and her son to make them divulge that information. He could well understand Renaldo's grief.

He glanced at Bianca, reunited with her Cesare, who had seemed overjoyed to see her. As she had seemed overjoyed to see her husband. But when he had held her in his arms she had looked over his shoulder at Warrey, and raised her eyebrows.

The manner in which he had got them out, Annaliese crouching in the back of the colonel's car, the way he had disposed of the driver with a single blow to the neck, the dominance of his personality, had made him almost a demi-god in the eyes of both women. Although Annaliese continued to leave no one in any doubt that she was the woman in possession. Which was just as well, he reckoned; the partisans had problems enough without a burst of jealousy on the part of Cesare.

As did he. Margo was officially dead, burned in a car crash. He did not know if London would act on his request for an exhumation. Besides, it was not necessary, as regards himself. He knew Margo was alive and well and currently in Italy, working for the SS. That utter bitch. But losing his temper was not going to help matters. She was here, and she was obviously giving the enemy all the help she could in catching up with him. He just had to stay one step ahead of her, and he had to make sure her presence did not get in the way of his job. In that respect, the capture of Marco and Signora Pescaro had to be turned to his advantage. "Our first duty must be to avenge your brother and mother," he told Renaldo.

"Can we not rescue them?" Cesare asked.

"It is something to be considered," John agreed, untruthfully. "But to do that, we must first of all find out where they are being held. And as they are probably being held in a military prison, we will need a great many men. Have you contacted the other leaders, Father Pasquale?"

"Some of them. But they are very nervous, after the recent German probes. And they are asking, is this not a result of your being here at all, Colonel Warrey?"

"It very probably is," John said. "But as I am here, and I am not going to go away, they will have to make the best of it. And the best is to strike against the Germans, as quickly and as effectively as possible. So, when will they come, these other leaders?"

"I will see what can be done," Pasquale said.

"Meanwhile, Renaldo," John told the partisan leader. "Thanks to Bianca's uncle, I have managed to make contact with my agent in Switzerland. He is organising a shipment of explosives across the border at Bormio. I wish you to take some men and go up there and pick up these goods. This is very important. We will need explosives if we are to free Marco and your mother."

And do a lot more besides, he thought.

John and Annaliese lay in a gully in the hillside, looking down on the spires of Trento, some distance away. They were totally concealed, as they needed to be, as overhead a reconnaissance plane slowly circled; the observer was almost certainly studying the hills with binoculars. That plane had been up there every day. But apart from that there had been little German activity since their narrow escape in Rivoli. Which was a sinister sign, as it could well mean they were planning another big sweep. There were troop movements along all the roads, but these were mostly heading south, where the Germans were preparing to attempt to stop the Allies crossing from Sicily; in the island the war had been reduced to mopping-up operations. But since Alexandro's attack, the columns were too well protected, usually by tanks, to be assaulted.

He simply had to know what was happening, and that meant sending someone into the town. He had chosen Trento, because Rivoli was too dangerous as long as Margo was there. As usual, Bianca had volunteered. She was in fact an obvious choice, as she knew the entire area very well, and yet was obviously too refined to be a woman of the mountains; decently dressed she could pass as a townswoman, and she had an identity card proving her to be a married woman. But John hated using her, especially as he could not be sure whether she undertook the task from sheer patriotism or from a desire to get away from her husband, if only for a brief while, or from a desire to please him.

He understood that he was forming a dangerous attachment to her, almost on the lines of his feelings for Soroya. He had never supposed he could ever replace Soroya, and 1943 was so different to 1940. In 1940 he had not been married. In 1940 he had never knowingly killed anyone. In 1940 he had been a tyro in the arts of espionage and raising mini-armies. Now he was regarded as one of Britain's most efficient and cold-blooded killers. And Aileen knew nothing of it. And Bianca . . . another difference between the Italian girl and Soroya was that Soroya had not been married, had in fact been given to him by a Senussi chieftain as his slave. Bianca was very definitely married, and in their mountain bivouacs he had more than once heard her panting as Cesare had wanted sex, and then memory had taken him back to that half-hour in Claudia's linen chest. He supposed his weakness for women would one day get him into serious trouble. As if it hadn't gotten him into serious trouble in the past.

"She is not coming," Annaliese said, with some satisfaction. "They must have captured her. What do you think they will do to her?"

"I have no idea," John said wearily.

"I have heard they stick an electric wire up your ass and then turn on the current," Annaliese said, with more satisfaction yet. "It makes your hair stand on end."

"I'm sure it would," John said. "There she is."

At least he hoped it was Bianca. A woman was certainly coming along the country lane, her basket on her arm. And a few minutes later he knew a flood of relief as her face became visible. "I must walk some more," she said as she drew level with their hiding-place. "Do not move for a while."

"Silly bitch," Annaliese muttered, but a moment later they heard and saw what she meant, as a motor cycle with side-car roared up the road. "We could shoot that," Annaliese suggested.

"And inform the whole world we were here?" John inquired. "We need to keep a very low profile until we are quite ready to move."

The motorbike pulled to a halt beside Bianca. John could not hear what was being said, but it was all very jolly. For a moment he thought she was about to be raped, as the man got out of the sidecar and began feeling her bottom, but after a brief exchange he got back into the sidecar and the bike drove away. Bianca watched it out of sight, then waved her arm, and John and Annaliese scrambled down from their perch. "That was a near thing," John said.

Bianca smiled. "Not really. I told them I have the clap."

"Do you have the clap?" Annaliese asked, innocently.

"You must show me what it is like," Bianca riposted.

"Ladies, please," John said, urging them both along the lane. "What's up?"

"Marco and Mama have been taken from Desenzano del Garda, and sent to Milan," Bianca said.

"They are still alive?"

"I think so. But there is talk that they have been very badly beaten."

"Milan," John said thoughtfully.

"It is a big garrison town," Bianca said.

"Don't you think we know that?" Annaliese demanded.

"As one grows older, one forgets things," Bianca pointed out. "I have been to Milan."

"So have I."

"I am going to have to knock your heads together," John said. They both giggled at that. "Milan is also a major rail centre, is it not?" he asked.

"Oh, yes," Bianca said. "Sometimes the Allies have bombed it. But I do not think they have been very successful. The trains are still running. Full of German soldiers travelling south," she added.

At least, John thought, if an attack on Milan could be disguised as an attempt to rescue Renaldo's mother and brother, he could be sure of their support. But he needed far more, and over the next week partisan leaders began to drift into the hills north of the lake. They came in ones and twos, suspicious, looking left and right at their compatriots, regarding John himself with a good deal of hostility.

"You are a famous soldier," Antonio said. "So these people say. But I have never heard of you."

"Stick around," John said. "How many men can you bring?"

"I have seventy men."

"And twenty women," put in his second-in-command, Dino.

"Fighting women?"

"They are armed. What is it they must do?"

"Kill Germans," John told him.

"Show us a German, and we will kill him."

"Hang about," John advised again.

At the end of the week he had a pledge of over a thousand men and women, all armed, and all anxious to fight. This was actually better than he had anticipated. All he was waiting for now was the return of Renaldo with the shipment of explosives out of Switzerland. By then Bianca had ventured as far south as Milan itself, and was able to confirm that Signora Pescaro and Marco were held in the SS prison there.

"And how did you find all of this out, eh?" Annaliese inquired, aware that Cesare was within earshot.

"People tell me things," Bianca said. "I have an honest face."

"What is the news?" John asked.

"There have been heavy air raids in the south," Bianca said.

"They have bombed Rome?"

"Not as yet, but this is expected. The raids have been against main rail centres, such as Foggia. But the coast has been bombarded by British battleships. There can be no doubt that the Allies mean to invade the mainland."

"Will the Italian Army resist them?"

Bianca shrugged. "At present the army is still in the war, on the German side, even though Badoglio has called for an end to Fascism. It is very difficult for them, with the Germans occupying all the key positions."

John nodded, thoughtfully. "Well, we must do our best to disrupt them. What else have you got to tell us?"

"That this Major Wiedelier, the SS commander in Tuscany, has returned to Milan, and the Englishwoman has gone with him."

"Holy Hallelujah," John said. "So they've stopped looking for me."

"And that is good, because I have a message for you. From my uncle, delivered to Carlo Trasacco. Uncle Boris has a very important wireless communication from the Allies, to be given to you personally. It is most urgent, and he wishes you to come to him at once. I will take you back to him."

John considered. But if the message really was urgent, he couldn't wait for Renaldo to return, hopefully with a transmitter of his own. There was no guarantee that he would.

"You cannot go back to Rivoli," Annaliese said. "It will be too dangerous."

"Not at all, if Wiedelier and Margo Cartwright have pulled out. Nobody knows what I look like." He thought it very unlikely the local SS would have a print of that photograph.

"So, another long walk," Annaliese complained.

"You are going to stay here," he told her.

"And let you go, with her?"

"Do you have any objection, Cesare?" John asked.

Cesare shrugged. "Are you not an honourable man?"

John swallowed at that.

"But why must I stay here?" Annaliese demanded.

"You will help to co-ordinate the movement of our people south, as they come in. Now, Cesare, Alexandro, Antonio, let us decide your movements. You will return to your people and prepare them. Hopefully, by the time I return, Renaldo will be back with the explosives. In the meantime you will start moving your people to the south. But you will all return here in one week's time, and I will give your final destinations."

They seemed enthusiastic. I have an army, he thought.

The Prisoner

John and Bianca set off as soon as it was dark, taking the route down to the river and the Trasacco farm. The partisans watched them disappear into the night, no doubt with mixed emotions, John thought. He could not escape the reflection that a large number of them still wished he would just go away or get himself killed. The idea of a massed raid on Milan, which could, perhaps, be linked to the rescue of Renaldo's mother and brother, was romantically splendid in the abstract, but there could be no doubt that a good number of the raiders would be killed or maimed, or that there would be large-scale reprisals by the Germans.

If this famous Warrey were to get killed or captured by the Germans before the raid could take place, well, they could go back to their old, very small-scale activities. He was equally concerned about the possible contents of this so urgent message Fabrico had received. As he had not yet obtained his own radio, the agent in Switzerland had no other means of contacting him, but contacting him at all was highly dangerous – for the receiver. And Home Affairs would know that people were on their way to the rendezvous – in fact, Renaldo should already have got there. His fear was that the message would tell him that his requested supply of munitions had been discovered and seized by the Swiss police.

He glanced at the woman. Like him, Bianca wore pants and a shirt under a windcheater; and she had a pack slung on her back. She was also armed with a tommy-gun, as was he, and they both carried Luger automatics, taken from the Germans, but this time John had decided that the weapons would be left, along with their

130

spare gear, at the farm to await their return. He wanted to avoid trouble. Bianca also wore a headscarf, from which her black hair drifted down her back. John wore a flat cap. Technically they were a farmer and his wife on their way to market, but they still intended to avoid encountering any German patrol.

She grinned at him as they trudged along. "One needs to be fit to be a partisan, eh?"

"You can say that again. Did anyone ever tell you that you are a very brave girl, Bianca?"

"Only you, Signor Warrey."

"Try John."

"I prefer Giovanni. That is good Italian, eh?"

"Then Giovanni it shall be." Actually, he preferred it too.

They walked some ten miles, then stopped to eat and bivouac for a few hours. Out here there was little risk of anyone coming along, so they did not even bother to stay awake, and were fast asleep in minutes, wrapped in their blankets. When John awoke it was daylight and the woman was gone, but she returned a few minutes later and prepared breakfast, which inevitably consisted of bread and sausage. "There is water over there," she said.

John washed himself in the small mountain stream, then joined her to eat. "It is going to rain," she said.

The sky looked clear enough at the moment, but he wasn't going to argue with her superior knowledge. Bianca packed up the gear, then knelt beside him where he was checking and cleaning their guns. "I would like you to kiss me," she said.

He looked up in surprise. "What brought this on?"

She gave a little shrug. "It is a feeling—" another shrug.

"I hope your feelings aren't accurate. You have a husband, Bianca."

"He beats me. Did you know that?"

"Why does he beat you?"

"He thinks it is the way to treat a woman. Very macho, eh? Do you beat your wife?"

"I don't think she'd go for it," John said. "But as you say, I do have a wife."

"Then we sin together, eh?"

It was not a time for argument, or indeed any disagreement between them. Supposing he wanted to argue. He took her face between his hands and kissed her on the mouth. Her arms went round him and he was rolled on to his back, the woman on top. Her hands were at his flies, and he pushed her away and sat up. She lay on her back, her quite beautiful face utterly calm. "You're a mountain of passion under that exterior," he remarked.

"And you are not. I want you, Giovanni. I have wanted you from the moment I saw you. Take me, now!"

"Ah—" think, Goddamit, because he did want to take her. He had wanted *her* from the moment he had seen her. And he dared not offend her, just in case she walked off and left him marooned in these hills. "Listen," he said. "We will have sex, when we have seen your uncle and received his message, and are on our way back."

"Why not now?"

"Because . . . I really couldn't concentrate, on the job in hand. It would not be good for either of us."

She considered this. "It would be good for me," she said at last. "I know this. But for you . . . I will wait until we have seen my uncle. But every day, every morning, you will kiss me."

"I think I can manage that."

"And you will touch me."

"Touch you where?"

She smiled. "I will show you." She unbuttoned her shirt, took his hand and put it inside her windcheater and then inside the shirt. Her flesh was chilled, the nipple hard; he could feel her heartbeat under his hand. He gave the breast a gentle squeeze, and she undulated, like a snake. And kissed him. "Tomorrow," she said, "it will be the other one. Now let us make haste." Whew, he thought, as he followed her through the trees, the river glistening on their left. He had managed to postpone the inevitable. But he suspected it was, inevitable. By that evening, after a very long day's walk, they had reached the farm, and were welcomed by Benito and his wife, and his son. "Tell me of this message," John asked Carlo.

"I do not know, Signor Warrey. I went to see Dr Fabrico, as I always do, and this is what he told me."

"Is this the first time you have been to the doctor since his . . . accident?"

"No, no, Signor. I went last week as well."

"And he said nothing about a message then?"

"No, Signor."

John looked at Bianca. "Sounds genuine enough."

"How did the doctor look?" she asked.

Carlo looked puzzled. "The same as always."

"Did he wear a bandage on his head?"

"A big piece of plaster, Signora."

"You have doubts about this?" Benito asked.

"One can't be too careful," John said.

"Is it possible to have a bath?" Bianca asked.

"Carita will show you. There is a pump by the well. You stay here," he told Carlo, as the boy started to drift outside behind the women. "He is precocious," he told John. "And that Pescaro . . . she is a lot of woman, eh?"

"Yes," John agreed.

He was allowed to have a bath after Bianca, but it was all very strictly controlled by Carita, as were their sleeping arrangements; she might not know about John, but she knew Bianca was a married woman.

"They are good people, but so old-fashioned," Bianca remarked, as they waited for the bus, having changed into town clothing; John even wore a tie, and Bianca a skirt. "And you have not kissed me or touched me this morning."

"It'll keep until we get to your uncle," John said. "But first, we'll just pay a call on your cousin, and make sure there has been no trouble since the last time."

They presented their passes, and had no trouble with the Fascisti police at the entrance to the town; the bus was in any

133

event crowded and the passengers were seen through in a hurry. They got down and strolled through the side streets until they came to Claudia's street. It was now late morning and people were searching for their aperitifs before lunch; the street was just about deserted, except . . . John grasped Bianca's arm and drew her back to the corner. "Copper."

"Eh?"

"There is a policeman just along the street."

"So? He has no reason to stop us."

"Not so long as we don't attempt to go into Claudia's building."

"Why should that concern him?"

"It is simply that he is standing where he can observe anyone going up those steps."

"He has stopped in the middle of his beat."

"I think it is too coincidental that he should have stopped exactly opposite her apartment building, and be waiting in the shadows. We have time. Let's go have a coffee." There was a street café just around the corner. They ordered coffee, and when it came, John remarked casually, "I used to know a woman who lived around here. Her name was Claudia Mirandola. You wouldn't know if she is still in this neighbourhood, would you?"

The waiter looked disapproving. "You knew this woman well, Signor?"

"Well, not really. We met once or twice, some years ago."

The waiter glanced at Bianca, not sure she should be involved in masculine talk. "You knew what she did, Signor?"

"Ah . . ." John also looked at Bianca. "I had heard."

"And you wish to see her again?" The waiter was now looking both scandalised and bemused; why should any man with such a beautiful woman as Bianca at his side wish to go looking for a whore?

"I might," John said.

The waiter sighed. "You are a man of much appetite, Signor. But you will not see Signora Mirandola again; she has paid the price, eh?"

"Eh?" Bianca sat up. "What do you mean?"

"Did you know her as well . . ." he glanced at Bianca's left hand. "Signora?"

"What do you mean by paid the price?" John asked.

"She is dead, Signor. Murdered. Strangled by one of her own clients."

"Oh, my God!" Bianca said.

"The wages of sin," the waiter said, piously.

"You say she was killed by one of her clients?" John asked. "Have the police arrested the man?"

"No, Signor." The waiter bent over the table. "The matter has been hushed up. They are saying it was a high official."

"A German?"

"Who knows, Signor? Or a Fascisti. It is best not to ask too many questions, eh?"

He went off to serve another customer, and John and Bianca looked at each other. "I am sorry," John said.

"I suppose it is an occupational hazard, murder, for a whore. As it is for a partisan," she said with her usual calmness.

"The question is, how does it affect us?"

"Why should it affect us?"

"Do you believe in coincidences?"

She shrugged. "They happen."

"Well, they shouldn't, if one wants to live a long life. Your cousin practised her trade without any problems until we entered her life, and now she is dead. What is more, the investigation is under wraps."

"You don't believe it was a high official, like the man said?"

"If it was," John said, "she wasn't murdered; she was executed." He drank his coffee, brooding.

"What do you want to do?" Bianca asked. "You think my uncle is involved?"

"I'm damned sure he is involved."

"He would never betray us," she insisted. "It would mean betraying himself."

"Not if he's agreed to lay a trap for me."

135

"I will cut off his balls," Bianca said.

"First catch your hare, as they say in my country." What a mess. It would be so simple to walk away from it. But if he was wrong, and there *was* an urgent message waiting for him . . .

"I will go and see my uncle," Bianca said.

"Too risky. Anyway, the message is supposed to be given to me personally." Something else he was beginning to worry about.

"There is no risk involved," Bianca said. "The Fascisti and the Germans do not know what I look like—"

"That colonel and his wife certainly do."

"Are they likely to be at my uncle's in the middle of the day? I will call on him, as his niece, and see what the situation is. If all is clear, I will signal you from the window, and you will come in and collect the message, and we will leave."

"And if all is not clear?"

"Then there will be no signal, and you will wait for me to leave. Then we can decide what we do next."

He gazed at her. "Did anyone—"

She smiled. "Yes. You did. Don't forget that you owe me a touch and a kiss."

At least there no policemen to be seen outside Fabrico's house, and as it was now lunch-time the street was deserted. Bianca squeezed John's hand, and left him in the shadows on the far side of the street, where he had waited with Annaliese on their previous visit, and then crossed herself. She moved with the utmost confidence, had taken off her headscarf, and allowed her hair to drift in the wind. She made an entrancing sight.

Which left him feeling very nervous. If anything were to happen to her . . . She rang the bell, and after a few minutes the door opened. And then closed again behind her.

Bianca stood in the darkened hallway, allowing her eyes to become accustomed to the gloom after the bright sunlight outside. The door had been opened by Carlotta, who was blinking at her, face rigid with dismay. "Signora Pescaro?"

Her voice was hardly more than a whisper. "You should not have come here. You—"

"Who is it, Carlotta?"

Carlotta's face closed, and she stepped away from Bianca. Bianca was aware that something was wrong, had a great temptation to open the door again and run for her life. But that would be to let Giovanni down, and in any event, it would betray herself. "Hello, Uncle Boris," she said.

Fabrico peered at her from halfway down the steps. "What are you doing here?"

"I have come to see you. I think you have something for me."

"Me? I have nothing for you." He came down the rest of the steps, and his eyes drifted to the door of his surgery.

Bianca's heart began to pound. "Then as I was mistaken, I will leave again. I am sorry to have bothered you."

She turned to the street door, and the surgery door swung in to reveal the two SS men. "I think you should stay, Signora," one of them said.

Bianca swallowed. "I have nothing to say to you."

"We think you do. Come in here."

Bianca glanced at her uncle, whose face was contorted with embarrassment, then entered the surgery. Fabrico followed. "This woman is your niece, Doctor?"

"Ah . . . yes. She is my brother's child."

"I see. Sit down, Signora . . . Pescaro, was it the maid called you?"

"That is my name."

"And your first name?"

"Bianca."

The officer sat on the desk, immediately in front of her. She found herself staring at his pants. She was trying to think, to compose her answers to all the questions which she knew were going to be asked, but she knew she was in the most terrible trouble of her life, and her brain seemed paralysed.

The officer picked up her left hand, looked at the ring. "And you are married. Would your husband be one Cesare Pescaro?"

"Yes."

"A known partisan leader. The brother of Renaldo Pescaro, the most wanted man in north Italy. After Colonel Warrey, to be sure."

Bianca did not rise to the bait. "I know my husband is a partisan. We are separated."

"Because you did not wish to be a partisan?"

"Yes."

"I think you are lying, Signora. You are a partisan, and you came here to receive a message for this Englishman, Colonel Warrey. Now is that not the truth?"

"I do not know what you are talking about," Bianca said, keeping her voice steady with an effort. "I came here to visit my uncle. Is that a crime?"

"By no means. When last were you here?"

"Ah . . . a month ago."

"That too is a lie. But we shall have the truth soon enough." He looked at Fabrico. "When last was your niece here, Doctor?"

Fabrico had also temporarily lost the power of coherent thought. But he could not betray his own niece. "If she says a month ago, it must be a month ago."

"I see. Tell me, Signora, where is Colonel Warrey now?"

"I do not know," Bianca said. "I do not know this man."

"I see. Well, I am going to take you down to headquarters to see if we cannot get to the truth of this." He nodded to his assistant, who picked up the phone and summoned a car. "I would like you to come too, Doctor."

"Me?" Fabrico's voice went up an octave.

"Yes. It will be necessary to make new plans, as this one seems to have failed. Stand up, Signora."

Bianca obeyed, with an effort; her knees felt weak. On the other hand, this officer, so smart and quiet and even good-looking, was behaving like a perfect gentleman. If only she could believe he would continue behaving like that.

"I am going to search you," the officer said, and took off his gloves. "Please stand quite still, and I shall endeavour not to embarrass you more than necessary."

Bianca stood still, as he slid his hands over her bodice and up and down her thighs. "Now part your legs," he commanded.

She obeyed, and his hands sought the inside of her thighs. But he did not touch her sexually, and the whole thing was very quick. If only her heart would settle down!

"Some of our people have been murdered by partisans carrying concealed weapons," he explained, pulling on his gloves. "I would not like that to happen to me. We will go now."

She expected him to handcuff her, but he did not do so, and she was allowed to lead them out of the house, where the Mercedes car was already drawing up; it could not have been very far away. She looked across the street without actually appearing to do so, but Warrey was not to be seen. She could only pray that he would get away. She did not suppose *she* would get away, could already feel the rope at her neck.

From the shadows across the street John watched in consternation as the people left the house. His first reaction was one of maniacal fury, a desire to rush forward and attempt to rescue the woman with his bare hands. And die, instantly, as would she. How he cursed the supposed safety of leaving their weapons at the farm. Then he saw that she was not handcuffed, and did not appear to be restrained in any way. She was being taken in for questioning, nothing more. If she could sustain her answers, they might well release her again. He had to wait, and see what happened. It was going to be a long morning.

Bianca sat opposite the SS captain in the car as it was driven to headquarters. "My name is Heinrich, by the way," he said. "As yours is Bianca, eh? I would like us to be friends, Bianca. I would like you to call me Heinrich, and I will call you Bianca. Would you not like to call me Heinrich?"

Bianca drew a deep breath. Her legs were pressed together, and were clammy with sweat. So were the hands she clasped on her lap. She did not dare look at Fabrico, seated beside her. "It is difficult to be on first name terms with someone who has just arrested you," she muttered.

"But I have not arrested you, Bianca. I am asking for your co-operation. And I am giving you a chance to prove your innocence, the truth of what you claim. If you can do that, then you will be as free as air, and you may return to . . . where do you live, by the way?"

Once again he had taken her by surprise. "I . . . I have an apartment."

"Oh, dear," he said. "I hope you are not saying you are a whore, like your late cousin." Bianca caught her breath. "Ah," Heinrich said. "You know about her."

"Only that she is dead."

"Yes. That was a pity, eh, Doctor?" Fabrico gulped. "But you are too beautiful to be a whore, Bianca," Heinrich said. "We have arrived."

The car had pulled into a courtyard, and uniformed guards were opening the doors for them. Heinrich gestured at an open doorway, and they were shown along a corridor and into a spacious office. Two young women, wearing white shirts and black skirts and stockings, sat at a desk on the far side, typing vigorously; they stood up and to attention as Heinrich entered. "At ease," Heinrich said. "Helga, would you ask Colonel Kolvig to step in here."

Helga moved to the door, and Fabrico gave a gasp. "Herr Captain—" he was shivering.

"Go on, Helga," Heinrich said, and sat behind his own desk; his assistant, who had been joined by another man, stood one to each side of Bianca and the doctor. The other secretary resumed typing. "You were going to say something, Doctor?"

"I—" Fabrico looked at Bianca. "I am sorry." He licked his lips.

"You are sorry for having lied to us," Heinrich suggested.

"Please, I have been co-operating. I have done everything Major Wiedelier wanted. I—"

"You have been lying to us," Heinrich said again. He stood up as Colonel Kolvig entered the room. Now it was Bianca's turn to gasp, She had not recognised the name, but she certainly recognised the man. Who was staring at her. "Thank you for coming in, Herr Colonel," Heinrich said. "I wished to ask you if you have ever seen this woman before."

Kolvig pointed; his face was turning purple. "She is the woman who assaulted my wife and me, with the man Warrey. My God—"

He took a step forward, his hand raised, and Bianca braced herself for a blow, but Heinrich checked him. "Forgive me, Herr Colonel, but she is our prisoner."

Kolvig glared at him. "Do you know what she did?"

"She undressed you, but only to your underwear. It could have been worse, Herr Colonel."

"You think this is a joke, eh? Well—"

"You wish her to be punished. She will be punished. And when she is being punished, you may come and watch, if you wish. Bring your wife. Thank you, Herr Colonel."

Kolvig continued to glare at him for several seconds, but as a regular army officer he knew the SS were a law unto themselves. He clicked his heels. "Heil Hitler!" He left the room.

"You seem to have made quite an impression on the poor colonel," Heinrich remarked, sitting down again, "I can well imagine. You would make an impression on me, were you to strip me to my underwear. Give Signora Pescaro a chair, Johann. I think she is about to fall down."

A chair was thrust into the back of Bianca's legs, and she sat heavily. She had indeed felt like falling down. "What are you going to do to me?" she asked.

"That depends on what you do for us, Signora. What I want is very simple: Warrey. The man is a dangerous *agent provocateur*. If he is not found, and put out of action, very quickly, he will cause a great many deaths. I think you know where he is. All you have to do is tell me."

"When you say, put out of action, you mean killed."

Heinrich shrugged. "That is not for me to say. My business is to capture him, alive if possible. Then it will be up to a military court. But I will not lie to you; if he is not wearing British army uniform when he is caught, he will be tried as a spy, and for that the death sentence is mandatory."

Bianca drew a deep breath. "Colonel Warrey is in the hills, with the partisans."

"Of whom you are one."

"No," she protested.

"Then how do you know where he is?"

A quick flick of the tongue; her entire mouth was dry. "I have heard this."

He studied her for several seconds. Then Fabrico made the mistake of coughing. Heinrich seemed to remember he was there. He turned. "You are a lying traitor," he said. "Why did you not tell us, a fortnight ago, when you were 'attacked', that the woman with Warrey was your niece?"

"Please," Fabrico said. "How could I betray my niece?"

"So you decided to betray us instead. That was a serious mistake, Doctor. You realise that your death sentence was only postponed so that you could help us?"

"Yes," Fabrico said. "And I have helped you, Herr Captain."

"You have betrayed us," Heinrich said. "The sentence will be carried out in one hour. In the public square. Johann."

The aide saluted, while Fabrico gave a stifled gasp, and then a scream. "No! Please! I will help you again. We can still trap Warrey. Please!"

Heinrich nodded to the second aide, who seized Fabrico by the arm and the nape of the neck, and marched him from the room, still screaming for mercy.

"Just like that?" Bianca asked. "You have such power?"

"As I reminded him, he was already condemned to death, for the murder of your cousin." He watched her expression. "You did not know this?"

Bianca was too clearly surprised, and horrified, to lie. "Uncle Boris killed Claudia?"

"Indeed. He tried to pretend it was a frenzied sex attack. But as he killed her out of hours, as it were – her hours – and did it only an hour after he had been interviewed by Major Wiedelier, it was obviously to protect himself from anything she might say. So you see, he deserves to die. We only kept him alive in the hopes of trapping Warrey."

He deserves to die, Bianca thought. Yes, he deserves to die. "And you have failed," she said.

"For the time being, perhaps. Although you will have to tell us where Warrey is. And I personally do not think we have failed at all. I would actually, again from a strictly personal point of view, prefer to have you sitting here than Warrey."

He got up, and came round the desk, and as at the surgery, sat on the edge, his knees virtually touching her shoulders. "Are you going to hang me too?" she asked in a low voice.

"It may well come to that; known partisans do not even need a trial. But not until I have finished with you." He reached out and put his hand to her head, let her hair drift through his fingers. "You are a striking woman, Bianca. Listen to me. Co-operate, tell me where I can find Warrey, better yet, help me find him, and I promise you that you will not die. You will go to a camp, where you will be humanely treated, and I may even be able to come and see you from time to time. Would you not like that?"

His hand drifted down the side of her face on to her shoulder, then on to the bodice of her dress; he gave her left breast a little squeeze. Bianca gasped. Warrey had done that, at her request . . . was it only yesterday morning? She had wanted so much more, and now she was going to get it . . . but not from Warrey.

"Leave the room, Gertrude," Heinrich told his secretary. She got up without a word, and closed the door behind herself. "It pleases me that you should be afraid of me," Heinrich said. "A frightened woman is far more compliant than a bold one. I wish you to be compliant."

Bianca knew an overwhelming desire to scream and scream and scream. But she gritted her teeth. This was all a part of the game he was playing, a game she had to play too, to the very end. "What we are going to do," Heinrich said, "is amuse ourselves. For the next hour. Then we will go and watch your uncle hanged."

"Do I have to do that?"

"Yes, you have to do that. A hanging, as we do it, is not

a pretty business; there is no drop. Seeing that, knowing it could be you standing there, and then hanging there, your legs kicking, may be good for you. After you have witnessed the hanging, we shall return here, and then I must ask you to get serious. Or I will have to get serious. You understand this?"

Bianca nodded without intending to. "I have several different things I can do to you," Heinrich said. "All of which would be amusing for me, and painful for you. I can, first of all, give you to my men for an hour. But you might enjoy that, even if you might feel a little battered at the end of it."

Bianca swallowed. "Or I could whip you. It is the approved method of dealing with women, as they are supposed to be less able to bear the pain and the humiliation than men. I can cane you, or I can use a flat strap . . . or I can use a whip which would cut your pretty little ass into a thousand strips. I can do that in the courtyard, with you tied naked to the beams, and with my men, and of course, Colonel and Frau Kolvig, looking on."

Bianca inhaled, noisily. "Or I can use simple and brutally old-fashioned methods, such as pulling out your toenails and fingernails. This is very painful, I am told, and it does have the drawback, like the bullwhip, of destroying beauty."

Bianca gasped. "Or, best of all, I can use electricity. I can attach the clips to any part of your body I choose, your fingers and your toes, your nose and your tongue, your nipples, your sex and put one up your ass. That will induce so much pain you will tell me anything I wish to know, and it has the great advantage of not in any way interfering with your physical beauty. Although I suppose your hair might turn white."

Bianca found that she was panting, and keeping still with an enormous effort. Why not leap up and hurl herself at him, and at least mark his face with her nails . . . before he pulled them out. But she knew she would not succeed. He was much the stronger, and all she would get would be a premature beating.

"Now, you see," he said, caressing her right breast. "I have put all my cards on the table. You know exactly what is going to happen to you if you refuse to co-operate. And believe me that I have told the truth when I say that at the end of it you will tell me everything and anything I wish to know. Does it not make sense to tell me now, and avoid all that pain and humiliation? Because once you have undergone that, you know, you will never be the same again. You will never have any satisfaction from holding a man in your arms. Even Warrey!"

Yet again he had surprised her. She had just been working out that he had just been indulging in psychological torture, that he was not really going to hurt her. But she could not stop her head from jerking, and colour from flooding her cheeks. Heinrich smiled. "As I surmised. You are his mistress. Well, well." He looked at his watch. "We still have half-an-hour. Take off your dress."

John stood in the crowd and watched Fabrico thrown from the back of the truck, immediately to be dragged to his feet by the Fascisti guards. The poor man was so terrified he could not stand unaided, and had to be half carried up to the scaffold. This appeared to be a fixture in the square, as the crowd which had accumulated round it seemed to be quite used to public executions. He heard the blaring of a horn and watched the onlookers part to let the command car through. Seated in the back were a German officer wearing the uniform of the SS . . . and Bianca.

John's eyes narrowed in the bright sunshine. She did not look as if she had been harmed . . . but her hair was less neat than usual, and as the car came to a halt no more than thirty feet from where he was standing, he could see that her clothes were dishevelled; her dress looked as if it had been taken off and put on again, hastily. Once again his blood began to boil, but he made himself stand still, and even retreat a few paces. If he could not help her at this moment, he could certainly harm them both were she to look round and see him.

But she was staring at her uncle, who was having the noose adjusted round his neck, opening and shutting his mouth as if he desperately wanted to speak. There was no hood, and at the signal the doctor was simply hoisted by two men pulling on the rope, which ran through a pulley at the top of the gallows. His face kicked and his shoulders strained as his face darkened, but it took him several minutes to die, John reckoned. The crowd watched in silence. No doubt most of them were Fascists. When they were sure the doctor was dead, they began to melt away. As he could not risk being isolated, John went with them, only pausing at the corner to look back at the command car, which was driving away.

What to do? Their visit had been a disaster, and he had not received that vital message. If there had ever been one. But his record of success and achievement rested on one simple fact: however fond he might have allowed himself to become of the women with whom he had worked in the past, or the men, he had never allowed their fates to interfere with his duty. He remembered wryly that he had even allowed himself to become fond of Margo Cartwright, although constantly being repelled by her abrasive personality.

Now, Bianca, a quite beautiful girl with whom he had known he was going to commit adultery, no matter how hard he tried to reject the idea, was gone, to a Nazi torture chamber, no doubt, and quite unthinkable pain. All he could do was avenge her. He presented his identity card to the German soldiers at the roadblock, and made his way out of town.

"You are telling me that you had Warrey in your grasp and you let him go?" Wiedelier was scandalised. And very angry. He shook the phone in his rage.

"Well, Herr Major, I never actually had him," Heinrich said. "He did not come himself for the fake message. He sent an assistant. The young woman of whom I was speaking, who has turned out to be the woman who was with him when he assaulted Colonel and Frau Kolvig – Dr Fabrico's niece. That lout has turned out to be even more of a traitor than we supposed."

"What have you done with him?"

"I have hanged him under the original sentence."

"Could you not have got more out of him?"

"In my opinion, no, sir. And we have the girl. We will get more out of her, I am certain."

"And you will enjoy it more," Wiedelier remarked. "I wish her sent to Milan. No, you had better bring her yourself. And Heinrich, I wish her to be in one piece when she gets here."

Heinrich replaced the phone, gazed at Bianca. "My boss wishes to question you himself," he said. "I am sorry about this."

"You mean he has even more obscene ideas than you?" she asked. She sat on a chair in front of his desk, wearing only her underwear. Heinrich had a great many fetishes.

"I should point out that I have done nothing to you yet, Signora. Save play with you a little. You should have enjoyed that. My boss, well, he does not like women. But he enjoys ill-treating them. As I say, I am sorry about this. Now I am going to lock you up for the night, and tomorrow morning we will leave for Milan. Dress yourself properly."

Bianca stood up, put on her dress. She was still having sudden fits of shaking, partly from watching her uncle hanged, and from knowing it was a very likely fate for herself, partly because this man had been so unusual in his love-making. She had supposed she would be making love with Warrey by now. But Warrey . . . at least he had got away. "Am I to be raped by your men?" she asked.

"Of course not. And please, Signora, I did not rape you. You were a consenting partner. Do remember that."

"I will remember that, Herr Captain," Bianca promised.

"Well, then, until tomorrow." He came round the desk, held her chin, and kissed her on the mouth. "I would like you to know that I have enjoyed today."

Bianca spat in his face.

The Raid

"What do you hope to get out of this girl?" Margo asked. She sat in the bright sunlight in the park overlooked by the Art Palace, and drank coffee. It was such a relief to be able to be out of doors and yet feel absolutely safe; Milan was the stronghold of the German Army in North Italy, and was probably the safest place in the country – if one happened to be a German or a German sympathiser.

"Perhaps it is what I hope to put into her, ha ha," Wiedelier remarked.

That would be a relief, Margo thought. Even if he had not laid a finger on her since that day in Rivoli, she lived in fear of another such dreadful experience. She said, "Even if Warrey was in Rivoli with her, when she was captured, he will be long escaped, and she will not know where he is."

Wiedelier snapped his fingers and a waiter hurried up with another brandy. "I think she will know certain things which may be of interest, things of which the Pescaro boy knew nothing. This Bianca Pescaro is obviously close to Warrey; Osterman is certain she is his mistress. She will know what are the goods he is expecting, which he called for by Fabrico's radio. She will also know the reasoning for this summoning of all the partisan leaders. There is obviously something being planned. After all, that is the reason for Warrey being here in the first place. He is planning a strike, and we must find out what it is. This girl will tell us."

"As long as I am not required to watch," Margo said. "But I still think you are going about it in the wrong way. Warrey is the key. As long as he is at large you will not have a moment's peace."

"You wish to go back to your idea of kidnapping his wife," Wiedelier said.

"It is the only sure way of catching him."

Wiedelier snorted. "You think it is a simple matter of snapping your fingers? Oh, yes, you say we got you out of England easily enough, but that was because you wanted to leave. Getting you into Eire and then back to Germany was no problem. No crime was involved, at least from the point of view of the British police, until you were already out of the country. And you were acting of your own free will, using such disguises as were necessary. This woman will be different. It will have to be a snatch, which is a crime. Then she will have to be kept prisoner, probably under sedation, until she can be got out. That is a dangerous business. It will have to be a submarine pick-up. That is both dangerous, for the submarine crew as well as our agents, and expensive." He shook his head. "And there is no guarantee of success." He pointed. "Oh, yes, *you* say Warrey is a romantic and gallant man, who would never sacrifice his wife. He appears to have sacrificed his mistress without a backward glance."

"We don't know she was his mistress, whatever Captain Ostermann thinks. I consider it unlikely. Is she not Signora Pescaro? That means she is the wife of one of the partisan commanders. Even Warrey would not risk upsetting his applecart by having it off with the wife of one of his commanders."

"Bah!" Wiedelier commented.

"So you will do nothing about my idea."

"I will consider it further, and then put it before my superiors. As I have said, I am not hopeful that they will agree. It is simply too expensive."

"Wars are expensive things," Margo remarked.

"The money still needs to be spent wisely. Now tell me, you claim to know Warrey; you have worked with him and you have observed his methods. Where would you expect him to launch his strike, presuming that we are right in assuming that he is about to make one?"

Margo shrugged. "I would say his aim must be to disrupt the movements of your troops and matériel. Which is the main rail centre in Northern Italy?"

"Milan. The Central Station, just a few blocks away."

"Well, then—"

"It is quite impossible for any partisan force to attack Milan. We are too heavily garrisoned, and the Central Station is guarded day and night. Anyway, it would serve no real purpose. Even supposing he managed to infiltrate the city and blow up the tracks, we would have them repaired again in a few days."

"Then he will not attack until the loss of those few days will have a serious effect on your war effort."

"What do you mean?"

"Well—" she considered. "What will you do when the Allies invade Italy?"

"Ha! Suppose they do."

"They will, Herr Major. That they are still sitting in Sicily is so that they can consolidate, and perhaps make other plans. You have not answered my question."

"I am not Field-Marshal Kesselring," he pointed out. "But military theory holds that an invading enemy must be checked, held, and thrown back at the earliest possible moment, before he can establish a beachhead."

"So, at the moment of invasion, you will send every man you can spare south, and every tank and gun as well, to meet them and check them and if possible throw them back into the sea. How will these men and tanks and guns get there as rapidly as possible?"

Wiedelier stroked his chin.

"So, you see, Warrey will attack the railway, I would say, the night before the invasion is to take place. A disruption to your troop movements of only three days, were it to happen at that moment, would be very serious, would it not?"

"Very serious," Wiedelier agreed. "You are a treasure, my

Margo. My problem is, I do not know the date of the projected invasion."

"This Bianca Pescaro might."

"Oh, come now, Margo. Do not spoil your brilliant analysis with absurdities. This girl is a peasant, the wife of a partisan. Do you suppose she is in the confidence of General Eisenhower?"

"If Osterman is right that she is Warrey's mistress, or even his close aide, which she certainly appears to be, she will be in *his* confidence. And he will have been given exact instructions as to when his attack is to be carried out. He may not have been told why, but *we* know it will be the night before the invasion begins."

"This is your theory."

"You just described it as brilliant, Herr Major. In any event, it is our best chance of both stopping Warrey and perhaps catching him, if you will not go along with my other plan. Make the girl give you the date of the attack. She will also confirm that it will be here. And then you have the whole Allied strategy in your lap."

Wiedelier continued to stroke his chin. "That would undoubtedly be a great coup. For me. And for you, Margo. Yes. We will see what this young woman has to tell us."

"Do you know," Margo said. "Perhaps I will attend, after all."

"My wife," Cesare Pescaro wailed. "My Bianca," he shouted. "Captured. They will rape her. They will torture her. They will cut off her breasts. Then they will hang her."

"She will have suffered, and died, in the name of Italy," Father Pasquale said.

The other partisan leaders, and there were several of them in the camp – including Alexandro – looked embarrassed. So was John, especially as he shared Cesare's emotions and could not reveal it . . . "I am sorry," he said.

"You did not defend her," Cesare shouted.

"I was unarmed and outnumbered," John said. "Again, I am

sorry. We are fighting a war. If it is any comfort to you, Cesare, I liked your wife more than any woman I have ever known. My grief is as deep as yours."

"Ha!" Cesare shouted. "You have had sex with her."

"I have not had sex with her," John said, for the first time heartily glad that he could tell the truth. "Where is Renaldo?"

"He went away and has not returned," Alexandro said. "Perhaps he has deserted us, eh? Has he not lost his brother, as well?"

"And our mother," Cesare moaned. "Our whole family, destroyed."

"But not you, eh, Cesare?" someone said, and laughed.

"We must not fight amongst ourselves," John said. "I sent Renaldo away, on a mission. He will soon be back."

He sat by himself to eat, and was joined by Annaliese. "This business is turning out badly, eh?" she asked.

"Not at all. It is a military exercise, and in military exercises there are always delays, casualties—"

"What did you mean when you said you loved Bianca more than me?"

"I did not say that I loved her at all," John pointed out. "I said I liked her."

"More than me."

"I never said that either. For God's sake give over. I am tired and depressed. I need to rest."

"You are depressed because she has been captured. What will you do now?"

"There is nothing I can do, about Bianca. We must carry on with our plan."

"How can we?" Annaliese demanded. "The Nazis are going to torture her until she tells them everything."

"Everything being what?"

"Well . . . what you are planning to do."

"She may know that we are planning to attack Milan, but she does not know when." Not even I know that, he thought.

"She will tell them where."

"Anyone with the slightest intelligence should be able to work out that when we strike, it will be at the Milan railhead. But they don't know how."

"We will all be killed."

"Some of us, certainly. You may remain behind with the women."

"Most of the women are coming. I will come too."

"Just remember that you volunteered." To his great relief he heard a shout. "Renaldo! Renaldo comes."

Renaldo listened to what had happened with a grave expression. "This is very bad," he said. "To have lost my mother, my brother, and now my sister-in-law . . . we *are* going to win this war, Giovanni?"

"It's our intention to do so," John said. "Now what have you brought me?"

There was less than he had hoped, but sufficient sticks of dynamite to destroy the railway station and a good area of track, he reckoned. With some left over for storming the SS prison. "Was there a message?"

"Yes," Renaldo said. "It says, unable contact by radio. Maximum disruption required two nine. Proceed as instructed. You know what this means?"

John nodded. "But you have brought me a transmitter?"

Renaldo unpacked the radio as if it had been an ingot of gold. But John felt the same way. "Gather up our people," he said.

When they were assembled, he stood in front of them, gazing at their bearded faces, the anxious women, the excited children. "We are going to attack Milan," he said.

"That is madness," Alexandro declared. "There are more Germans in Milan than any other city in Italy."

"Which is why they will least expect an attack," John said. "Our objective is to rescue the Pescaros from the SS prison, but as we are going in anyway, we will also blow up Milan Central Station. We are going to carry out the attack one week from today, on the night of Thursday, 2 September. That means you, Renaldo, and you, Antonio, will start moving your people now, to infiltrate the city. You will move in ones and twos so as not to arouse suspicion. I am told there are several safe houses available." He looked from face to face.

"There are places," Antonio said.

"What about my people?" inquired Alexandro. He might not like the idea of attacking Milan, but he did not intend to be left behind.

"You are going to be with me, Alexandro," John said.

"Well, well," Wiedelier said, walking slowly round Bianca, who stood, handcuffed, in the centre of the room. "I can see why you were reluctant to give her up, Heinrich. Have you had her?"

"Well . . ." Heinrich shifted his feet.

"Oh, I do not blame you. I might even have her myself. She is a beauty." He put the ferrule of his swagger stick under Bianca's chin, to raise her head.

She gazed at him without expression. She had expected torture for so long it had almost become a state of mind. But where she had quickly worked out that Heinrich liked to talk about it but would never do it, was not actually a sadist, who had only slapped her face when she had spat at him, she knew this man was entirely different. This was the real thing.

Heinrich glanced at Margo, standing by the door of the interrogation room. He had met her in Rivoli. But was she really intending to stay?

Wiedelier himself released the handcuffs, and Bianca rubbed her wrists together. "Undress," Wiedelier said. "Let me look at you."

Bianca obeyed. She knew she could not fight them. It was a case of submitting and hoping to get away with as little pain as possible.

"Magnificent," Wiedelier said, walking round her again, and this time flicking her buttocks with his stick. Bianca breathed, slowly and evenly. "You are a married woman, I believe," Wiedelier said.

"Yes, Herr Major."

"Have you children?"

"No, Herr Major."

"Perhaps you will never have children, now. Do you regret that?"

"Yes, Herr Major."

Wiedelier stood in front of her, fingered her breasts. Heinrich was embarrassed, because of the presence of the other woman.

"Now, I will tell you what I wish you to tell us," Wiedelier said, still holding Bianca's nipple. "We know that you are Colonel Warrey's aide. You have been identified as being with him when he assaulted Colonel Kolvig. We also know that you are the niece of the executed traitor Boris Fabrico. It is a reasonable deduction, therefore, that you are in Warrey's confidence and know his plans."

"Colonel Warrey does not confide in me," Bianca said. "I do what he tells me to, nothing more."

Wiedelier squeezed, and she gave a little gasp of mingled pain and outrage. "Do not attempt to play games with me, Signora," Wiedelier said. "We know Warrey is in Italy to lead a partisan revolt against the government. We know he is at this moment preparing to carry out an attack on . . . Milan."

Bianca's head turned, involuntarily. Wiedelier smiled. "You see? You know that too. All we require from you is the date."

"I do not know the date," Bianca said. "He has not told me. I do not think he knows himself, yet."

Wiedelier took her chin in his hand, moved her face slowly to and fro. "You are going to tell me the date," he said. "Even if you scream it with your last breath, you are going to tell me. Why not save us all a lot of bother and tell me now?"

"I do not know the date," Bianca panted.

Wiedelier considered her for a few moments. Then he said, "Very well. If this is your wish. Put her on the boards."

Two of the SS men moved forward, seized Bianca's arms. She did not resist as they marched her across the floor and placed her back against the huge X formed against the wall by the wooden boards. Her arms were extended along the two upper beams and secured by the wrists, her legs were similarly extended and secured by the ankles. Her feet were just off the floor, and she hung there by her wrists, her breasts heaving as she panted. One of the orderlies placed a table in front of her, and the other placed on the table a control box with a wind-up handle. From the box protruded two wires, ending in alligator clips. Then they stood back, to attention.

Wiedelier picked up the clips, one in each hand, and stood immediately before Bianca. She closed her eyes, but opened them again when he jabbed her in the stomach. "Do not go to sleep, my dear," he said, running the end of the clip up and down her chest and stomach, circling her breasts. "Where would you like me to begin?"

The whistle blared as the train pulled into Bergamo Station. The Fascisti guards on the platform stirred and began moving up and down, but they were not very interested. This was a branch line hiving off from the main Milan–Brescia railway to serve the towns north of the city, and seldom carried anyone of importance. Today there were quite a few passengers on the platform, waiting to board. It was late afternoon and they would expect to be in Milan by dusk. Presumably some were returning to the city from work, others were looking for a night out – the martial law of a few weeks earlier had been relaxed, at least here in the north.

The driver leaned out of his cab to greet the soldiers, then continued to look back along his little train as doors banged and various people got in and out. He grinned at the big, good-looking man and the even better-looking woman who walked up the platform towards him, hefting their bags. The first-class carriage was immediately behind the caboose, and he had no doubt they were first-class passengers; they were both very well dressed, the man in a suit with a fedora pulled down over his eyes, and the woman in a smart frock and high-heeled shoes.

To his surprise, they continued past the first-class carriage and came right up to him. "Good evening, Signora, Signor," he said, lifting his cap. "You are going to town?"

"We hope so," John said, at the same time stepping into the caboose, drawing his pistol and thrusting it into the driver's midriff, while Annaliese stood behind him to prevent anyone seeing what they were doing. "We wish to travel with you," John said.

The driver stepped back, and Annaliese joined them in the caboose, still making sure they were obscured from the platform. "Just do as we say," John advised, "and you will not get hurt. But we will shoot you, if we have to."

The man swallowed, and they heard the guard's whistle. "Time to go," John said.

The driver worked his levers, and the train moved out of the station. "Are you in communication with the conductor?" John asked.

"There is a telephone," the driver said.

"Right. Now, do you stop again, before Milan?"

"We stop in Monza."

"I wish you to stop first, in Usmate."

"We do not stop in Usmate at this time. It is not on this schedule."

"My friend," John said. "I wish you to stop there."

"Then we will be over our schedule for Milan."

"It will only be a short stop," John assured him. The driver muttered, staring along the track. John grinned at Annaliese.

"Are we on our schedule?" she asked.

He looked at his watch. "Just."

"They will hang you," the driver remarked. "You cannot steal a train."

"We are only borrowing your train," John explained. "However, I am sure they will hang us if they can. It is time to slow."

"I will have to whistle."

"Then whistle."

"The stationmaster will wish to know why I have stopped, out of schedule."

"I don't think he will," John said.

The driver glanced at him, and the train began to slow. The phone buzzed. "Tell him to come up," John said.

"Why are we stopping?" the conductor asked. "It is not on schedule."

"Come up," the driver said. "There is a problem." Usmate was now in sight.

The conductor opened the door in the rear of the caboose. "What is the—" he gulped as Annaliese thrust her pistol into his ribs.

"Just behave yourself," John told him. "Like your friend."

With a screeching of iron on iron the train drew to a halt. The platform was crowded, but there were no soldiers to be seen, nor was the stationmaster visible. The waiting people, men and women, crowded on board, carrying suitcases of varying sizes. "All right," John said.

The driver released the brake. "They will hang you," the conductor said.

"That's a cliché," John pointed out.

The door opened, and Alexandro came in. "That was easy, eh?"

"What did you do?"

Alexandro grinned. "We slit their throats. The station is now closed for the night. They will not be found until morning."

John thought he was being optimistic, but he didn't need until morning; another two hours would do.

"When we get to Monza," the conductor said. "We have to stop. Then—"

"I know," John said. "Take off your jacket and cap. I think they'll fit Alexandro. By the way, what is your name?"

"Pietro," the guard said.

Alexandro crammed himself into the tunic, put on the cap; he had shaved for this occasion. "This is the big one," John reminded him.

Annaliese's hand crept into his as the train slowed again. But it was now seven o'clock, and there were few people on the platform other than the Fascisti guards. Alexandro stepped down confidently, whistle in hand. Two people got off the train, and the doors banged. The stationmaster looked out of his office door. "Who are you?" he asked. "Where is Pietro?"

"Pietro has been taken ill," Alexandro said. "I am a stand-in."

The stationmaster went back inside. "He will telephone, to find out if that is true," Pietro said.

Alexandro blew his whistle and stepped back into the train.

"Where will he telephone?" John asked.

"Bergamo."

"And Bergamo will tell him you were all right when we stopped there. What will he do then?"

"He will telephone Milan Central, to tell them something is wrong."

"How much further to Milan Central?"

"Ten minutes."

"Time enough," John said.

The lights of the city were glowing in the near distance. The train slowed and the whistle blew. It was just dusk. The train eased into its allotted track, slowing all the time. "Are you going to kill us?" Pietro asked.

"That is not our intention," John said. "However, there is going to be a lot of shooting. I suggest you both lie on the floor and stay there."

"What about our passengers?"

"I strongly recommend they do the same thing," John said. "Go tell them."

The train was stopping. There were two soldiers on the platform, but as the train came to a halt half-a-dozen more ran up the stairs: the stationmaster in Monza must have acted very promptly.

"Now," John shouted. "Go, go, go!"

Alexandro blew a fanfare on his whistle. The first passengers were just getting down, and were hurled left and right by the partisans in their midst, who leapt from the train, tommy-guns and revolvers pulled from their discarded suitcases to spray the platform with bullets. Soldiers fell left and right and alarm bells and sirens began to sound. "Lie down!" Pietro and the driver were shouting through the now open door at the back of the caboose. "Lie down!"

Some of the passengers had already been hit. The rest hastily lay on the floor of the carriage with their hands over their heads. Even as they did so, there was a massive explosion from further in the city. Renaldo and Cesare and Antonio were doing their stuff. "Keep going," John told Alexandro, and leapt down on the track side of the train, carrying his haversack of explosives. Annaliese jumped down beside him, tommy-gun held in both hands.

Guns exploded and bullets sang left and right, ricochetting off the various trains. Other passengers screamed and threw themselves down to avoid being hit. From the city there came the wail of more sirens.

John leapt over the track and raced at the control centre. A man appeared in front of him. "Halt!" He levelled a rifle and Annaliese cut him down with a burst from her gun. More shots were fired, and she replied, then gave a gasp and went down on her knees.

"Take cover," John shouted, but he was not going to stop now. He reached the control centre, looked up at the windows, and saw a man looking down. He drew his pistol and fired. The man disappeared, but the window was still open. Even while firing John had unfastened his haversack with his left hand, and now he drew the grenade, pulled the pin with his teeth, and changed it to his right hand before tossing it through the window. There was a startled exclamation from above him, then the bomb exploded. John ran round to the door, hurled it open, and looked at the scene of carnage inside, with two men clearly dead and three more both wounded and shocked.

There was no time for sentiment; the equipment had to be destroyed. John drew another grenade, threw it in, and stood against the outside wall as there was another devastating explosion. He ran back down the steps, exchanged shots with someone on the far side of the track, and ran to the main Rome train, which was standing four tracks away. This had been abandoned by the passengers waiting to travel south, and as instructed, was surrounded by Alexandro's men, engaging in a gun battle with both Fascisti guards and German soldiers who were pouring into the station. "We will not hold them," Alexandro panted, lying down to fire his tommy-gun.

"Long enough," John said, opening his haversack to pack his explosive charges under the engine.

"You are an expert," Alexandro said admiringly.

"I was trained to it," John told him. And have practised often enough, he thought, as he remembered blowing up the bridge outside Benghazi. With the Senussi! But these fellows were just as good. "Cover me," he said, and extended the wire. "But when I shout go, go like hell." He ran back almost to where Annaliese lay, leaping over the tracks, set the box down, connected the detonators. "Go," he shouted. "Go, go go!"

Alexandro's men raced away from the train. One or two had fallen, but they had given a good account of themselves. "Are you all right?" John called to Annaliese. There was no reply. "Shit," he muttered, and watched the German soldiers, who had taken over from the Fascisti, running forward as they saw the partisans retreating.

He pressed the plunger, and the station was filled with a huge explosion. The engine seemed to leap from the track, breaking up as it did so. Men were hurled left and right, and John had to hold on to the nearest rail to stop being thrown several yards. But he was first to recover, and taking advantage of the stunning effect of the explosion, he scooped Annaliese from the ground and ran towards the other side of the station, where more partisans were still engaged in a gun battle with the Fascisti. "Go, go go," he shouted, panting now as the woman was a dead weight. A dead weight! He dropped to his knees beside the nearest track, laid her on the ground. Shit, he thought again. After so much.

It was now quite dark, and all the lights in the station had gone out. He peered at her face, felt at her blouse; it was a mass of blood. Her face was ugly, the mouth open, the eyes staring. Noise boomed and crashed around his head, men shouting, others screaming, some shooting, explosions still going off. But most of the surviving partisans had left the station. He laid Annaliese down, and bending double ran through the darkness. Someone shouted, and fired at him, then he was behind a train and out of sight.

A few minutes later he was outside of the station, mingling with a vast crowd that had gathered, shouting information, rumour, gossip. Several armoured cars had appeared, and even a few tanks, and a cordon of soldiers pushing people back, forcing them to jostle together. Several people gave John curious glances, at least partly because of the blood on his clothes, but none were prepared to betray him at the moment. He willingly went with the crowd which was being herded down the Via Vetruvio; that was the right direction for SS headquarters. But at the corner he separated from the crowd, and hurried down a side street, hands thrust into his pockets. "Halt there!" A Fascist patrol.

John ducked into a doorway, drawing his pistol as he did so. The two men appeared in front of him, and he shot them both before they could present their own weapons. There was so much noise going on he doubted the shots were noticed by anyone else.

He gained the square behind the headquarters, where there was a huge crowd milling about what suggested a pitched battle. The gates had been blown in and Renaldo and Cesare had clearly led their people inside, but had any got back out?

"Colonel!" He turned his head, sharply, and saw Antonio.

"What has happened?"

"I do not know. I am to cover their escape."

"When?" John wondered. Then he saw the partisans returning. People broke and fled left and right as Renaldo shot his way out. German soldiers also scattered, but now there were tanks as well, firing into the building, regardless of the certainty that some of their own people had to be inside.

Renaldo was carrying a woman over his shoulder. Cesare followed, also carrying someone on his back. Behind and around them their men continued to fire indiscriminately, at the Germans and into the crowd. "Now's your time," John said, also opening fire.

Antonio waved at his men, who had been mixing with the crowd, and now drew their weapons to begin shooting. "Withdraw," John snapped.

The partisans dissolved into the side streets. Renaldo and Cesare had already vanished into the darkness. John found Antonio beside him. "Have we won?" the partisan leader asked.

John gave him a savage grin. "In a manner of speaking."

The bedroom door crashed open, and Margo, who had been under the bed, looked up in alarm. The night was filled with noise, sirens, alarms, bells, gunshots, shouts, screams. She looked at Wiedelier. "What has happened?"

"What?" he shouted. "The swine. The bastards. They have dared to attack my headquarters. They have broken in and rescued the prisoners . . . those of them that were alive, anyway. They have blown up the railway station—"

"But . . . how? You had it totally surrounded."

"They came in by train. From Bergamo, would you believe it? Oh, I am going to have some executing to do. Those bastards!"

Margo slowly crawled out from beneath the bed and sat on it. She had not felt so shaken since that desert crash the previous year. The violence of the assault . . . but Warrey had also been involved in that crash. "Warrey!"

"Of course, Warrey."

"Have you got him?"

"I do not know. We're rounding up people now. Quite a few of the bastards were killed. So were quite a few of my people.

But the deaths are not relevant. It is what he has done. Quite apart from the damage to our prestige if they can just come in here and steal our prisoners . . . the railway is destroyed. The control box is destroyed."

"This is what I said would happen," Margo reminded him.

"Bitch!" He slashed his hand across her face and she fell over the bed, tasting blood. The phone jangled. Wiedelier snatched at it. "Yes." He listened, then slammed it down. "British warships are bombarding Reggio di Calabria and Salerno." Margo sat up, wiped blood from her mouth. "We will make them pay," he said. "Oh, we shall make them pay. I will take hostages, and I will shoot them—"

"That will not get you Warrey," Margo said, pushing herself up the bed to avoid another blow.

He glared at her, then picked up the phone. "Get me Berlin," he said. "I wish to speak with Reichsführer Himmler. Personally."

John sat on the hillside above Lake Garda, and stared at the glistening waters. He was still exhausted, after the five days of hiding in the hills and mountains to get here. He was also somewhat numbed. Experienced as he was, ruthless as he considered himself to be, that had been the most violent action in which he had ever taken part. And it had cost so much. Annaliese! And he did not know how many other of his close associates.

Alexandro sat beside him. "A great victory."

"I suppose you could say that."

"But you lost the woman, eh? No matter, Don Giovanni, we will give you another woman. Luana! You would like Luana?"

"Did she survive?"

"Luana is one of those who always survives."

"I'll think about it," John said. He didn't want Luana, or any woman. Apart from Bianca. Bianca! Because there she was, standing in front of him.

He stood up, peering at her. It was Bianca, most certainly. The face was the same, the black hair flowed past her

164

shoulders, even the expression remained as icily calm as he remembered. But the eyes had changed. The eyes were those of a woman who had looked into the pit of hell, and seen what lay there.

She stood alone, although she was surrounded by the rest of the partisans. Even her husband stood a little distance away. John went to her. "Are you all right?"

"Yes," she said, in her usual low voice.

Cesare joined them. "They tortured her. They—"

"Colonel Warrey knows what they do," Bianca said.

Cesare's shoulders slumped. "My woman," he moaned. "My wife. Degraded by those thugs."

"If it is that hard to bear," Bianca said, "then I can no longer be your woman, be your wife."

Cesare stared at her for several seconds, then turned and walked away.

"I am sorry," John said.

"For what? You know I did not love him."

"I am sorry for what happened. You saved my life by refusing to tell them where I was in Rivoli."

"Yes," she said. "Now you must save mine."

"Another day, another dollar," Bridget said, getting down from the command car she had just parked in the neat row outside the headquarters centre. It was a bleak early autumnal day in Scotland, with the promise of rain. But then, it had rained yesterday as well.

Bridget was Irish, and had a wry sense of humour. She was a somewhat large young woman, raw-boned but not unattractive of face, with a mass of thick red hair which even cut short simply would not stay confined within her peaked cap. Aileen Warrey thought she probably looked better in her ATS uniform than she ever had in civilian clothes.

"There's a dance on tonight, at the Royal Hotel," Bridget confided, as they walked back to the barracks together. "It's to celebrate the Italian surrender. You going?"

"I don't have a pass this weekend," Aileen confessed,

"For Jesus' sake, we'll get you one," Bridget said. "That's going to be no hardship. You haven't taken up a pass since coming up here. You're a model soldier. But even model soldiers need to let their hair down, sometimes."

"Well—" Aileen said, hesitantly.

"There's always the chance we could get laid," Bridget said. "There's a new outfit moved into the district. Yanks. They'll be there. No brass. This is an enlisted men's do."

"Do you want to get laid?" Aileen asked.

"I'm panting. Shit, it's been a long year." She glanced at her companion. "But you're still luvvy duvvy with that husband of yours, eh? For Christ's sake, how long have you been married?"

"Eighteen months, all but," Aileen confessed.

"And he's been away ninety per cent of that time. Now, how many women do you suppose he's shagged in that time?"

Aileen bit her lip. She wanted to respond, angrily, declare her certainty of Johnnie's utter fidelity . . . but she knew that wouldn't be true. He had never confessed to any affairs, and she had never probed; with her he had always given a very good imitation of being in love. But she was sure the affairs had been there. Johnnie was too good-looking, had too much of a naturally easy way with women, not to have succumbed.

She didn't hold it against him. They *had* only had five weeks together in the past seventy-odd, and she had never been that enthusiastic about physical matters, afraid of giving vent to the feelings that had occasionally surged inside her. Although she and Johnnie had grown up together, virtually, it had been as best friends more than mutually attracted bodies. It was even possible for her to feel guilty about their having married at all. She had pushed it through, when it would have been far more sensible for them to have waited until the shooting, and the separations, were over. And he, always the perfect gentleman, had obliged.

As he had felt obliged to have sex with his wife? Because, she suddenly realised, he had never been that enthusiastic, either. Yet she felt he had been unfaithful to her. Was that because she had lain there like a sack of coal? That hurdle could be overcome. But suppose he really did not find her very attractive? Either way, what could be wrong in going out dancing with a lot of strange men? Especially on such a great day, which would surely bring the end of the war a little closer. So that she could have her bottom squeezed and her breasts fondled and might even get kissed? She felt she could stand a bit of that, with someone she hopefully would never meet again. There was absolutely no need to go the whole hog and, as Bridget would have it, get laid. "You're on," she said.

The dancing was of the wild and vigorous variety, with the women being thrown to and fro as if they were sacks of potatoes. Some of the men were quite adept and performed extravagant manoeuvres like sliding their partner between their legs while never letting go of her hands or losing the rhythm of the music. Aileen, wearing a dress for the occasion, found it all a bit much, especially when her partner, a large sergeant, threw her right over his shoulder, skirt flying about her waist, before expertly catching her again and setting her on her feet. But as he had caught her by the thighs while her skirt had still been up she felt she was getting to know him rather too well. "Whew!" she gasped. "I'm quite dizzy."

"Sure is hot," the sergeant agreed. "Let's take a walk." Before she could think of an adequate reply, she had been ushered through the black-out curtain and then the door, on to the porch. "That's better," the sergeant said, and led her down the steps.

I don't want to be doing this, Aileen thought desperately. But at the same time, she didn't want to be rude. "I don't even know your name," she said.

"Dick. Dick Haddon. And you're Aileen, right? I heard that other girl say it."

"Aileen," she agreed. "My husband calls me Ally." Which was quite untrue, but she had to get John into the frame.

"Ally," he said. "I like that. Ally." He was still urging her onwards, towards a small copse of trees which stood in the centre of the park opposite the hotel.

That ploy had been a dismal failure. "Don't you think—" she said, and then found herself in his arms, being kissed quite fiercely, far more passionately than John had ever kissed her. "Oh," she gasped, when she got her mouth free, but by then she was worrying about his hands, one of which was resting on her breast, lightly; the other was gripping her buttock, very hard.

"You really turn me on," Dick said.

"Ah—" Aileen tried to think of something to say, and then realised they weren't alone.

There were three men standing round them. "Excuse me," one of these said, "would you be Mrs John Warrey?" His English was perfect, but there was a slight accent. "One of the ladies at the dance pointed you out to me," he explained.

"What the fuck—" Dick released her to turn to face the intruders. But as he did so, one stepped up behind him and threw an arm round his throat. He made a startled noise, which ended in a higher-pitched sound. Then he was released, and crumpled to the ground. Aileen stared in horror as the man drew the knife from Dick's back and wiped it clean on the sergeant's tunic.

"We wish you to come with us, Mrs Warrey," the spokesman said.

"You—" Aileen opened her mouth to scream, and he caught her throat.

"Now," he said. Aileen kicked at him, but he side-stepped her flailing feet. One of his aides had opened a little attache case, and now he poured some of the contents of a bottle on to a cloth. Aileen inhaled the odour of chloroform and wriggled even more desperately, but then the hand holding the cloth was placed over her face, and after another moment's struggling she subsided.

The leader looked at his watch. "We have very little time," he said in German. Between them they lifted Aileen's body and carried it to a car waiting on the far side of the park.

Justice

'The tree of liberty must be refreshed from time to time with the blood of patriots and tyrants. It is its natural manure.'

Thomas Jefferson

The Bait

"**M**rs Warrey," said the young man, speaking perfect English. "Welcome to Germany."

Aileen stepped on to the dock, cautiously. She was still uncertain in her movements, both from the amount of sedative drugs she had been fed and from the motion of the submarine. She was still uncertain what had happened, and why. Memory was a series of vague glimpses into a world that she had never suspected to exist.

She remembered the American sergeant, Dick somebody, collapsing dead at her feet; she had never seen a dead body before, much less a man killed virtually in her arms. Then she remembered nothing more until she had found herself on a lonely, wind-swept and rock-filled shore, somewhere still in Scotland, she surmised, but on a west-facing coast. There had been several men around her, and a winking light out to sea. She did not think they had molested her in any way, save by the very act of kidnapping her and carrying her unconscious body, but as soon as they realised she was fully awake they had chloroformed her again, despite her protests.

Then she had woken up on board the submarine. The captain had been a grave young man, bearded but handsome, who had indicated that she was actually in his bunk. He spoke very little English, and she spoke no German, so communication had been difficult. She did gather than he had no idea why she had been kidnapped, and was only obeying orders, orders which he had not liked, as taking his boat that close inshore to Britain was a highly hazardous occupation. "Important," he had said, pointing at her. She wished she knew why.

171

She also wished she could get the image of Dick out of her mind. A man had been murdered, just so these thugs could kidnap her. An ATS driver. It made no sense. She was also desperate for a bath; she still wore the dress from the dance, stained with Dick's blood, and had not changed in twenty-four hours. Nor was she allowed to change again. "Deutschland," the captain said.

The dance! Bridget! And all the others? What would they be doing? They would have found the sergeant, stabbed in the back, and with her disappeared. They might even suppose she had killed him. They would certainly have no inkling of what had really happened.

But now at last she was in Germany, although she had no idea which seaport. And here was a young man, good-looking and polite and wearing plainclothes, who was speaking perfect English. Oddly, she was not afraid. She couldn't think of any reason to be. She was a humble sergeant. True, she was married to someone in Intelligence, but so were quite a few other women. She knew absolutely nothing about John's work. "Why am I here?" she asked.

"We have a job for you to do," the young man said, ushering her to a waiting car. There were only seamen and sentries on the U-boat dock, nor could she see anyone beyond the gates; it was past midnight, and this was clearly a very secret operation.

"Just like that?"

He sat beside her. "As you say."

"And you think I will be prepared to work for you?"

He smiled in the darkness. "You have to do nothing, Mrs Warrey. Save be what you are: Mrs Warrey."

Aileen wished she could think straight. "Is it something to do with my husband?"

"I am not at liberty to say. Why do you not just relax. I am going to take you to an hotel, where you may have a bath and a meal and a change of clothing. Then we are going on a long journey, you and I. I hope it will be a pleasant one."

Aileen soaked in a hot tub. She was not particularly tired, as

172

she had spent the last three days mostly sleeping; she had not been allowed to leave the captain's cabin, even though she had gathered, from the noise and the fresh air, that they had made most of the journey on the surface. Now her only problem was the continued fuzziness of her brain, a hangover from the chloroform and the drugs she had been fed.

She was accompanied in her hotel room by two women, who she gathered were members of the Gestapo, although they were not wearing uniform. Nor were they the least unpleasant or aggressive. They were both blonde and attractive, smiled a lot, and one of them spoke a certain amount of English. "Do you know why I am here?" Aileen asked, when she got out of the bath.

"You are here," the woman said. "Now, these clothes. You try, eh?"

There was quite a selection, made with an eye to her build and height. Between them the two women sorted out a trim suit, a skirt and blouse, and a dress, all of which fitted her fairly well. There were also underwear and stockings, and even a pair of low-heeled shoes. "Now you are ready," the woman said. "Which of these outfits would you like to wear?"

Aileen chose the suit. She supposed she had to co-operate as long as necessary, both to avoid any ill-treatment and because any sort of resistance would be pointless. Patience, she told herself. She had always been a patient person.

She was given a meal of bread and sausage, and a cup of rather poor coffee, and then again delivered to her escort. "My name is Carl, by the way," he said. "You may call me Carl. May I say that you are looking very nice?"

"Thank you. And where are we going now, Carl?"

"Italy."

Once again she was totally surprised. "Am I allowed to ask why?"

"You can ask whatever you like, Mrs Warrey. Unfortunately, I am not able to answer you. My orders are to deliver you to Milan. That is all I know."

Italy, she thought. Italy had just surrendered, and had indeed changed sides. Only a couple of days ago. She had rather lost track of the days, but there was no way her kidnapping could be related to the Italian surrender, because it had been so carefully and elaborately planned that it must have been organised some time ago, and the surrender had only been announced . . . the day of the dance. Or had the Germans known it was going to happen? But whether they had or not, there was no way it could be related to her.

They reached a railway station and boarded a train. It was just dawn on a wind-swept morning. Carl showed her to a first-class compartment. "You understand that we must spend the next twenty-four hours in here," he said. "And that I must accompany you everywhere, during that time. Everywhere," he repeated, for emphasis.

"I understand," Aileen said.

"Good. It would be very helpful if you were to co-operate fully in this. Otherwise I will have to put you under restraint. I would not like to have to do that."

"Thank you."

He sat opposite her, and the train began to move. To her surprise he did not draw the blind, but allowed her to look at the houses, many of them bomb-damaged, and the people, very much the worse for wear. But soon they were out in the country, where conditions looked better. She kept expecting him to make an advance, but he did not, although from time to time he made polite conversation. When she needed to use the toilet, he went with her, but remained in the corridor, with the door between them closed.

I should be working out ways to escape, she thought. That is my duty as a soldier. But there did not seem the slightest chance of escaping. And even if she could escape Carl, what would she do then? She spoke no German, had no money, and would be picked up again within five minutes. And then, as he had threatened, she would be put under restraint. There seemed no point.

The train rumbled through the German countryside and

various towns all day. They changed once. In the afternoon she could see mountains in the distance. "The Alps," Carl explained. "They are still a long way away."

They had dinner served in their compartment, with a bottle of hock, and he grew quite jovial. The compartment was not a sleeper, so Aileen took off her shoes and curled her feet on the seat beside her; Carl spread a blanket over her. She remained terribly conscious of his presence, especially after he had turned down the light, but his manners remained impeccable, not at all what she had heard of the Gestapo.

When she woke at dawn they were winding their way through the peaks. "This line was blown up by the partisans, only a couple of weeks ago," Carl said, chattily, as he shaved in the basin. "But it has been repaired, as you see."

Aileen smiled politely, and hoped the partisans were taking the day off. And then, Milan. The Central Station had also been blown up, or bombed, quite recently, she estimated, judging by the amount of damage. But it was being repaired, even if, she also estimated, it was only operating at half capacity.

Carl opened the door for her, and she stepped down. Two black-uniformed soldiers were waiting for her. "Here we must say good-bye," Carl said.

"Oh." She felt sorry to lose him. "Will I see you again?"

"I doubt it. I will wish you good fortune. Remember, Mrs Warrey, co-operate as you have done on this journey, and no harm will befall you."

The SS officers escorted her out of the station to a waiting car. There were lots of people about, on their way to work, she supposed, and considerable traffic. No one paid her any great attention; they were more concerned with gossiping about the considerable amount of damage that had been done to several of the buildings around the station. Conspicuously absent were any Italian soldiers, but she knew the Germans had taken over the entire country since the surrender, and disarmed and imprisoned as much of the Italian Army as they could lay hands on. The new attitude was reflected in the squad of armed men who patrolled the streets, and the fearful glances of the passers-by.

She was driven to an hotel in the centre of the city. Here the swastika flag fluttered in the breeze, and there were armed sentries on the door. Her guards, who had not spoken during their brief journey, opened her door for her, and indicated that she should get out. She went up the steps and into the lobby, where there were more armed and uniformed men – and a woman, tall and thin, with good features but an unpleasant twist to her lips, and red hair, obviously long but presently confined in a bun. She wore a dress and was the only civilian to be seen. "Aileen Warrey," she said in English. There was no trace of an accent.

"That's me," Aileen said, determined to be as cheerful as possible. "Are you English?"

"I was. Margo Cartwright."

She paused, waiting for a reaction. But Aileen had never heard the name. "But . . . if you're English," she said, "what are you doing here? What am I doing here?"

"My name means nothing to you?" Margo asked.

"Should it?"

"Your Johnnie plays things even closer to his chest than I supposed," Margo remarked. "Come." She led Aileen to the stairs.

"Please," Aileen said. "Do tell me what's going on. Do you know Johnnie?"

"He and I have both worked for the SOE," Margo said.

"Special Operations Executive? No, no, that's not right. He's in Intelligence, but—"

They reached the first landing, and Margo led the way along the corridor. "John Warrey is one of His Majesty's most distinguished field agents," she said. "He specialises in leading guerilla resistance to enemy forces. He did this very successfully in North Africa, and now he is doing it here in Italy."

She paused before a closed door. Aileen had also stopped. "John? Here in Italy? Working with the partisans?"

"Again, far too successfully," Margo said, opening the door.

"A couple of weeks ago he blew up Milan Central. Did you not see the damage?"

"John did that?"

"He's good at blowing things up. He and I blew up a lot of things in the desert."

"I don't understand," Aileen said. "You and John have worked together? Then why—"

"I changed sides," Margo said. "This is Mrs Warrey, Herr Major."

Aileen gazed at the man in the black uniform. He looked quite pleasant. "Charmed, I'm, sure," he said in English. "Tell Otto to bring in his equipment, will you, Margo." Margo left the room. "I trust you had a pleasant journey, Mrs Warrey?" Wiedelier asked.

"It wasn't unpleasant," Aileen said. "Save that a man was killed—"

She paused, but Wiedelier did not change expression. "There is a war on," he pointed out.

"But I don't know why I am here at all. And nobody will tell me."

"Well, you see, your husband has been proving a great nuisance to us," Wiedelier said. "He has been killing a lot of my people—"

"John? Killing people?"

"You did not know this? Come now."

"I did not know this," Aileen said. "John has never killed anyone in his life."

"My dear woman, you are an innocent. Colonel Warrey has probably killed more Germans and Italians, by himself, than any other soldier in this war."

Aileen gulped. "So you see," Wiedelier explained, "it is very necessary for us to put him out of action. Ah, Otto. Set yourself up."

Aileen gazed at the photographer, who carefully brought his equipment into the room. "We require some photographs of you," Wiedelier explained. "What they call in America, mug shots, eh? Sit down."

Margo was holding a straight chair. Aileen sat in this, suddenly feeling quite breathless. John, a mass killer? She just couldn't believe that. But these people were so terribly serious. The man Otto was arranging his tripod, and was now hidden beneath his black cloth. "Do not smile," Wiedelier said.

The camera flashed, and again. "Now the sideways shots," Wiedelier said.

Margo turned Aileen's head left, and then right, for the photos to be taken. "Now the two of you together," Wiedelier said.

Aileen turned her head in surprise, and found Margo's face next to hers. Again the camera flashed. "Now a group shot, I think," Wiedelier said. He stood behind Aileen, and Margo stood beside him. "Excellent. It is necessary, you see, Mrs Warrey, for your husband to be in no doubt that you are actually in our possession. Very good. Now we must make him anxious. Take off your clothes."

"Do what?" Aileen demanded.

"Strip, darling," Margo said into her ear. "We must remind Johnnie of what he is missing."

"I absolutely refuse. You have no right—"

Wiedelier snapped his fingers, and Margo opened the door, to admit two SS men. Wiedelier gave a command in German. Aileen did not know what he had said, but there was no mistaking the intention of the men as they advanced towards her.

"No," she said. "Please. I will do it."

Wiedelier nodded.

"But—" Aileen bit her lip. "Could they leave again?"

"They will stay," Wiedelier said. "In case you change your mind. Besides, why should my men not have a little enjoyment?"

Aileen looked at Margo for help, but Margo merely smiled at her. Cheeks flushed, she took off her jacket and let her skirt fall, unbuttoned her blouse and laid it on the chair, hesitated. Surely that was enough.

"Everything," Wiedelier commanded. Aileen released her

suspenders and rolled down her stockings, then slid her cami-
knickers from her shoulders and past her thighs. The garment
gathered about her ankles and she instinctively closed her hand
over her pubes. "Hands behind your head," Wiedelier said.

Aileen closed her eyes as she obeyed. But she was to be
spared nothing. "Eyes open," Wiedelier said. Aileen obeyed,
and the camera flashed, and again. She found that she was
panting. "Just a couple more," Wiedelier said. Aileen realised
he was now standing behind her. He put one arm round her
waist, settling his hand on her breast, and with the other himself
grasped her pubes.

Her knees gave way; only one man had even touched her
there, and that had been John – and she had been reluctant
to have it happen. But she did not fall, as Wiedelier was
holding her up. And the camera was flashing again. "Very
good," Wiedelier said. "In fact, excellent. Have those developed immediately, Otto, and sent to my office. If they are
any good, I will need some of them blown up." He gave
Aileen a squeeze and released her. Now her knees did give
way, and she slid to the floor, on her knees. "I leave her in
your care," Wiedelier told Margo. "Remember that this is your
project. Remember also that we may need her for a personal
appearance." He signalled his men, and Otto packed up his
equipment, then all the men left the room.

Aileen listened to the door close. "May I get dressed now?"
she asked in a low voice, and looked at Margo's shoes and legs
as she stood above her.

"I don't think that will be necessary," Margo said. "I like you
the way you are."

John Warrey climbed the hill above the partisan encampment,
carrying his radio. He did this most days, listening from as high
up as was possible for any message from Switzerland. Because
of the mountains, VHF reception was not always very clear. But
the past few days had been peaceful, at least for the partisans.
They reckoned they had scored a tremendous victory in their
raid on Milan, and he was not going to argue with that, even

179

if their casualties had been heavy, and the casualties amongst the civilian population had been heavier yet, as the Germans had ruthlessly taken hostages and shot them in reprisal. But it had been a necessary part of the war, and now that Italy had surrendered the Italians were in any event a conquered people.

And the Allies were now firmly ashore, in the toe and at Salerno, which was not all that far south of Rome. With the Italians out, it would now be a straight fight with the Nazis. No one could doubt that the going would be tough, as the Germans poured men and matériel to the south – the disruption of the Milan railway network had served its purpose at the time of the invasion, but that had soon been repaired.

The publicity value of the raid had probably been more important than the actual effects. Renaldo was confident there would be more recruits now, for the partisan bands. John hoped he was right, even if he wasn't quite sure how they were going to cope, logistically. Renaldo was happy enough; he had his brother back, even if Marco was in a continuous state of shock, starting at the slightest touch. Cesare was not happy, because he had lost his wife. They had both lost their mother. One man's loss, John reflected, and looked back down the hillside at the woman patiently climbing behind him.

Bianca followed him everywhere. He presumed she was in as great a state of shock as Marco. But she concealed it better, save for her fear of being out of his sight. Sometimes he wondered if it was less shock than a determination that, as he had been responsible for what had happened to her, it was his duty to care for her for the rest of her life. He couldn't argue with that. He had not asked her for any details about what had happened, because he knew the methods employed by the SS. He knew she had been raped, by at least one man, perhaps by Wiedelier himself. He knew she had been subjected to all of Margo's bitter inhumanity. He knew where they would have attached the electrodes, and he knew, because he had had to undergo similar treatment in his training, the pain that had torn through her body, added to the humiliation of being a woman tortured by men. That she so desperately wanted to sleep every night in his arms, and have sex with him every night as well, was because she was determined to regain her womanhood, and having been rejected by her husband, to be *his* woman in all things. He didn't know how he could refuse her any of that, after what she had suffered, even if she had not been a beautiful woman.

Shades of Soroya, he thought. The two women were entirely different. Soroya had been all energy and bustling determination, switching from bubbling exuberance to simmering anger in an instant. Bianca was utterly quiet, slow and thoughtful in her movements, seldom smiling but equally seldom showing anger. But that she possessed the anger, and the determination, could not be doubted. There was another difference, from his point of view. Soroya had come into his life before he had got married. Bianca . . . that future was very cloudy.

He found his favourite position and sat down, extending his aerial, switching on the set, and listening. But there was only static at the moment. Bianca caught up with him and sat beside him. She lay back on the grass, her hands beneath her head, her blouse inflating slowly as she breathed. There was hardly a cloud in the sky, and little breeze. The sun remained warm, even in September. "On a day like this, it is difficult to realise there is a war on," she said.

"What would you be doing if there wasn't?" he asked.

She smiled. "What I am doing now, Giovanni. Lying beside you."

He had no reply to make to that. Presumably she knew, as well as he, that this had to come to an end one day. All the world hoped it would be one day soon.

"Duce," said the set. "Duce. Home Affairs."

Bianca sat up. This was the first time she had actually heard the radio working. John thumbed the switch. "Duce," he said.

"I am to offer you our congratulations," the voice said. "Your coup was brilliant."

"Thank you," John said.

"Now as to the man himself. He has been rescued from his garrison by German commandos."

"Say again?" John requested.

"Musso has been taken from his prison at Gran Sasso in the Abruzzi mountains by a commando force led by Otto Skorzeny. This is a considerable coup for the Germans, and the Italian Fascists."

"Yes," John agreed, feeling his muscles tighten. He had a pretty good idea of what was coming next.

"Our information is that he has been taken to Germany for a meeting with Hitler," the voice said. "But also that he will not stay there. He will be returned to north Italy to reconstitute the Fascist state up there. We do not wish this to happen."

"Understood," John said. "Do you mean you wish him taken prisoner or disposed of by executive action?"

"Executive action would be best," the voice said, "as if he is taken prisoner again the Germans will simply come after him again. Understood?"

"Understood."

"We will keep you informed of his movements and where he can be located on his return. But we are informed that his headquarters will be somewhere close to Lake Garda, perhaps Desenzano. We expect this to be quite soon, so you must start moving your people immediately. This operation must be undertaken the moment the target becomes available. Do not begin any other operations before then. Out."

John switched off the set, closed down the aerial.

"You are to kill Mussolini?" Bianca asked. She had picked up quite a bit of English from their relationship.

He nodded. "If it can be done."

"It would be a suicide mission," she pointed out.

"Could be." He had undertaken suicide missions before. Only then, as in the attempt on Rommel's life, he had sent others to do the job. But this would have to be personal.

"I will come with you," Bianca said.

He glanced at her. "I don't think that would be a very good idea," he said. "You don't want to be taken by the SS again."

"I do not wish to live if you are dead," she said.

"Let me work on it. But for the time being, do not mention

this to anyone. Anyone." He stood up, took her hand and stood her beside him.

She leaned against him. "Now you do not wish sex."

"Let me work on that too. I've a lot on my mind. Down."

He pushed her down again as the airplane came into view. It was a reconnaissance machine, and circled slowly over the valley below them. John took out his binoculars to study it, for it seemed to have spotted something, and he would have thought the encampment was too well concealed in the trees. Then he realised it was dropping what appeared to be leaflets. It did this for several seconds, then flew on to the next valley. Now it was too far away to be properly made out, but from the way it was again circling John deduced it was again dropping . . . leaflets?

"What is it, do you think?" Bianca asked.

"Maybe they're announcing Il Duce's rescue, and the setting up of the new Fascist State," John said. "We'd better get down there."

They scrambled down the hillside, had not reached the camp when they saw Renaldo coming towards them, waving several pieces of stiff paper. "They have gone mad," he said. "The Germans have gone mad. They are sending us pin-up pictures." He held out the photographs as John and Bianca got up to him.

John took the first one, stared at it in horror. Bianca had taken the second one. "This is the man and the woman who tortured me," she said. "But I do not know the other woman."

Renaldo chuckled. "They do." He offered the third photograph. John realised he had never seen Aileen so naked before. "You know this woman, Giovanni?" Renaldo asked.

"Yes," John said. "I know this woman." His first reaction was one of total shock. But that was already being overtaken by a slow-burning anger. Aileen was such a total innocent, of everything seamy in the world. To think of her in the hands of a man like Wiedelier, and a woman like Margo . . . the whole set-up had to be Margo's creation, an outpouring of that tortured mind.

"She is important to you?" Bianca asked.

"Yes," he said. "She is important to me."

"So they hope you will try to rescue her," Renaldo suggested. "Then they will capture you or kill you."

"Yes. Let's get back to the camp."

The first essential was to keep calm. Think as a soldier and not as a man or a husband. The Germans had Aileen. She might be already dead, executed after having her photograph taken. Even if she was still alive she could already have been raped and tortured. Was that a reason to abandon her? Was he as little a man as Cesare? On the other hand, if she was still alive, whether she had been raped or tortured or not – and the woman in the photographs had not appeared to have been ill-treated in any way – then rushing madly into the blatant trap would not help either of them.

There was also the point that he had been given specific orders, not to undertake any other action until Mussolini had returned to Italy, and when he did return, to go for Il Duce rather than any personal matters. Home Affairs had not mentioned personal matters at all. Perhaps he did not know of them. More likely he had been instructed to ignore them. Because he expected Warrey to ignore them too? At least until after Mussolini had been dealt with?

Where did that leave the man and the husband?

"We strike again, soon?" Alexandro asked.

John had insisted the various bands split up again after the Milan raid, to make them the more difficult to find. In fact the Germans hadn't looked very hard; they had been too concerned with disarming those elements of the Italian Army still behind their lines, and in rushing men south to fight the Allies. But Alexandro came over to Renaldo's camp as often as he could; he worshipped John as much as anyone else, now.

"Soon," John told him.

"Where this time?"

"I will tell you when it is time." These men, and women, had fought for him, and killed for him, and died for him. Yet he could not altogether trust them, because each had his or her own idea of the society they wished to have after the war was over; they were united only in their desire to be rid of the Germans. Thus he could not risk one of them sneaking away with the information that the great Warrey was planning the assassination of II Duce, who he knew was still a much revered figure to many of the partisans.

"It will be something big?" Antonio asked, eagerly.

"It will be something very big," John said.

"That woman is your wife," Bianca remarked, as they huddled together beneath their blanket. The days might still be warm, but the nights were growing increasingly cold.

"Yes," he said.

"What will they do to her? She has no information about us to give them. They will execute her."

"If they were going to execute her," John said, "they will already have done so. They are hoping that the photographs will be sufficient to make me try to rescue her."

"Are you going to do that?"

"No," John said.

She rose on her elbow to peer at him. "You do not love this woman?"

"As a matter of fact, I do. But I can do nothing about her until I have completed the Mussolini mission."

Bianca lay down again. He supposed she was for the first time realising the true nature of the man to whom she had tied herself. Because he had rescued her? After having allowed her to sacrifice herself in the first place? But rescuing Bianca, and Marco, had been to make sure the partisans followed him. He could not expect them to risk their lives for a woman none of them knew.

"You do not wish sex?" she asked.

"Not right now."

"Will you ever wish sex again, Giovanni?"

He kissed her forehead. "I'm an optimist."

"One week," Wiedelier said, striding up and down his office as he normally did when agitated. "One week, and nothing."

"He is a strong character," Margo said.

"This was your idea. It cost a great deal of time and money."

"And it will work, Joachim. Warrey is, as I have said, a strong character. And an intelligent one. I would say that he has decided that having kidnapped his wife, and photographed her, we then executed her. So while he may be planning vengeance, he supposes it can be achieved in his own time. What we need to do is let him know that she is alive, but that she will be executed, on a given date, if he does not surrender."

Wiedelier paused in front of her chair, and she braced herself for one of his sudden attacks. "Will he not assume that also is a trick, and that she is already dead?"

"Not if we show the world that she is alive. I suggest that we take her to some place like Rivoli, and display her in public there. Warrey has friends in Rivoli—"

"I thought we had executed them all," Wiedelier said.

"I shouldn't think we have. Expose Aileen Warrey in Rivoli, and make the announcement of her date of execution. That will bring him in."

Wiedelier stroked his chin. "It had better. Berlin is beginning to ask questions. We will try this one next week."

Margo raised her eyebrows; today was Tuesday. "Why must we wait until next week?"

"Because Il Duce returns to Italy tomorrow. To create a new Fascist state. We will all be on parade."

"We understand that he will make his headquarters in a town called Salo," Foreign Affairs said. "Not Desenzano. Do you know this place? It is a small town on the south-west shore of Lake Garda, a few miles north of Desenzano."

"I know Salo," John said.

"Then this should make it easier for you."

"Yes," John said thoughtfully. "You say he arrives tomorrow?"

"That is correct. He will take up residence, and the day after he will make his announcement of the new Fascist State. You have carte blanche as regards method and timing, Duce, but speed is important."

"Understood," John said. "Over and out."

John had already moved the main body of the partisans down from the hills and along the west side of the lake. They followed him without question, although he had not yet told them their destination – for the most part they thought it might be Brescia. But for all their faith in his leadership, he knew he had to pick his people very carefully. And plan very carefully.

"We are going to attack Salo," he told the partisans.

"What is there at Salo?" Renaldo asked.

John knew there were already rumours circulating; he had to tell them part of the truth. "It is where the new Fascist State headquarters are being set up," he said. "We must destroy them, to show Italy, to show the world, that Fascism is dead."

"But will not Il Duce be there?" Renaldo asked. He was astonished, but also a little pleased, John thought.

"Yes, he will. But as a figurehead controlled by the Nazis. Our orders are to attack and destroy his communications system before the town can be fortified."

Renaldo stroked his chin. "To attack Il Duce himself—"

"I am beginning to think you are a Fascist at heart," John remarked.

"He made the trains run on time," Renaldo pointed out.

"I'm sure we can find someone else to do that," John said.

"It will mean a pitched battle, and many lives will be lost," Cesare grumbled.

"If you do not have the stomach for it, forget it," John said.

"To attack the beast in his lair," Alexandro said. "Ah, that will be something. Why do we not just kill the bastard?"

John grinned. "It may come to that. Then do I assume you are with me?"

"Me and all my people, Giovanni. It is what Premier Stalin would wish us to do."

"Hurrah for Premier Stalin," John said.

"Tell us what you wish of us," Alexandro said.

"Between you and me," John said. "We *are* going to kill Mussolini."

The Failure

From earlier reconnaissance, John knew it was not possible for a large body of men to infiltrate Salo, simply because the town was not big enough and there was no safe house. In any event, it only needed one good shot to carry out the execution; John knew he had to be the man. Help, in the form of a diversionary attack, was only needed to get away afterwards.

Salo was actually situated up a small inlet off the lake, but the lake represented his way out, if everything went according to plan. Studying the town from the hills above through his binoculars, he could make out the hive of activity on the western side, where men and machines were tearing up the ground and walls were already beginning to appear, "They obviously mean to turn the town into a communications centre as well as a garrison," he told Renaldo and Cesare. "This is what we have to destroy. Causing trouble in the town itself will only be a diversion."

Renaldo nodded, gloomily.

"So you will take your people to the north and west of the town and attack those building works," John said. "You will use grenades and destroy as much as you can. Understood?"

"You will come with us, Giovanni?" Cesare asked.

"Alexandro and I will cause a diversion in the centre of the town. Now, it is very important that we both move at the same time. Check your watches. Eleven o'clock tomorrow morning. Not a moment before, and not a moment after."

The publicity hand-outs, which had been easy to obtain, had announced that Mussolini would make his address from the

189

balcony of his hotel, overlooking the town square, at eleven o'clock on the morning of Wednesday 15 September.

"Will Bianca go with you?" Cesare asked.

"I think it would be best for Bianca to stay here with the other women."

Cesare nodded. "That is good. She has suffered a great deal, through working for you, Giovanni."

It was the first time he had mentioned the relationship between John and his wife. "I know this," John said.

"When the war is over," Cesare said, "you will take her away, and care for her?"

"I shall try to do so, yes."

"But this woman whose picture we have, is she not your wife?"

"It's a damned complicated world," John said. "Let's get the war over first, eh? And sort out our personal relationships after."

Cesare grinned. "You are the commander, Don Giovanni."

"I do not trust him," Bianca said. "He hates you."

"So did Alexandro, when we first met," John pointed out. "Now he is my most faithful follower, even more so than your brothers-in-law."

"That was when you first met," Bianca argued. "But you and Renaldo and Cesare are now old friends, are you not? So it seems. And you did not make off with Alexandro's wife."

"Did I make off with you?"

She snuggled against him. "It just happened. But I wanted it to happen. I do not wish anything to happen to you, Giovanni."

"And nothing will. Cesare may hate me, as you say, but I don't think he will do anything about it until the war is over."

Margo opened the door and gazed at the woman on the bed. She seemed to have known her forever. Because she had known Warrey, for so long, and so well, from time

190

to time. "Get dressed," she said. "We are taking a journey."

Aileen sat up, cautiously. She existed in a constant apprehension of some kind of physical assault, as much from this woman as from any of her male captors. Margo had a way of looking at her that made her skin crawl. Yet no violent or sexual finger had been laid upon her throughout her brief captivity, and she continued to be well fed and kept in comfortable surroundings. She was being saved . . . for what? She could not resist the question: "Have you captured Johnnie?"

"It will happen soon," Margo said. "You wish to be there when it does, do you not? It may be the last time you will ever see him alive."

"What will they do to him?"

"They will ask him to tell them the disposition of his guerilla forces," Margo said.

"He will never tell them that."

Margo smiled. "I think we may be able to persuade him." Aileen shuddered. "And then they will hang him, publicly, I imagine in the square in Milan."

"And me?"

"Would you not like to hang beside him?"

Aileen licked her lips.

Margo chucked her under the chin. "You'd make a pretty pair. But I might be able to save you that ultimate humiliation."

"Why should you do that?"

"Because I think I could become quite fond of you."

"I'd sooner be in bed with a rattlesnake," Aileen said, loading her voice with as much venom as she could.

Margo's eyes blazed with anger, and she almost swung her hand. Then she checked, and smiled. "Wiedelier says you must not be marked, until after we have captured Warrey. But when we have done that, I will ask him to give you to me."

"Has this man been searched?" Wiedelier inquired.

191

"Most thoroughly, Herr Major," Heinrich said.

Wiedelier leaned back in his chair and surveyed the somewhat dishevelled and definitely frightened man standing in front of him. "Well? What have you to say to me?" He spoke Italian.

The man licked his lips. "I have a message for you, Signor Major."

"A message from whom?"

"From Cesare Pescaro."

Wiedelier sat straight, slowly. "The partisan leader?"

"Yes, Signor Major. Signor Pescaro wishes me to tell you that it is the intention of the partisans to launch an attack on Salo tomorrow morning, as Il Duce announces the formation of his new government."

"What sort of an attack?"

"It is to destroy the communications."

Wiedelier stroked his chin. "Who will lead the attack? Warrey?"

"Warrey will be in the town itself, Signor Major. He says his function will be to carry out a diversion, but Signor Pescaro suspects he has designs on the life of Il Duce himself. The attack on the communications is to be led by Cesare and his brother. But they do not intend to carry out this attack. Is it not Warrey you wish?"

"Repeat," Wiedelier said. "You are saying that Colonel Warrey will be in Salo tomorrow morning, trying to get close enough to assassinate Il Duce?"

"Yes, Signor Major."

"Thank you," Wiedelier said. "That is very useful."

The man licked his lips. "Signor Pescaro said you would reward me, Signor Major."

"Of course. Hang this carrion, Heinrich."

The man stared at Wiedelier in consternation. "He said—"

"He clearly takes me for a fool," Wiedelier said. "Do it indoors, Heinrich, and dispose of the body."

Heinrich gulped, and signalled his men.

"When do we leave?" Margo asked. "I have told the woman to dress herself."

"Well, you can tell her to undress again, if that is what she wishes."

"Is she not coming with us?"

"It is no longer necessary," Wiedelier said. "I have made other plans."

"Major Wiedelier. Il Duce," said the aide. "And Signorina Margo Cartwright."

Margo was taken aback. She had only ever seen photographs of Mussolini before, in full, glittering uniform and rows of medals, with his chest thrust out as far as his jutting jaw, and his round Fascisti cap on his head. But here was a broken old man, badly in need of a shave, wearing an ill-fitting uniform, constantly trembling, and always glancing right and left at the aides surrounding him, either needing their constant support or fearing an attack.

His Italian aides were little better, a highly nervous group of men. Unlike the Germans, who *were* in glittering uniforms, and exuded confidence and arrogance. "Major Wiedelier is in charge of anti-subversion measures in the north, your excellency," the staff officer said. "And Signorina Cartwright is his assistant."

Mussolini's eyes flickered over Margo. She had read enough about the erstwhile dictator to know that he had a reputation for being unable to keep his hands off any woman, but she doubted even the Venus di Milo come to life would have much effect on this man. "Anti-subversion," he said, his voice sharp. "Partisans. Anti-Fascists. You must stamp them out, Major."

"I am doing so, your excellency," Wiedelier assured him.

"The people are waiting to be addressed, your excellency," said the staff officer.

"Is it safe?" Mussolini asked.

"I guarantee it, Duce," Wiedelier said.

Mussolini shuffled towards the double doors leading on to the hotel balcony, and his entourage followed. Margo glanced at Wiedelier, uncertainly. He had not told her what had caused his change of plan, nor indeed what his new plan was. Now she saw him give a nod to Heinrich, who was waiting on the far side of the room, and the captain immediately slipped out of a side door. Then they followed Mussolini to the doors, which were opened to expose the balcony, where a loudspeaker had been fixed up, and a newsreel cameraman was already filming as Il Duce emerged.

Mussolini hesitated as he emerged into the daylight, then squared his shoulders and went forward. As he did so, from the forecourt of the hotel several tanks rolled out on to the street, sending the large crowd scuttling for safety. The tank guns slowly lowered and ranged the square. "You'll pardon me, Duce," Wiedelier said. "I will speak first."

John and Alexandro had infiltrated the city at dawn. Their papers had not been checked very thoroughly, because the announcement of Mussolini's arrival had brought people from all the districts surrounding the lake to Salo to see their once-hallowed leader. They had mixed with these crowds, as anonymously as possible. John had brought with him his favourite Mauser hunting rifle, the one he had used in Switzerland, broken into several parts and carried in the haversack worn by most men from the country, and supposedly containing only food. Now it was just a matter of finding the best vantage point. And then getting out again. But this had been organised as far as was possible. Salo used the lake as a receptacle for its sewage, and the system led directly to the water's edge. If they fired as soon as the diversionary attack commenced, and then acted quickly enough, in the confusion John anticipated they would reach the water through the sewage system, and Pasquale would be waiting for them in a boat, having been ostensibly fishing. It was a desperate plan, but John had been involved in so many desperate plans in his brief career he was beginning to have faith in them

The square was quite large, but with the rifle that was not relevant. "That one," John said.

The building was situated exactly opposite the hotel that was Mussolini's headquarters. It was tall, and contained several apartments, and like all its neighbours, was as yet unguarded. But it was still very early in the morning, and the Fascisti police were all still asleep or breakfasting. John and Alexandro stepped into the foyer. "Signors?" asked the concierge.

John had already scanned the name board. "We have business with Signor Petritoli," Alexandro said.

"He is expecting you?"

"Of course," Alexandro said. "It is the top floor, is it not?"

"The top floor." The woman looked uncertain, and John grinned at her.

"We shall not be long," he said.

"You wish to buy something?"

"If he has anything to sell, why not?"

"It would be good if you bought something," she said. "Then he would be able to pay the rent, eh?" She reached for the house phone.

"Good point," John agreed. "Do you think she will call the police?" he asked, as they climbed the somewhat rickety stairs.

"There is no reason for her to do that," Alexandro said, puffing. "What do you think Petritoli is selling?"

They reached the top landing, knocked. A moment later the key turned, and the door swung in, to reveal a young man wearing a beret and a painter's smock over his clothes. "Signor Petritoli?" Alexandro asked. "We have come to look at your work."

Petritoli nodded. "Justina telephoned. I was not expecting you."

"We have just heard of you," Alexandro explained.

Petritoli stepped back, and there was a flurry of movement from behind him. The young woman who had been reclining on the settee was hastily pulling a sheet over her nudity. "Don't mind us," Alexandro said.

John also entered the studio, and closed the door.

"What would you like to see?" Petrotoli asked. "Nudes, or landscapes. I do them both."

"We have not actually come to buy," Alexandro said. "We wish the use of this room, for a few hours."

Petritoli looked from one to the other, and then at John's bag. "Over there," Alexandro said. "Both of you. Do as we say, and we shall not harm you."

Petritoli looked at the bag again. "You are mad," he declared. "This town is filled with soldiers, Nazi and Fascisti."

"We have allowed for that," Alexandro said. "Sit together, against that wall."

Petritoli looked at his model, then shrugged. He sat on the floor, against the wall. Daintily she sat beside him. Equally daintily, Alexandro removed her sheet. "I am going to tie you up," he explained. "That way no one can suppose you were in collusion with us, right?"

The young woman swallowed. She naturally was an attractive sight, or she wouldn't have been an artist's model, John reckoned. But he had more important things on his mind, as he began putting the gun together. "Mad," Petritoli said again. "You will be killed."

"As long as we are out of here when we are killed," Alexandro pointed out, "it will not matter to you." He made them sit back to back, then bound their wrists together, behind their backs, then their ankles, then passed the cord round and round their waists, and secured that. "Now I must gag you also," he said. "I am sorry, but there will be no time afterwards." He completed his task.

By then John had assembled the rifle and loaded it, and was standing by the window, which looked directly down on to the balcony of the hotel opposite. "Ten to ten," he said.

Alexandro sat on the floor, produced a pack of cards, and began playing patience. John prowled around the studio, looking at the paintings; they weren't very good. Petritoli and his model shifted their positions from time to time, as well as they could. At a quarter to eleven both men stood by the window, looking down on the square, now crowded with people. The Fascisti guards were taking up their places round the square, in the doorways of the buildings. Now, if it was going to happen, they would be betrayed by the concierge. But as Alexandro had said, there was no reason for her to do so, as she had accepted their story that they were dealers come to look at Petritoli's work.

John studied the hotel, watched the cameraman fiddling with his equipment, then the double doors above the balcony swung open, and several men emerged. Mussolini was in their midst. Moving hesitantly. Wiedelier was to one side, Margo immediately behind him. I can get them all, he thought.

He looked at his watch: four minutes to eleven. Then he saw the tanks, rolling out from the hotel forecourt. The rumble of their engines seeped up to the artist's studio, and was included in a far louder rumble from behind them. "They are surrounding the square," Alexandro said. "They know we are here. We have been betrayed."

John hesitated, while all manner of possibilities ranged through his mind. He hates you, Bianca had said. Then what of the diversionary attack? He looked at his watch again. Two minutes. Then he looked back at the balcony.

Wiedelier had taken Mussolini's place before the loudspeaker. "Warrey," he said, his voice booming across the square. "We know you are here, Warrey. You cannot escape. The town is surrounded. Show yourself and surrender, and there will be no bloodshed."

"Shit!" Alexandro growled. "It is gone eleven. Where is the attack?"

"There is not going to be an attack," John said, his voice almost a snarl. "As you said, we have been betrayed."

Mussolini had retreated to the back of the balcony. John levelled the rifle, sighted, and fired. But as he did so, a man stepped in front of the Duce. The bullet crashed into his skull and he spun round and fell, his brains scattering. Mussolini also fell, seeking shelter behind the dead body. Instantly all was uproar, men drawing their pistols and firing wildly, the tanks firing with more purpose, into the building from whence the shot had come.

197

John fired again, still seeking Mussolini, but only hit some-one else. Then the building shook as a shell crashed into the lower floors, while the soldiers in the square formed up for an assault. "We must go," Alexandro said.

All of these lives, for nothing, John thought bitterly. "Release them," he snapped.

Alexandro drew his knife and cut the bonds on Petritoli's wrists. "Free yourselves and get out of here," John told them.

"We will be killed," Petritoli wailed, while the model revealed a good pair of lungs as she screamed the moment he dragged the gag from her mouth.

"You'll certainly be killed if you stay here," John said, as the building shook again from the impact of another shell. "Let's go."

Alexandro opened the door, pistol in hand, and they dashed on to the stairs. These were already filled with people seeking to escape the doomed building, shrieking their terror, while pieces of plaster showered down from the ceiling and the stairs themselves were trembling. "Out, out," Alexandro bawled, pushing people left and right. They saw the guns and screamed even louder, but parted before the two armed men.

John and Alexandro reached the bottom hallway just as the front door was thrust open by several German soldiers. Alexandro fired into them, emptying the pistol magazine, and they fell away to either side of the steps. Alexandro and John ran the other way, threw open the back door, and emerged into a narrow yard. "Over there," Alexandro ran at the far fence and scrambled over. John followed, and received a sudden jolt, somewhere in his back.

For the moment he felt no pain, but he knew he had been hit, and he thought it might be serious. Then he was tumbling down on the far side of the fence, while bullets whined in every direction as the Germans took over the house. Now they were in another back yard, and a woman was leaning out of a window above them, shouting incoherently. "She will pinpoint us," Alexandro said, hastily cramming a fresh magazine into his pistol. John steadied himself, levelled the rifle, aiming to miss the woman but hit the window frame, and fired. The woman gave another scream and disappeared.

But now the Germans were at the fence behind them. John sent his last two bullets at them, and thought he had hit someone from the shout of pain. Then he threw down the rifle and drew his own pistol. "Through there!" Alexandro pointed at a gate. "But . . . you are hit!"

"Go, go, go," John said.

Alexandro ran for the gate and threw it open with his shoulder. John followed, starting to feel dizzy. Alexandro put his arm round his waist to steady him. "Listen," he said, "there is a manhole. Get down into the sewer and go to the lake. It is not far. Pasquale will find you."

"And you?"

"I will discourage them."

John hesitated. But in a very short time he knew he was going to be useless if not dead. "It makes more sense for me to stay," he said.

"That is no sense at all," Alexandro said. "You are our leader. You must survive. Now go. Give my regards to Comrade Stalin."

John hesitated a last time. But, if he could survive, it *was* more important for him to do so than Alexandro. "I shall remember," he said, and lifted the manhole cover.

"How could this happen?" Mussolini demanded. He was still shaking. "Those men, those—"

"Brigands and outlaws, your excellency," Wiedelier said. "We are rounding them up now."

"But they nearly shot me!"

"They did not shoot you, Duce. They shot at you, which is an entirely different matter. We had to expose you, briefly, to make them reveal themselves. In particular the man Warrey. We have him now. Do you wish to see him?"

Mussolini shook his head. "I wish him executed."

Wiedelier nodded. "You can look on his dead body instead."

"To think," Wiedelier mused, "that that caricature of a man supposes he can again rule Italy. Come."

Heinrich entered the room, and saluted. "All is now quiet. There has been considerable damage, and I am afraid three people were killed when the house was bombarded. Seven were wounded."

"I have no doubt they were all traitors. Our people?"

"We have five dead and three wounded."

"And Warrey?"

Margo, seated beside her master, found she was holding her breath. "There is no sign of Warrey, Herr Major."

Slowly Wiedelier sat straight. "What did you say? The town is surrounded. He cannot have escaped."

"I think he is dead, Herr Major."

"Then where is his body?"

"In the lake, I think. There is a man you should see."

Wiedelier frowned. "A partisan?"

Heinrich nodded. "Warrey's right-hand man. So he claims. And it is possible he may be telling the truth. He has been identified as Alexandro Fittipati, leader of a Communist partisan group. We know that Warrey has been using the Communists."

Wiedelier got up, picked up his hat and swagger stick. "I will see this man. You come with me, Margo. You may be able to catch him out."

The basement of the hotel was being used as a temporary morgue-cum-hospital. Here the wounded were laid out. The stench was unpleasant.

"This is the man, Herr Major," Heinrich said. "He was certainly with Warrey when they attempted to escape."

Wiedelier stood above Alexandro, who lay on the bare floor, his body a mass of blood. As far as Margo could see, no attempt had been made to tend his wounds or ease his pain. "You are dying, Fittipati," Wiedelier said.

"But I took some of your bastards with me, eh?" Alexandro asked, and actually managed a grin.

"Some," Wiedelier said. "Do you wish to die in much more pain than you are now suffering?"

Alexandro shrugged, and his face twisted in agony. "If I am going to die, it does not much matter how."

"Tell me where Warrey is."

"Warrey is dead."

"We have not found his body. Where did he die?"

"Maybe in the sewer, maybe he got to the lake. He was badly hit. He knew he was dying. I told him to try to get out, but I knew he would not make it."

"Why did you not go with him to the lake?"

"Because I had been hit too. I have not the strength of mind that Warrey has. I could not move." Another twisted grin. "I could only shoot."

Wiedelier considered him for several seconds. Then he turned to Margo. "What do you think?"

"I think he could be telling the truth," Margo said. "But it might be a good idea to drag the lake."

Wiedelier looked at Heinrich, who shrugged. "I will do so if you wish it, Herr Major, but I should point out that the lake is very deep, even close in to the shore. And that there are strong currents. I think it is very unlikely that we will recover a body."

"Do it anyway," Wiedelier said.

Wiedelier gave Margo a glass of schnapps, took one himself. "If Warrey is dead, then we are to be congratulated. We may commence by congratulating each other."

"Thank you. Is my work here finished, now?"

"No. I think you should stay here, until we are quite sure that he is dead. Until we have looked on his body. Anyway, where would you wish to go?"

"Somewhere far away from the Allies."

"This is far enough. They are not going to find it easy to come up the peninsula. We have established so many defensive lines they will still be there next year. No, no, you will stay here. I have become used to having you about the place."

"And Warrey's wife?"

"She has become entirely redundant. You may dispose of her." He shook his head. "All of that time and money, for nothing."

"I would like her kept alive," Margo said in a low voice.

Wiedelier refilled their glasses. "For what purpose?"

"Just . . . company."

Wiedelier subjected her to one of his stares. "You mean, sexually? You? But of course, I should have known."

"I just wish to have her," Margo muttered. "She is English, as am I. I have no one to talk to."

"The decadent English female," Wiedeliar remarked. "Of course you may have her, Margo. To do with her whatever you wish."

The fishing boat came into the shore, at a deserted bank well north of Salo. It was the appointed place, and the partisans were waiting for it. "Quickly," Pasquale said. "The colonel is badly hurt."

Warrey was only just conscious. The day had descended into a vast, pain-filled blur. The sewer and the rats, the outfall and the plunge into the surprisingly cold water, the effort to keep afloat, the sight of the fishing boat, all drifted in and out of his memory like a dream. Then Pasquale's face, as he bound up the wound. "I do not think it is fatal," he said. "But it is bad. And you have lost a lot of blood."

Now he was carried ashore and looked at Bianca, leaning over him, her face wet with tears. "Alexandro?" Luana was beside him, anxious.

"Do not ask questions, now," Pasquale said. "He is too weak. Where is the cart?"

They carried John to the cart. He could not stop himself moaning with pain. "We must give him something," Bianca said. "Mix this."

Bottles of sedatives were poured together, taken from his own First Aid kit, and a moment later he felt a prick in his arm. He only hoped the needle was clean.

When John awoke the movement had ceased, and he was lying on a blanket on the ground, surrounded by anxious faces. The pain had receded, a little, but it lurked, waiting to return. "Soup," Bianca said, feeding him.

He drank, greedily. "How is it?"

"A great hole, four broken ribs . . ." she made a face. "What happened?"

"We were betrayed. They knew we were coming."

The partisans exchanged glances. "What happened to Alexandro?" Luana asked.

"Dead, or taken."

"My Alexandro!" she screamed.

John had not been aware the two had a relationship. "He sacrificed himself that I could get away," John said. "I shall not forget that."

"And Mussolini?" Pasquale asked.

"I didn't get him. The whole thing was a catastrophe." And for a lot of innocent people, he thought. I didn't even get Wiedelier, or Margo. He was not used to failure, or at least, such complete failure. He had also failed to get Rommel when sent against the German general – clearly assassination was not his forte – but he had at least caused a great deal of disruption behind the German lines in North Africa.

"Who did this thing?" Pasquale asked.

"I have an idea," John said.

Moving slowly, because of John's wound, the partisans retreated north of the lake and across the Adige to the mountains; the Fascisti, and the Germans, were out in force, scouring the entire lake area. But the band was now very small, and Pasquale, who had assumed command, kept one step ahead of their pursuers. For John it was a continuing agony. Bianca and the priest had bound him up as best they could, but he could still feel the broken bones grating, and he remained weak from loss of blood. Coherent thought came and went. "You should be in hospital," Bianca told him.

"Listen, we must try to smuggle you across the border into Switzerland."

"That will be very difficult," Pasquale said. "The Germans have at last worked out from where we are getting our supplies, and have closed all the mountain passes."

"I couldn't go, anyway," John muttered. "I still have a job to do here."

Bianca grunted in disapproval, but she didn't really want him to go.

"Where are Renaldo and Cesare?" John asked. Two weeks had passed since the abortive attempt on Mussolini's life, and Renaldo's people had not returned.

"I think they must be all dead, or captured," Bianca said.

Maria Theresa burst into tears, and Marco looked as fierce as a twelve-year-old boy could.

But there had been no diversionary attack.

"You still have not told us who you think betrayed you," Bianca said.

"I will deal with the matter when I am fit again." There was so much to deal with. Principally Aileen. But she was beyond his reach. He could not ask these loyal people, who now consisted mainly of women and children, to attempt another assault, and suffer more horrendous casualties, to save his wife, when he could not lead them. He did not even know if she was still alive.

"I will find out," Bianca promised. She did not go herself, but sent Luana, who was an expert at infiltrating the towns. She was gone several days. While she was away, John tried to contact Home Affairs, but could not raise a reply, and he dared not use the set for more than a few minutes at a time, in case the Germans traced the signal.

After a week, Luana returned. "Nobody knows what has happened to your woman, Giovanni," she said. "It is supposed she has been executed since the Salo raid."

She is dead, John thought. So what have I got left, but vengeance?

"But I heard something else," Luana said. "They were talking of a raid on a German outpost north-west of the lake."

"Who did this?" Pasquale asked.

"They say it is the band of Renaldo."

"Renaldo? Was he not destroyed at Salo?"

Luana shrugged. "I can only repeat what I was told."

Pasquale looked at John. "He acted without orders."

"Yes," John said. "I would say we have a split. What we need, Pasquale, is more men."

"Your husband seems to have more lives than a cat," Margo remarked, kicking off her shoes and stretching herself on the bed beside Aileen.

Aileen had sat up at her entrance. Now she hastily moved to the far side of the bed. But her heart was pounding. "You mean he is alive?"

"I suspect he is, although Wiedelier is certain he is not. But we have been unable to find his body. They say the lake is renowned for keeping its secrets. But until it gives up this one, I am stuck in this hellhole for the foreseeable future. But if he is alive, I don't think he is showing too much regard for you, my dear. He knows we are holding you. He must suspect the worst as regards your treatment. Yet he still seems to prefer fighting his little war, ignoring your situation entirely. I do not think that is very gallant. If I were you I would be very angry about it."

Alison had in fact been thinking about it; she had little else to think about. But she was still only slowly coming to terms with the knowledge that John was apparently a famous undercover agent; she had always found it odd, and regarded it as due to the back-scratching element of the armed services, that he should have picked up two medals merely for correlating intelligence reports. Now . . . according to this woman, he was a ruthless and even savage killer. A government assassin, who only a few days ago had gone after Mussolini himself, and who had killed God alone knew how many men, and women, in North Africa.

Admiration for what he was, so successfully, had to be greater than revulsion for what he did, also successfully. To think that the quiet, thoughtful man she called her husband, with whom she had shared just five precious but essentially dispassionate weeks over the past year and a half, went out to kill whenever he was not at her side!

She knew he was fond of her. But she had never supposed he was wildly in love with her. Theirs had been a typical genteel middle-class marriage. But for the war they would have lived entirely unexceptional lives, with John going to the architects' office every morning, while she perhaps had coffee with a friend, playing tennis or walking on weekends, attending or throwing the odd cocktail party, really letting their hair down on New Year's Eve with perhaps an illicit extra-marital kiss or two, perhaps in the course of time becoming parents, and then growing old gracefully together, while never exceeding the bounds of propriety as dictated by their class and their heritage.

Why, during their still few bouts of love-making, when he had touched her bottom or between her legs the hand had always been hastily withdrawn with a silent apology! The perfect gentleman.

"You know, of course," Margo said, "that he has always had a woman in tow. He likes working with women, I think because they always fall in love with him. When I think of the Arab bints who used to follow him around like bitches on heat . . . I do not suppose these Italian woman are any different. Doesn't that make you jealous?"

Yes, Aileen thought, it makes me jealous. Not of the women, but of what I might have received, at his hands, had I been able to serve with him. "Did you once follow him around as well?" she asked, innocently.

Margo's face became distorted with anger, just for a moment. Then she said, "Come here."

Aileen hesitated, then moved back across the bed. She didn't want to have SS men called in here to manhandle her. And besides, she was aware of an emotion she had never experienced before. Or if she had, it had been immediately suppressed. Now, suddenly, suppression of emotion was the very last thing she felt like doing.

Margo held her hand. "So," she remarked, "you are becoming fond of rattlesnakes." She ran her hand over the bodice of Aileen's dress. "Tell me about John," she said.

The Reunion

A s winter set in, the Allied armies steadily progressed up the peninsula. Naples fell on 1 October, and two weeks later Badoglio formally declared war on Germany. This made no immediate difference to the situation in the north, as Mussolini's New Fascist State was firmly established, under German control. And as the weather worsened, the Allied advance slowed, until in January 1944, when it came up against the hugely fortified German position at Cassino, south of Rome, it ground to a halt altogether in the rain and the mud. Mussolini, meanwhile, was pursuing a policy of vengeance, executing as many of his old comrades as he could lay hands on, including such once faithful supporters as Marshal di Bono and his son-in-law Count Ciano.

This witch hunt was useful for John and Pasquale, as they received a considerable number of new recruits, many of them deserters from the Army, but it was a stagnant and frustrating period for all of them. John was particularly concerned about his inability to make contact with Home Affairs. He knew from his radio that the Germans had reported him dead, and it seemed obvious that Cox had accepted that and withdrawn his Swiss-based support. With his own short-wave set he was unable to reach anyone else to correct the situation.

He would in any event have been unable to undertake any large-scale operations, both because of his wound and because of his shortage of *matériel*. The wound healed slowly during the winter, aggravated by their constantly having to keep moving to avoid German patrols. Yet he could feel himself growing stronger. But with no support from across the border there was little he could do about the lack of ammunition and explosives. "You should not fret so," Bianca told him, as they huddled in their blankets in an Alpine cave, listening to the wind howling outside. "The Allies are winning. We have but to wait for them to reach us."

"I was sent here to fight a war," John grumbled. "Not hide in a cave." Without her constant loving care, and Pasquale's unchanging encouragement and faith in the ultimate victory, as well as the priest's real talent in managing their people, John felt he would not have survived, certainly mentally. His mind was a turmoil of guilt, at having been able to do nothing about Aileen, and of the relative failure of his mission. The Milan raid had been a great success, and had certainly assisted the Allied invasion, but the cost had been exorbitant, and in personal terms as well. He could not be sure whether or not he had ever intended to get together with Annaliese; he was not sure he had even liked the woman. But she had fought at his shoulder, and died, virtually at his shoulder.

He could only find solace in Bianca's arms, in the strange mixture of hardness and softness of her naked body, in the eagerness with which she reponded to his touch. Had he found a replacement for Soroya? He doubted he could ever do that. But for the moment she was his only comfort.

They heard nothing of Renaldo and Cesare either. But as they also did not hear that they had been killed or captured, they had to suppose they were still operating. Maria Theresa fretted. "I must go to my husband. How can he exist, without his wife?"

"I would say he is existing very well," Bianca commented.

"Ha," Maria Theresa commented. "What do you think, Marco?"

Next day they left, to search for their family.

"It is necessary to plan for the spring," Pasquale said. "Our people are restless. They wish to attack the Germans. Or the Fascisti. They wish to attack something. When will you be well again?"

"In the spring," John promised.

His best bet, John supposed, would be against the railways, as another raid on any town was simply not practical; he lacked both the men and the firepower. And in the spring, as he had promised, he felt strong enough to resume operations; his broken bones seemed to have mended, even if they gave him a twinge from time to time.

He now had a force of some hundred men, women and children, a far cry from the fifteen hundred he had been able to use in the Milan attack, but they were armed, and were sufficient to remind the Germans that he was still alive, and maybe reopen communications with the Allies. But he still lacked sufficient explosives to carry out a major attack. "We will have to hijack a train," he said. "And then tear up the track, and so derail it."

Pasquale scratched his chin. "It will be very difficult."

"It's the best we can do. I thought you wanted action?"

"I think we should attempt to contact Renaldo."

"You reckon? After he deserted us at Salo?" He still preferred to keep his thoughts on the betrayal to himself.

"I have been thinking about this," Pasquale said. "Renaldo was always an admirer of Mussolini. That he why he was against the attempt to assassinate the Duce. That is why he would not fight. But now that Italy is in the war, on the Allied side, I believe he may change his mind, and come in with us again."

John shrugged, and winced. "Just so long as the next time he obeys orders."

Pasquale went off.

Two days later the sentries reported several men approaching the encampment, which was still situated in and around the cave in the hillside. John immediately supposed they might be Renaldo's people, and perhaps Renaldo himself. Or Cesare. He got up, strapped on his pistol, leaving it concealed beneath a blanket thrown over his shoulder. But for the time being he remained in the cave.

"I have come to take command," announced the newcomers' leader; it was not a voice John recognised. But the visitors were surprisingly spruce, and very well armed.

"We have a commander," Bianca told him.

The newcomer snorted. "Some itinerant priest?"

"Our commander is Colonel Warrey, the man who led the raid on Milan."

The newcomer frowned. He was a little man, with a pointed beard and heavy eyebrows. "Colonel Warrey is dead."

"That is not so," Bianca said.

John got up and moved to the front of the cave. He was fully dressed, although he knew he had lost a lot of weight, and his beard had grown again, to a considerable length. "I am Warrey," he said.

The newcomer peered at him. "The Colonel was badly wounded in the attack on Salo," Bianca explained. "But he is well again now."

"He does not look well to me," the newcomer remarked, and approached the cave. "I am Colonel Valerio. I have been sent by the Council to take command in this area."

"Council?" John inquired.

"The supreme Communist Council in North Italy. The Council is concerned that this area has shown little activity against the Fascists during the winter."

"We have been inactive because the Colonel was wounded," Bianca said, hotly.

"But now he is well again, he says," Valerio pointed out.

"Yes," John said. "I am well again. And ready to undertake an offensive. But you are welcome to serve with us, if you wish, Colonel Valerio."

Valerio stared at him. "I will command."

Shades of Alexandro. But Alexandro had turned out well in the end. "No," John said. "I am in command, and will remain so."

"I was sent by the supreme—"

"I was sent by the Allied High Command," John said, drawing the bow a bit but this man could not possibly know any different. "By General Eisenhower himself." Drawing the bow tighter yet.

Valerio continued to stare at him for several seconds, his hand hovering by the revolver at his belt.. But he was in a difficult position, as he had only seven men, and he was in the midst of close to a hundred partisans. John decided to end the confrontation, one way or the other. "If you do not think I am well enough to lead," he said, "Watch." He had practised constantly during the winter, and the pistol, which had remained concealed beneath the blanket, was in his hand and levelled before the Communist leader could blink.

Valerio gave a little gasp and stepped backwards, while the partisans clapped. "He shoots even better," Bianca said

Valerio glanced at her, then at his companions, then at John again. "Tell us what you plan to do, Colonel," he said.

"I am leaving Italy," Wiedelier said. "Would you not like to leave Italy?"

"Would I?" Margo cried. "Oh, thank God for that." The Allies advance might currently be held up before Monte Cassino, but she did not doubt they would break through once the weather improved. "But why?"

"My superiors have at last accepted the fact that Warrey is dead. All partisan activity here in the north has subsided. I have therefore been recalled for special duties in France. There seems to be no doubt that the Allies will attempt to invade France this summer, and with my special knowledge of handling subversive activities I am required there. I could take you with me."

"Oh, please." Anything to get out of Italy.

"Well, then, we shall leave next week."

"And the woman?"

"Warrey's wife? I told you, Margo, she is redundant. If you enjoy possessing her, that is up to you."

Margo was not embarrassed. Nothing that this man could do or say would ever embarrass her, now. "Can I not take her to France as well?"

"Like a toy poodle?" He shrugged. "If you wish. But she is your responsibility. If she becomes a nuisance, I will have her shot. Or sent to a concentration camp. She would probably prefer to be shot."

"She will not be a nuisance," Margo assured him.

"Germany?" Aileen asked. "I don't want to go to Germany."

"Well, you can't stay here on your own," Margo told her. "You either come to Germany with me, or it is a bullet in the head."

"And what happens to me in Germany?"

"Actually, I am going to France. You'll like France."

"I've been to France," Aileen muttered. What had she become, simply in her determination to stay alive, to wait for Johnnie to come for her? But he had not, and the Germans were now sure he was dead. While she . . . had become a kept woman, in the most ghastly of fashions. She was a pampered pet. In the nine months of her captivity her hair had grown out from its Army crop into the luxuriant black silk of her girlhood. She was well fed and well wined, every day. She had been bought the best clothes available from the dress shops of Milan. And every day she descended further down the slope to hell.

So what was left? Suicide? Only if she could take Margo with her. She was determined to do that, but . . . It should be simple enough; there were always weapons lying about the rooms they shared in the hotel. Her problem was that she knew nothing about weapons, and she did not know if she had the guts to kill. Whereas Margo knew everything about weapons, and Margo certainly knew how to kill, and she was the bigger, stronger woman. Am I that weak, she wondered? That afraid? Oh, Johnnie!

"We leave a week tomorrow," Margo said. She stood in the centre of the room, looking about her, hands on hips. "I will be so glad to see the back of this dump."

John had not yet chosen a target, much to Valerio's annoyance,

when Luana returned from one of her prostituting visits to
Rivoli. "I had a German officer," she announced.

"And did not drive a knife into his ribs?" Valerio demanded,
contemptuously. He and his men were certainly disruptive
elements in the partisan camp, but John did nothing about
it, because they were by far the most eager of his people
to resume the fight. More importantly, the Communists had
brought with them several sticks of dynamite, not sufficient
for a major assault, but certainly sufficient to blow up a train.

"Then I would not be here, stupid," Luana said. "He gave me
information."

"What information?" John asked.

"He told me that Major Wiedelier is returning to Germany.
Tomorrow week."

"Wiedelier? You are sure? What of the Englishwoman?"

"He did not mention her."

"But where Wiedelier goes, she will go too," Pasquale said.
He had returned from his visit to Renaldo's camp, which was
situated some distance away. Renaldo had been as surprised as
anyone to learn that John had survived Salo. He had promised to
co-operate in any projected attack. John had not commented on
this, but he had no intention of ever trusting Renaldo again.

"I have heard of this Wiedelier," Valerio said. "He is good
riddance."

"Wiedelier," Bianca said. "I would like to have Wiedelier."

Valerio laughed. "What would you do to him?"

"I would tie him on his back, naked, and drop burning coals
on his prick until he was a eunuch," Bianca said in a low voice.
Even the partisans were shocked into silence. John squeezed
her hand. "You do not know what he did to me," Bianca said.
"The way he played with me, the electricity he pushed into my
body—"

She had never spoken of her treatment by the SS before. Now
her fingers were like talons, biting into John's flesh. And what
had Wiedelier done to Aileen, before he had shot her? "I think
we will make that train our target," he said. "You are sure of
the date, Luana? Tomorrow week?"

Luana nodded.

"And the route?"

"They will take the train to Monza and thence up to Como and into Switzerland for Munich."

The map was spread. "Como is a hundred kilometres," Valerio said.

"So we leave immediately," John said. "We will stop the train outside Monza; there is no need to go to Como."

Wiedelier and the two women boarded the train at Milan Central at seven o'clock in the morning. It was gloomy, both from the early hour and the overnight rain. The train was carrying quite a few German personnel north. Rats deserting a sinking ship, Aileen thought; she knew where the Allies were. They were coming, even if dreadfully slowly.

Wiedelier naturally had a compartment to himself, with the women. Their scanty luggage was placed in the overhead racks, and then, as always, he subjected Aileen to several long stares as the train started moving. "What do you think about, Frau Warrey, sitting there so silently?"

"I was wondering what you think about, Major Wiedelier, knowing that the war is lost for you, that the Allies are slowly crushing you to death, the Russians in the East, the British and the Americans in the south, and soon in the west as well. When they have won, and are dictating peace terms in Berlin, you will be charged with war crimes." She glanced at Margo. "And you will be tried as a traitor, and shot."

"Stop it!" Margo shouted. "Stop it!" she shrieked. "You are a bitch!" She began swinging her hands, slapping Aileen to and fro. Aileen tried to roll with the blows, but tasted blood as her lips were cut.

Wiedelier watched them for several seconds, before he said, "Cease!" Margo subsided, chest heaving, cheeks red. "If she upsets you so much," Wiedelier said, "why do you keep her?"

My God, Aileen thought, it was her life they were discussing, as if she were some object of dubious value.

"I will make her suffer," Margo said. "Suffer!" she shouted.

Slowly Aileen wiped her lips, looked at the blood on her hands. There was so much more she could say, to drive this woman again into a frenzy of terror, at what she had done, what she had become, the ghastly mistake she had made in selling out to the enemy. But that would only earn her another beating. It would keep.

"Then let us try to have a civilised journey," Wiedelier said.

The train rumbled on, made its usual stop at Monza, where several people got on, carrying their items of luggage, mostly shoulder bags or handbags. Then they were away again, moving north towards Como. The guard looked in, clipped their tickets. He was an Italian, and looked nervous.

"In another hour we shall be in Switzerland." Wiedelier looked at his watch. "Early for schnapps, eh? We will have a drink then."

The train pulled into Desio Station. This was a small place, but the platform was crowded. "Where are all these people going?" Margo asked. "They cannot be going to Switzerland."

"Probably up to Como," Wiedelier suggested.

Aileen looked out of the window. Odd, she thought, most of these passengers were also carrying little bags; they looked remarkably similar, in their body language, to those at Monza. Then she saw a quite strikingly beautiful woman, tall and slender, with the pale features of a Madonna, shrouded in long, silky black hair . . . very like her own, she realised. "Isn't she gorgeous," she remarked, without thinking.

Margo looked in the indicated direction, and gave a strangled shriek. "Bianca Pescaro!"

"What?" Wiedelier jumped up and turned to the window. As he did so, Aileen realised that the man beside the woman Margo had denounced was John. His face was half concealed, but there could be no doubt of it.

Margo was reaching for the window, but Wiedelier pushed her away. "Stay here." He opened the door to run along the corridor. Instantly there was a burst of firing. The people on the platform scattered, those obviously innocent seeking shelter, the others, led by John and the woman, running towards the

216

train, discarding the handbags from which they had taken a variety of weapons.

Now the shooting became general. Margo dropped to her hands and knees. "Get down, you stupid bitch!" she shouted. "Do you want to get killed?"

"John," Aileen said. "That was John!"

Margo got up again, her face the picture of consternation. "Warrey is dead," she snapped. "Dead, dead, dead!" A bullet shattered the window, and she went down again. Then she crawled to the open door into the corridor, and disappeared.

At last Aileen forced herself to the floor. She had no idea what was happening, save that she was in the middle of a gun battle. But John! Alive, and again attacking the Germans. She could not believe it. But she had seen him! She crawled to the doorway, looked out. The corridor was empty. But as she hesitated, uncertain what to do, two German soldiers ran into it, from the front of the train. "Take cover, Fräulein," one shouted, not knowing who she was.

Aileen ducked back into the compartment. As she did so, one of the men spun round and hit the floor of the corridor in a flurry of blood. The other stepped into the compartment beside Aileen, pistol drawn, watching the doorway.

"Down here!" John's voice! The soldier raised his pistol, and Aileen scrambled to her feet and shoulder-charged him from behind. She seemed to bounce off him, but he lost his balance and staggered forward, through the doorway and back into the corridor, immediately to be struck by several bullets and fall beside his comrade.

"Johnnie!" Aileen screamed. A moment later she was in his arms.

"They told me you were dead," she sobbed.

"And I supposed you were dead. But here—"

"They were taking me to Germany. Oh, Johnnie—"

"We'll speak of it later," he said. "Where's Margo?"

"I don't know. She crawled out of here. She's somewhere on the train, I should think."

He peered at her face. "Your hair . . . and you've been beaten."

"I haven't had a haircut in ages. As for the bruise . . . I had a fight with Margo." She gave a wry smile. "Or she had a fight with me, would be more accurate." Margo, she knew, was going to lie between them like a bolster. Margo, and how many others? But for the moment she was too happy to care.

"We'll get her," John said, and gave an order in Italian to the men behind him. "Now let's get out of here; this train is going to blow."

"My bag—"

He snatched it from the rack, put his arm round her shoulders as they went along the corridor. This was littered with bodies, mostly German soldiers, but there were also some partisans. Other partisans were looting the dead of their weapons and ammunition. John opened the door for her, on to the platform, and then helped her down. The platform was guarded by armed partisans, both men and women, but there was a crowd of onlookers beyond the barriers. And beyond them, the sirens were wailing

"They'll have people here any minute," John said. He held her hand to lead her along the platform to the end, and then down on to the tracks. These were being torn up by another body of partisans. John gave more orders in Italian, and they downed tools and hurried for the trees and the hills.

Aileen could not believe she wasn't dreaming. Last year her entire world had been turned upside down, when she had been kidnapped. Now it was being turned upside down again, the other way. But this was John, a masterful, dominating man she had never known, holding her hand. She stumbled beside him, into the trees, and up the slope beyond. "That woman who was with you," she gasped.

"Later," he said. There was going to have to be a great deal of explaining, later.

More and more men and women were now joining them, shouting and cheering. But some were disconsolate. "They can't find Margo," John said. "Now there's a pity. But—" he

218

pointed through the trees, at Bianca, waiting for them. She was accompanied by several men, and in their midst was Wiedelier. He had lost his jacket and his cap and his waistbelt, and had clearly been beaten.

"I claim him," Bianca said. "For what he did to me."

What had she said she would do to him? "Bring him along," John said. "Whatever we decide to do to him, we haven't the time to do it here."

Bianca looked at Aileen, and Aileen immediately knew who she was, even if she hadn't been able to understand the exchange. So she gazed back, knowing there would have to be a confrontation, some time. Whenever they got where they were going.

"Let's move," John said.

Margo reached the end of the carriage and dropped down to the ground. There was shooting all around her, but it seemed no one had seen her, save for three German soldiers crouching beside where she fell. One of them she recognised. "Help me," she gasped.

"Help you, Fräulein?" the sergeant asked. "We are trying to help ourselves." Then his gaze softened. "Get out. Make for the woods and follow the track back to Monza. Tell them what happened here."

Margo crouched as she ran through the trees, keeping the track on her right. Her shoes came off and she ignored them, staggering and wincing as her stockings were torn to shreds by the rough ground. She had run about two hundred yards when she heard the explosion behind her and was flung on to her face by the blast. She rolled over and sat up, staring back at the train, which was burning fiercely, listening to the distant shouts. But the firing had died down. Wiedelier! What had happened to Wiedelier? Without Wiedelier she was nothing.

What do do? She heard sirens wailing, and now more shots. The Germans were counter-attacking. But to go back, if Wiedelier had been killed, would be to expose herself to prison at the very least. Only Wiedelier knew who she was, why she was. And if Wiedelier was dead . . . Heinrich Osterman! Heinrich knew. But Heinrich was back in Milan.

Somehow she had to get back to Milan. Heinrich would be glad to see her, if she could tell him that Warrey was still alive. And Heinrich, unlike Wiedelier, was a gentleman, and certainly not a pervert. She made herself move again, down the track, towards Monza. It was several miles away, and her clothes were torn and her body ached. But she would get there, and she would get back to Milan. It could be no more difficult than surviving in the desert.

Planes ranged overhead, tanks crashed through the under-growth and clawed their way up and down the hills and through the valleys, hostages were taken and shot . . . but the partisans had as usual melted away into the mountains.

Not fully fit after her months of captivity and lack of exercise, Aileen was exhausted by the end of the first day, could do nothing more than collapse on the ground, regardless of the damage done to her smart dress; it was in any event torn in several places. John had to shake her awake to make her eat and drink. "I think I'm dreaming," she said. "I think that all the time. Oh, Johnnnie—"

He squeezed her hand, and she realised he had not yet kissed her. Well, she supposed, kissing in these circumstances was hardly appropriate. It would work out. It had to, now they were together, fighting . . . or at least, running, for their lives. But did she want to be kissed by a man known as a mass murderer? Could she ever wish to have sex with him again? Perhaps he understood her feelings, which was why he was giving her time. Or perhaps he was no longer interested in her, if he had that beauty to warm his back. "Where are we going?" she asked.

"To the area north of Lake Garda. That is our base."

"And you have been there—?"

He grinned. "Getting on for two years. I'm sorry I couldn't tell you."

"Or about North Africa?"

"That too. Who told you about that? Oh, of course, Margo." His face was serious. "Was it very bad?"

"Sometimes. Johnnie—"

"I shouldn't have asked that. Some things are better kept to oneself."

"No," she said. "It's something we have to talk about."

"Not now," he said.

They dared not risk a fire, and their food was cold and hard. Aileen realised that the quite large number of partisans at the railway station had dwindled to a group of no more than twenty, the others hiving off to diffuse the pursuit. But this group retained Wiedelier as a prisoner. He was the only one. "Do you wish to speak with him?" John asked.

Aileen shuddered. "What will happen to him?"

"He will be executed; he has wronged too many of these people. Especially Bianca. She was his prisoner for several days, and he tortured her, quite savagely. But I am going to try to have it carried out in a civilised manner."

"Bianca," Aileen said. "Is she—?"

"She is close to being my second-in-command," John said. "After Father Pasquale."

With which Aileen had to be content for the time being. There was so much about her new existence that was completely strange to her, a far greater contrast between the life she had always known and imprisonment by the Germans. Merely sleeping out of doors was new to her; even in her training in England they had always had the use of at least a pup tent. Performing one's necessaries was another first, for she dared not go too far from the encampment. But seven of the group were women.

Including Bianca. She was by herself a little way from the camp when Bianca joined her. "You speak Italian?"

"A little," Aileen said,

"Warrey's wife," Bianca said, "You have caused him much grief."

"I know," Aileen said. "And what have you caused him?"

221

Bianca's face was serious. "As much happiness as is possible."

I should hate you, Aileen thought. But you are so beautiful. And to think of you, at the mercy of Wiedelier – then perhaps I should hate John. But John had only done what came naturally. "Then I thank you," she said.

Bianca raised her eyebrows. "Has he told you of me?"

"No," Aileen said. "Should he have?"

"When he is ready," Bianca said, and fingered the material of her dress. "This is very fine. Do you have other clothes like this in your bag?"

"Yes," Aileen said. "Would you like to see them? Have some? You would be welcome."

"You do not have to be my friend," Bianca said, and returned to the camp, to sit before Wiedelier, and stare at him.

Wiedelier was very afraid. He knew he was to all intents and purposes already dead. It was the manner of the dying that frightened him. He was acutely uncomfortable, his hands tied behind his back. The women tended him, taking down his breeches to allow him to pass water, giggling and cackling to each other as they handled him, fed him, and gave him water to drink. Only Bianca did not smile or laugh or jeer. She did not even touch him. She just sat and stared at him, while he licked his lips. "You will kill me, with those eyes," he said.

"Oh, yes," she said. "I am going to kill you. Slowly."

Aileen almost felt sorry for him. It had to be a fate he had always feared. She could not imagine what his feelings might be, knowing he was in danger of being tortured to death.

She had no indication of what the sleeping arrangements might be, and in any event John allowed them to rest for only a few hours before urging them on again; the valley behind them was filled with noise as the Germans sought them. They marched all night, steadily climbing. At dawn she could go no further, and again collapsed. John called a halt, and the women prepared a meal. "She will not survive," Bianca said.

"She is stronger than she looks," John said.

"What will happen?" she asked. "To us. To me."

He sighed. "Right this minute I have no idea."

"She is your wife. But you are not a Catholic. You could divorce her."

"Do you think you and I could make a go of it? As husband and wife?"

"Have we not shared everything? Or is it because I was tortured by Wiedelier? Was she not also tortured by him?"

"I suppose it's possible. She has not spoken of it."

"I did not speak of mine, for a long time. Do you love her?"

"She is my wife."

"That is not an answer. Is her sex as good as mine?"

Another sigh. "No, Bianca. I do not think there is a woman in the world whose sex is as good as yours."

"I will make you very happy, for the rest of your life," Bianca said.

"I do not doubt it. But will I make *you* happy?"

"Oh, yes."

"There are things . . . I do not wish Wiedelier to be mutilated."

"He deserves it."

"No doubt he does. But we're trying to be civilised."

"Civilised," she scoffed. "There can be no civilisation in a war. It is a business of killing, destroying,"

"True enough. But we must see what we can do, when possible."

"Will you stay with me, afterwards, if I do not cut him up?" Bianca asked.

"Listen, let's win our war first, and worry about afterwards, afterwards. But I will not stay with you *if* you cut him up."

She gazed at him for several seconds. Then she said, "Will you share my blanket, tonight?"

"I think we should sleep separately, for the time being."

"You will not go to your wife?"

"No. She has a lot of adjusting to do."

Bianca nodded. "Well, then. Tomorrow."

When they awoke the following morning, John was summoned by Pasquale to look at Wiedelier. The SS officer lay on his back, a knife thrust through his throat, pinning him to the ground. He had not been mutilated.

"Did she do it?" Aileen asked, as they trudged through the valleys.

"Of course."

"And you can still—" she shuddered.

"Do you know what he did to her? Perhaps he did the same to you."

"He never touched me," she said in a low voice.

He glanced at her, surprised.

"What will you do with Margo, when you capture her?" Aileen asked.

She had betrayed herself. "I imagine we will hang her," John said.

"We have the Englishwoman, Herr Captain," said the lieutenant.

Henrich Osterman raised his head. He had been studying the report of the attack on the train. The partisans seemed to have found a new leader. "What Englishwoman?"

"Major Wiedelier's assistant, Herr Captain."

Heinrich got up and went into the antechamber. It was difficult to recognise the huddled woman in the torn clothes, smothered in dust and mud, seated in one of the chairs, as Margo Cartwright. "My God! You were on the train."

Margo hardly seemed to hear him. She was shivering, although it was warm inside SS headquarters in Milan. "She was picked up by a patrol outside Monza," the lieutenant said. "She was in a very bad state."

"She is still in a very bad state," Heinrich pointed out.

"I gave her some schnapps, but she would not eat."

The attack on the train had been three days ago. "Have Dr Feldmars come in immediately," Heinrich said. He lifted Margo from the chair and took her into the office, laid her on the settee. "Tell me what happened. Did the partisans capture you?"

She licked her lips. Heinrich went to his desk, took out a bottle of brandy, and filled the cup. Margo drank this, and seemed to feel better. "Warrey," she said.

Delirious, he thought. "But you got away," he suggested.

"Warrey led the attack."

Heinrich frowned; she was speaking quite lucidly. "Warrey is dead, Margo."

She sat up. "He is alive, I tell you. He led the attack. He and that renegade priest, and that bitch of a Pescaro. I saw them all. They got Wiedelier."

Heinrich knew that at least was true; Wiedelier's body had not been found. "And the other Englishwoman?" His tone was only slightly contemptuous.

"I don't know. I think they must have got her as well. But Warrey! Warrey is alive and again leading the partisans."

"If this is true, I must inform Field Marshal Kesselring at once." He stroked his chin. "I suppose I will have to inform Mussolini as well. This is a bad business. Come," he called as there was a knock on the door. "Ah, Herr Doctor. Kindly examine Fräulein Cartwright."

The doctor made a face but pulled up a chair and sat beside Margo. Heinrich returned behind his desk and started to telephone. By the time he had finished, Feldmars had completed his examination. "There is nothing the matter with her a hot bath and a square meal will not set right. She has several cuts and bruises, and her feet are in a bad state. I will take her down to the hospital and attend to her."

"And then I will be well enough to travel again?" Margo asked.

"Why, certainly," Feldmars agreed.

Margo looked at Heinrich. "I want to get out of here as soon as possible. Please get me out of here, Herr Captain."

"I'm afraid that is not practical," Heinrich said. "I have just been ordered to keep you here until Warrey has been captured and executed. That is our first priority, Margo. Warrey!"

The Justice

John and Father Pasquale lay together on the slopes of the hill some ten miles north of Lake Garda, and with their binoculars studied the troop movements beneath them. The Germans were moving masses of men south to maintain their defence of Cassino, and to continue their attacks on the Anzio bridgehead. They had little to spare for seeking and destroying the partisans, and were more inclined to launch sudden probes into the hills. But these were generally seen long before they could be dangerous.

It was now late spring, and delightfully warm. "It is time for us to be doing again," Pasquale said. "Valerio is restless."

"Valerio is a dangerous man," John remarked.

"Nonetheless, he is right. We must attack something." Pasquale glanced at John. "It is time to forget your domestic problems, Giovanni."

John snorted. But he knew the priest was right. It had been a difficult month. Having executed Wiedelier, Bianca had withdrawn into a world of her own. She knew John condemned her for what she had done, so coldly and efficiently and mercilessly. But because she had not avenged herself as she had wanted to, she had no doubt that he would in time forgive her and return to her side. She rated Aileen as nothing.

While Aileen continued to flounder out of her depths, confused and disturbed by the life they were living, so unlike anything she had ever known, the food they ate, when they could get it, the rough clothing that was all she had to replace her tattered garments, trying to care for her hair, now as long as Bianca's, the communal intimacy of the partisan encampment

226

. . . and most of all by the fact that John had not yet slept with her.

Because he was the most confused of them all? Or because he knew that whichever way he turned would be final? He kept telling himself that he should be overjoyed to have his wife alive and well . . . and he was, for her sake. He was relieved that she had neither been raped nor tortured, although just what else had happened to her he could not be sure. But he had known Margo for a long time.

To go to her would mean a total rejection of Bianca. Aileen could not be asked to accept a *ménage à trois*, and Bianca would not forgive him. And she remained his surest support in his dealings with the partisans. They respected her, for having survived the SS.

He had even asked Pasquale for advice. "Aileen is your wife," the priest had said. "You have no choice. Bianca must understand this."

"Do you think she will?"

Pasquale had stroked his chin. Now he remarked. "There is a bridge ten miles away, over which these troop columns must pass. You know about bridges?"

"I've blown one," John said, remembering that horrendous night outside Benghazi.

"If we blew this one, it would slow up the transfer of troops to the south."

John nodded. "Good thinking. But it will have to be carefully done; we have only half-a-dozen sticks of dynamite left."

"Can we not obtain some more?"

"By raiding a German arms dump? I don't think that would work out very well; they're too well protected. We're in what is called in England a chicken and egg situation."

"I do not understand."

John grinned. "Well, Father, you can't have a chicken unless you have an egg to hatch; but you can't have an egg to hatch unless you have a chicken to lay one, right? We can't carry out a proper raid on the Germans until we get some explosives; but we can't get any explosives until we carry out a raid on the Germans."

"Ah," Pasquale said. "I will go and see Renaldo. He may still have some."

"And you think he will give them to us? He was supposed to join us last month, and he never did."

"I will see what can be done," Pasquale said.

It was necessary to tell Valerio what they were planning, if only to keep him happy. "But this has to be strictly between you and me," John said. "And Father Pasquale, of course."

"You do not trust my people?" Valerio demanded.

"I don't trust anyone, old son," John said.

"You are planning something," Bianca said, as she and Aileen prepared their evening meal. Remarkably, the two women seemed able to work together. But that, John reminded himself, was almost certainly because he had shown no favouritism towards either.

"That's my job," he reminded her.

"You're going to attack again?" Aileen was anxious. She spoke English.

"As soon as certain dispositions have been made, yes."

"Do you have to? Can't we just sit here and wait for the Allies to get to us?"

"We're fighting a war," he said. "I'm sorry you got mixed up in the nasty side of it. But it has to be fought."

"What is she saying?" Bianca asked.

"Nothing of importance," John told her.

Pasquale returned three days later. To John's surprise he was accompanied by Renaldo, together with Cesare and three other men. All six were in a state of high excitement. "The Allies have broken through at Cassino," Pasquale said. "The Germans have abandoned the monastery, and have ceased counter-attacking at Anzio. They have evacuated Rome and are retiring north."

"Holy Hallelujah," John said.

"But that is not all of it," Renaldo said. "The Allies have landed in France, in Normandy. A huge invasion force. There is a great battle going on. But the Allies will win, eh?"

They had to, John thought.

"Surely now we do not have to attack them, here," Aileen said.

"It is more than ever necessary to attack them, here," Valerio said. "We must hit them while they are in disarray, eh? Have you brought the dynamite, Renaldo?"

Renaldo's face closed. "It is in a safe place. First you must tell me what you want it for."

"I am not going to tell you that, yet," John said. "Because if I do, I suspect the Germans will find out about it."

Renaldo glared at him. "Are you calling me a traitor?"

"Yes," John said.

Renaldo licked his lips, glanced left and right. "You have no proof."

"I have proof enough."

"Bah," Cesare said. "I told you we should not have come." He looked at Aileen. "I am told this woman is your wife."

"She is my wife, yes," John said.

"Then you are finished with *my* wife. You can give her back to me."

"No," Bianca said in a low voice. "You cannot do this, Giovanni."

It was John's turn to look left and right. But the partisans, while they would not force him, would not support him either. It was a personal matter between himself and Cesare, and they had long been uneasy about his relationship with another man's wife. He glanced at Pasquale.

His friend's face was grave. "He has the right to ask for his wife to be returned to him, Giovanni. And you have no right to refuse him."

"He will beat me," Bianca said. "He will mutilate me. He will kill me."

John gazed at her. The most beautiful woman he had ever known, who had been so very good to him, and who had

229

sacrificed herself for him. Then he looked at Aileen, who hardly seemed to be breathing. Of course she would wish the relationship ended. But he simply could not do it, this way. "Bianca stays here," he said.

"You have no right," Renaldo said.

"I have every right to protect my people from a pack of traitors," John said.

"You accuse us—" Cesare began.

"Yes," John said. "I accuse both of you."

They glared at him, then looked at each other, then at the waiting partisans. "I demand satisfaction," Cesare said.

John hesitated. As commanding officer, he had the right to refuse. But heads were nodding. "You shall have it. Name your weapons."

Cesare grinned. "Knives, Giovanni."

John swallowed. He should have anticipated that: knives were the one weapon of which he knew almost nothing.

"Knives," Renaldo shouted.

"Knives," Valerio agreed.

"Oh, my God." Aileen clutched John's arm. "Please, Johnnie. He'll kill you."

"Hopefully not." He looked at Cesare. "First blood?"

"No, no," Cesare said. "To the death."

John turned to Pasquale. "It is his right," the priest said. "Now I must give you absolution."

Cesare knelt, and listened to the priest's low voice. Then Pasquale turned to John. "I am a Protestant, as you know, Father," John said.

"Nevertheless, my son, you would do well to listen to what I have to say." John gazed into his eyes, then knelt. Pasquale bent low over him. "I have seen Cesare fight before," he whispered. "He is ambidextrous. He will attack you with the knife in his right hand, and at the last minute switch it to his left. God go with you."

John took off his jacket, tested the ground with his boots. Cesare had kicked off his shoes and was barefoot. Valerio gave John his own knife, a wicked weapon with a blade a foot long.

"Use it well," he admonished. "I would not like to lose you, Giovanni."

John grinned at him, glanced at the two women, who had insensibly drawn closer together – were he to die they would both be in a perilous situation – and had been joined by Luana.

Cesare's knife was hardly less long, and he moved confidently, from right to left, holding the weapon in his right hand as Pasquale had warned, but with his left hand also thrust forward. How incongruous, John thought, that in this year of 1944 I, a colonel in the British Army, should be facing this barbaric rite of death? But then, he reflected, was not warfare itself a barbaric rite of death?

Cesare moved forward at considerable speed. John easily side-stepped him, and had the opportunity to thrust at the momentarily exposed side of the partisan, but could not bring himself to do so. Cesare turned, eyes blazing pin-points of angry concentration, and advanced again, this time more cautiously. Then he thrust, but John caught the blade on his own. Steel scraped against steel, and the two hafts came together with a thud, Cesare's face very close. Now he suddenly snapped his teeth at John's nose. John's head jerked and he tried to disengage, but lost his footing, and had to stagger to regain it, In that moment Cesare had, as Pasquale had predicted, whipped the knife from his right hand to his left, and was again thrusting.

This time John went down, evading the thrust but landing so heavily that the knife flew from his hand. Desperately he rolled to regain it, but before he could do so, and while his back was turned to Cesare, the Italian had leapt on him and was driving the blade downwards. John felt no immediate pain, but instead a sudden awareness of weakness. And he knew there was going to be another, fatal, blow. But before he could either receive it or gather his wits there was a shriek from Cesare, and he fell to the ground beside John.

John rolled away, regained his knife, and sat up. But Cesare was dead, blood flowing from his mouth. There was a great deal of shouting, and the morning was beginning to swing around

John's head, as it had on that day in Salo: he had only just recovered from that wound. Aileen was kneeling beside him, tears streaming down her face. "Oh, Johnnie, Johnnie! You're hurt." She was tugging at his torn shirt to get at the wound.

"I don't understand," he muttered. "You—"

"Bianca," she said, tearing the shirt into strips to bind up the cut. "It doesn't look too deep. But you're losing blood. Lie down."

"Bianca!" He shook his head to clear it, focused on the Italian woman. She had been seized by Renaldo's men, and her arms bound behind her back. But her head was still high.

"Murderess!" Renaldo stood in front of her. "Husband killer! You all saw it," he shouted. Once again, nods of agreement. "She must be hanged," Renaldo said. There was some shuffling of feet, but no one argued. "Now," he bawled. "Take her to that tree. Prepare a rope."

Bianca was bustled towards the tree while two men tied a noose. Valerio stroked his chin, but did not interfere. "Oh, my God," Aileen muttered, completing the improvised bandage.

"Father, you must stop them," John said.

"No one can stop them now," Pasquale said. "She murdered her husband. I can but give her the last rites."

"Help me up," John said.

"Johnnie, you're badly hurt," Aileen protested,

"Help me up." With her help, he reached his feet, looked left and right, but could not see his discarded pistol. So he stepped up to Valerio and plucked the pistol from his holster. "Hey," Valerio shouted.

"You going to stop me, or support me?" John asked.

Valerio gazed at him, then grinned. "I will not stop you."

John staggered towards the tree. The rope had been looped over a branch and was dangling beside Bianca's face. She had closed her eyes, but her head was still up. Renaldo himself fitted the noose round her neck, and pulled it tight. "Dream of me," he snarled, and signalled the three men holding the end of the rope.

"Wait there!" John shouted. They all turned to look at him.

Bianca opened her eyes. "That woman is guilty of nothing," John said.

"She murdered her husband," Renaldo snarled,

"She executed a traitor, on my orders," John said.

"A traitor? You make these accusations—"

"You and your brother were intended to launch a diversionary attack at Salo. What happened to that attack?"

Renaldo licked his lips. "The Germans were too strong—" but he was aware of the restlessness around him.

"Then explain how the Germans knew Alexandro and I were in the square," John said.

"Because of that my old friend Alexandro was killed," Valerio said, following John towards the tree.

"You—" Renaldo changed his mind about what he would have said. "Nothing can change the fact that this woman killed her husband."

"Nothing can change the fact that this woman executed a traitor," John said. "As I do now." He levelled Valerio's pistol and shot Renaldo through the head.

The partisan leader fell to the ground, and the echoes of the shot faded into the mountains. No one moved, and there was no other sound above the soughing of the wind. Then John said, "Release that woman and bury those men. You—" he pointed at Renaldo's three men, who seemed petrified with fright. "You will take my people to where the dynamite is hidden."

Bianca was released and brought to him. The partisans were looking thoroughly shame-faced. "I owe you my life," he said.

"More than once," she reminded him. "Now let me see to your wound."

"Aileen has bound it up."

"And you are about to faint," she pointed out. "Come and lie down."

John looked at Valerio, who grinned. "By all the saints in heaven," he said. "I am glad you are fighting for us and not against us, Don Giovanni."

"No doubt it is the will of God." Father Pasquale sat beside John.

"That I should be preserved to lead you?"

Pasquale sighed. "That you should be preserved, for whatever end He has in mind for you."

John moved, restlessly. He was running a fever, and his wound ached abominably. Once again he was immobilised. And now he was alone, save for the priest and the women and children; Valerio had taken the partisans to destroy the bridge. But he was still in command. He felt sure even of Valerio's unquestioning obedience now. What had Cox told him, last year? To kill whoever opposed him? He had postponed doing that, for a year. But it had come down to it in the end. "I don't think you approve of me, Father," he suggested.

"I think that in many ways you are an heroic figure, Giovanni. But there are two sides to every coin, is that not true? One day your weakness for the flesh will bring you down."

John grinned. "You don't think it's already done so?"

As it had nearly done more than once in the past. But in the past, at least before Salo, he had managed to avoid serious wounds, and the incapacity that went with them. Now they were coming too regularly, and he was virtually at the mercy of the three women, each of whom wanted him, for a reason of her own.

He didn't really care to think what Luana wanted, or indeed might be like. She had attached herself to him following Alexandro's death, simply because she needed to be attached to a man. Bianca just wanted to be his woman. Aileen wanted to be his wife. At least they did not squabble about it. Aileen might not like Bianca, but she understood that had the Italian woman not interfered he would be dead. She also understood that John had had to save her from being hanged, if only out of gratitude, even if she had clearly been shocked by the way he had executed Renaldo.

For all of those reasons, no doubt it was a relief to her that he was in no condition to have relations with any of them, so that the question of sexual jealousy, who he would eventually turn to, had been put on the back-burner. But the end of the war was rushing at them, when all personal as well as public problems would have to be resolved. He was not sure he wanted that to happen.

And if it was happening, it was happening very slowly. The Allies, now greatly reduced in strength as all spare men and *matériel* were wanted in France, pushed north to what the Germans called the Gustav Line, along the River Arno. They occupied Pisa, but attempted no further advances for the time being. The Germans, and the remnants of Mussolini's Fascisti army, were well dug in, but as they also had been denuded of men and *matériel* for the defence of the Reich itself – from both east and west – they could not undertake a counter-offensive.

Of Margo and anything the SS might be doing in Milan, there was no word.

Mussolini continued to rule after a fashion, at the behest of his German masters, and to indulge in lavish affairs of state. But he had to know he was living on borrowed time. "He is the man we want," Valerio said, sitting by the fire in the mouth of the cave into which the cold weather had driven them; the snow was clouding down. "I would like to execute him, personally."

"Chance would be a fine thing," John said. His wound had taken longer than he had hoped to heal, complicated by their lack of medicine. But he was nearly fit again, and he would be by the spring, for the second year running, when next it would be practical to mount another offensive of their own. Meanwhile . . . news drifted in, either from deserters come to join them or from Luana's visits to towns along the lake. Of how by Christmas the Allies were at the Rhine, although their attempts to cross had been for the moment checked. But no one doubted they also would make it in the spring, as the Russians were virtually in Warsaw.

Luana also reported that Margo was still in Milan, and was now the property of Captain Heinrich Osterman, of the SS. No doubt she now felt safer there than in Germany, John thought. But he did not suppose she could be very happy. As for what would happen when the final collapse came . . .

"Heinrich Osterman," Bianca said. "He is the man who raped me."

Once again she was brooding on vengeance.

"Do you ever wish to see Margo again?" John asked Aileen. She gave a little shudder. "I'm not sure."

"What would you do with her? Or to her?"

She glanced at him. "It's like with you and Bianca. In a way. I hate her, for what she did to me, what she tried to make me. But . . . I know if she hadn't been there, when the ploy of kidnapping didn't bring you out, Wiedelier would have had me shot out of hand."

"You understand I had to go after Mussolini, as I had been ordered."

"Yes," she said.

He wondered if she did. "And then I was wounded, and . . . we thought you were dead."

"I have said I understand."

"You realise that Margo will be executed, after the war, as a traitor?"

Aileen nodded. "It's such a beastly business. And yet—" she flushed. "I'm not sorry about anything that has happened, John. I know that if I had been left by myself in England, looking at things from a distance, I would never really have understood what it is like, to kill and be killed, to live like an animal, to do so many horrid things . . . and yet be able, from time to time, to feel . . . happy, I suppose. I don't imagine I have ever been so fit."

"So, no regrets at all?"

"Oh, I have regrets. I could wish . . ." her gaze drifted to Bianca, peeling potatoes a few feet away.

"Listen," he said. "We are going to be together when this is over. We are going to be man and wife. We are going to have that child."

"And Bianca?"

Bianca's head moved; she could not understand English, but

236

she knew her name had just been used. "She will accept it," John said. "After the war is over. Can you accept what has happened between us?"

"I don't know," Aileen said, seriously. "I can understand it. But accepting it . . . ask me when the war is over."

The partisans carried out a series of raids in the spring, with considerable success; the German and Fascisti grip on Tuscany was weakening with every day. By now John had even managed to reopen radio communication with the Allies in Pisa, and received instructions. "It is again Mussolini we wish," said the voice. "We realise that Salo is very strongly defended, but we believe the defences will be breachable if your assault is carried out in conjunction with our next offensive."

"Is there going to be one?" John asked.

"Very soon, Colonel. Prepare your dispositions, then wait for the single call sign, X, and act. You will have air support. How many days will you need from X?"

"Three," John said.

"Confirmed," said the voice.

"Sounds promising," John told Valerio. "How many men do we muster?"

"One hundred and sixty-three men," Valerio said. "And thirty-five women capable of bearing arms." He glanced at Bianca and Luana, but not at Aileen, who he obviously discounted.

"We could do with more men," John said. "What about Renaldo's people?" They had heard nothing from them since the execution of the two brothers.

"Do you think they will fight for you?" Valerio asked.

"If it is to be the last fight, I think they will, or they may find themselves out in the cold when it is over."

Father Pasquale nodded. "I will go and see them, and put them in the picture."

"He is a good man," Valerio remarked, after the priest had left.

"But you would abolish him," John suggested.

Valerio smoked his pipe. "I do not know about that."

"Is not one of the essential tenets of Communism to abolish the Church and all organised religion?"

"You are thinking of Russian Communism," Valerio said. "The Italians are too religiously minded to stand for the abolition of the Church."

"Were not the Russians very religiously minded before the revolution?"

"Of course. And they still are. But the Russian Church, the Orthodox Church, is different to the Roman Catholic. The Russian Church has always been subservient to the tsars. The patriarchs have always been the tsars' men, mostly chosen by them. So, to the Russian peasant, the Church has always been a kind of supreme body, to be respected, to be feared, to be obeyed, but as an instrument of the government rather than something to which he personally belonged. When someone, in this case Lenin, came along and told them it was no longer necessary to respect and obey either the tsar or the Church, it was easy for them to accept that. Here in Italy it is different. The Pope is independent of the state. And the people feel a part of the Church. It rules their lives, certainly, but it is also there for them to turn to in their hour of need. And it is flexible. Father Pasquale is a living example of that."

"It is clearly something about which you have thought a lot," John said. "So, if you were to launch another revolution, after the war, to turn Italy into a Communist state, you would retain the Church, and the Pope."

"Of course. There would have to be some changes, of course, but I think it would work."

"And you do mean to attempt to take over the country," John suggested.

Valerio's eyes were hooded. "Let us first discover what is left to take over, when the shooting stops, Don Giovanni."

Which made it extremely likely, John thought, that Valerio might be the next person he would be required to destroy; the pair of them had worked so closely together for the past six months he was not sure he could do that.

A week later Pasquale returned, with some ninety partisans, men and women. "Renaldo's people?" John was astonished.

"They are now led by a man called Arnulf," Pasquale explained.

John looked them over. They were well armed. But he quickly spotted both Marco and Maria Theresa amongst them. "Those also, will fight under me?"

"They have said they will," Pasquale said. "At least as long as there is fighting. Afterwards—" he sighed. "You have made many enemies, Giovanni."

Perhaps predictably, Maria Theresa sought her sister-in-law, and sat with her, muttering. Maria Theresa had turned, in the space of a year, from a bubbly girl into a very sombre woman. "What does she say?" John asked Bianca.

Bianca made a moue. "She would like to kill you. But she will not," she hastily added, "as long as you are our commander. She wishes to kill Germans more."

"You'll keep an eye on her, I hope."

"Why should that girl wish to kill you?" Aileen asked.

"She's Renaldo's widow."

"Renaldo—" Aileen stared at him in consternation.

"Yes," John said. "The man I shot for treason."

He tuned in every day, as instructed, but another three days passed before he received the single message: X. Instantly he summoned Valerio, Pasquale and Arnulf. "We are going to move down the west side of the lake and seize Salo," he told them. They were struck dumb. "Our target is Mussolini and his government."

"But Salo is a fortress," Valerio protested.

"The Allies have crossed the Arno and are advancing. They have promised us air support. We will attack after Salo has been bombed. Valerio, you will take your people west of the town and attack the barracks." He grinned. "This again will be a diversionary attack, but should the opportunity present itself, you will press home. Father, you will take our people and attack the waterfront. Arnulf, your people will attack the town itself."

"That will be the most dangerous," Arnulf protested. "And the most costly."

"You will be proving yourselves," John said. "I will lead you."

"You?" All three men spoke together.

"There can be no mistakes this time," John said.

"That is crazy," Aileen protested. "You don't know how many of those people still hate you for killing Renaldo and Cesare." She glanced at Maria Theresa, watching and listening, even if she could not understand English.

"This is the best way to find out," John said. "I will have Bianca to watch my back. You will remain here. I will leave sufficient people for you to be safe."

"No," she said. "I am coming with you. I can protect you better than Bianca."

"Have you ever fired a gun in anger?"

"I have not," she said. "But I will if I have to."

He gazed at her for several seconds. "I don't want you to be killed," he said. "Or even hurt."

"Snap," she said. "But if we go, we go together."

"She will be a liability," Bianca said.

"Somehow I don't think so," John said. "Anyway, she's coming."

He gave Aileen a choice of weapons, and she opted for a tommy-gun, which could do the most damage with the least expertise. He wondered if she would have the nerve to actually squeeze the trigger. But perhaps it wouldn't be necessary.

The partisans moved out of the hills the next morning. It took them two days to work their way down to within striking distance of Salo, and John had great difficulty in persuading them not to attack the various columns on the road, all heading north. The end was in sight. Once in position, they waited another twenty-four hours and then saw the long line of bombers winging up from the south to drop their deadly cargoes on the little town and the surrounding fortifications. They could hear the noise of the explosions and they could see the columns of smoke rising from the collapsed and burning houses, even if they could form no impression of what conditions might be like beneath the blanket of explosives. "I never knew there were so many planes in the world," Bianca said.

The bombers were finished, and John sent runners to his commanders to tell them to advance. Then he led his own centre body forward, hurrying down the road they knew so well. Soon they encountered a stream of refugees, leaving the town for the supposed safety of the hills. They stared at the partisans, hurrying by, and the partisans stared back. Undoubtedly most of these people were Fascist supporters, but there was no time to deal with them now.

An hour's rapid walk brought them to the outskirts of the town, and they paused to gaze at the blazing inferno. "We're more likely to get burned to death than shot," John said. "Stay close," he told Aileen.

Cautiously they picked their way into the town. Buildings were still collapsing, entire walls falling outwards to crash into the streets. The apartment building from which he had attempted to shoot Mussolini looked no worse than any of the others as it burned; he wondered what had happened to poor Petritoli and his attractive model? Across the square the Fascist headquarters also burned, its flags crumbling ashes. John led the rush through the lower gateway into the courtyard, saw a row of exploded trucks and tanks. But there was no human being alive, although there were several bodies scattered about the yard.

"Upstairs!" Again he led the way, tommy-gun thrust forward, Aileen at his shoulder, Bianca and Luana and Maria

Theresa behind, while Arnulf and the rest of the partisans spread out through the town. Now they were in as great danger as on the street, for much of the upper floor was burning, and with every gust of wind clouds of choking smoke swept across them, causing them to cough and spit. But again, only dead bodies.

John paused for breath, looked at Aileen. Her face was blackened with smoke, and her hair was wild, but she looked surprisingly alert, even if she must have seen more corpses today than in her entire life.

"The cellars!" Arnulf was in the yard, waving his arm. His men were already breaking down the doors, which were red hot. John dashed down the stairs as the doors were thrust open, allowing a gush of smoke to emerge. He checked in consternation at what he saw, for the cellars had been used as a hospital, and were crowded with dead or dying men, mostly, he suspected, Italians, lying on the floor on filthy blankets, and however bad their wounds, dying of smoke inhalation.

"Here is one alive," Arnulf shouted, and John hurried to his side.

The man was coughing and clearly had only minutes to live. John knelt beside him. "Il Duce," he said. "Where is Il Duce?"

"He is not here," the man panted. "He went to Milan. Milan. He went to Milan."

John and Arnulf looked at each other. "We march on Milan," John said.

It was necessary to regroup his little army, and then make camp for the night south of the stricken town. "Are you all right?" he asked Aileen, as they sat together for their evening meal.

She shuddered. "I never want to experience that again. Will it be like that in Milan?"

"I'm afraid that will be extremely likely. Only more of it. How many times did you fire your tommy-gun?"

She shuddered again. "I never fired it at all. How long have you been doing this sort of thing?"

242

"Since 1940, really."

"And I never knew."

"Would you have liked to know?"

She glanced at him, then sighed. "No. I don't think I could have married you, had I known. But . . . wouldn't that have been better for both of us?"

It was dark now, and behind them the shattered town still glowed. Valerio and Pasquale joined them. "There was almost nothing to do," Valerio said. "They all surrendered as soon as they saw us. Now they want to fight with us. There must be more than a thousand of them. And they have good weapons."

"Can they be trusted?" Pasquale asked.

Valerio looked at John.

"I think it would be safer for us to manage on our own," John said. "Take as many of their weapons and as much ammunition as you need, destroy the rest, and tell them to wait here for the arrival of the Allied soldiers. It cannot be more than a day or two, now."

"But we will go to Milan?" Valerio checked.

"Tomorrow," John promised.

Aileen spread her blanket beside his. "How long will it take, to reach Milan?"

"That depends on whether or not we can raise some transport. Then it is a matter of hours. If we have to walk it, a few days. But I think we'll find some transport along the way."

"And then?"

"Once we capture Mussolini, we make contact with the Allies, hopefully. And hand him over for trial."

"And then?"

"I would say our part in the war is over. Yours, certainly."

She looked as if she would have asked another question, then changed her mind, lay down, and composed herself for sleep. The bivouac had become a vast snore, their campfires burning down, while the fires in the town continued to blaze. Around them were a variety of sounds, from the barking of hungry dogs to the bleating of terrified sheep, and a good deal of human noise as well, as refugees continued to cram the road.

One of the sentries awoke John at two in the morning. "We hear engines, Giovanni."

John sat up. Aileen appeared to be fast asleep. He could hear nothing significant himself, but he was willing to concede that most of the partisans had better ears than himself. "Where?"

"You come."

John got up – he had been sleeping fully dressed down to his boots – buckled on his gun belt, and followed the man through the camp to where it overlooked the road. After the earlier crowds this was now almost deserted. "You hear?" the man asked.

"Can't say I do," John said. "But if it's motor transport, we must have it. Turn out the camp, but quietly."

"Afterwards," the man said.

John turned sharply, stared at the pistol directed at his stomach, saw Marco and Maria Theresa emerging from the gloom behind their messenger. "There must be no noise," Marco said.

"Do you really think you can get away with this?" John asked. "You are surrounded by my people."

"We shall not wait to see them, tomorrow," Maria Theresa said. "You killed my husband."

"And my brothers," Marco said.

"Use the knife," Maria Theresa said. She was also armed with a pistol, as was her brother-in-law. But Marco now holstered his gun, and drew his knife.

John licked his lips. There was a gun in his holster, but quick as he was he knew he would have no chance against two already presented weapons – and his flap was buttoned. So . . . scream? That would not save his life, and in the confusion that would follow the assassins would easily make their escape. But just to die, with the end in sight. He drew a deep breath . . .

"Stop there," Aileen said, out of the darkness.

Maria Theresa turned, pistol thrust forward. "Look out!" John shouted.

Aileen squeezed the trigger of her tommy-gun. Maria Theresa collapsed like a discarded sack as the bullets tore into her stomach. The man levelled his pistol, but John was already throwing himself sideways, grasping his thighs in as rugby tackle and bringing him down. Aileen was firing again, this time at Marco, as he lunged at her with his knife. He went down.

Maria Theresa was rolling on the ground in agony. Aileen stood above her, while around them the camp came to life, people shouting, some even firing their guns, as they ran towards the source of the trouble. Aileen dropped to her knees beside the stricken girl. "I did not . . . oh, my God!" John knelt beside her, took the tommy-gun from her hand. "I had to," she whispered. "Johnnie, I had to."

"You saved my life." She raised her head; even in the dark he could see the tears streaming down her cheeks. Then she was in his arms.

Bianca stood above them, then knelt herself, beside her sister-in-law. "Help me," Maria Theresa gasped, blood mixing with the froth coming from her lips.

"Nobody can help you," Bianca said.

Pasquale was kneeling by Marco. But Marco was dead. Now he knelt beside Maria Theresa. "Why did you try to murder the Colonel?" he asked.

"I had to avenge my husband. Cannot you understand that, Father?" Her voice was breaking.

"It is very sad," Pasquale said, and gave her absolution. Then he looked at John. "Let us hope the feud is over, now." He looked at Bianca in turn.

Bianca looked at Aileen. "It is over," she said, and walked into the darkness.

"God," Aileen said when they regained their bivouac, after having waited for Maria Theresa to die. "I've killed two people, Johnnie. Two people."

"You did what you had to do," he said. "That is what warfare is all about. Supposing you wanted me to live."

"Oh, John . . . please say we're done with it now."

He sighed. "I can't say that, Aileen. We still have a job to do." He took her in his arms, and for a few seconds they were almost lovers again. Then they both realised it was not going to happen. Perhaps it was Maria Theresa. He hoped it was. But he felt they both knew better.

Next day the partisans ambushed a German column attempting to flee to the north, and found themselves in possession of several trucks and cars. Now they made good progress, careering down the road, each car and truck overloaded with people, hanging out of the sides, firing their rifles and revolvers into the air. The city was in sight when they were halted by a roadblock. "Let us through," Valerio shouted. "I am Colonel Valerio. This is Colonel Warrey. We have business in Milan."

"I am under instructions from the Allied general to keep the city clear, pending the arrival of his troops," said the guard commander, importantly. "What business do you have?"

"We seek Il Duce," Valerio told him.

The commander snorted. "You will not find him in Milan. He left hours ago,."

"To go where?" Pasquale asked.

The commander shrugged. "Who knows? He left with a German column, to go north. Into Switzerland, eh?"

"You let him get away?" Valerio was aghast.

"How was I to stop him? It was a strong column. We will get him. The Swiss will hand him over."

"There is no guarantee of that," Valerio said. "*We* will get him." He pointed beyond the barrier to where a side road led north. "Let us through and we will take that road."

The commander hesitated, then ordered the barrier opened. Valerio and his people drove through. John braked his car beside the commander; with him were Pasquale, Aileen and Bianca – Luana had gone with Valerio. "Are there still Germans in the city?"

The commander grinned. "They are all prisoners, or dead."

"Does that include the SS?"

"Oh, the SS left with Mussolini. I saw them go. There was no prospect of them surrendering; they would have been torn to pieces."

"Did they have the Englishwoman with them?"

The commander nodded. "There was a woman with them."

"Then we will follow Valerio."

The commander shrugged.

Once again the barrier was raised, and they drove through. Valerio and the several other trucks that had followed him were already out of sight, but they could see his dust on the unmade road. John drove as fast as he dared, while the hills rose about them. The women clutched their weapons and looked to either side; they might come on fleeing Germans at any moment; Pasquale, unarmed, seemed more relaxed than any of them. Then they heard shots from in front of them, and a moment later saw Valerio's trucks, parked at the roadside, while the partisans milled around. Lying in front of them were several dead people, and several more with their hands on top of their heads.

John braked. "Why have you stopped?"

Valerio pointed at a small farmhouse, single-storied but with stone walls. "He is in there, with his mistress, Clara Petacci."

There was no sign of life from the farmhouse. "Where is his escort?" John asked.

Valerio shrugged. "According to these people . . ." he pointed at the prisoners, "the Germans abandoned him and drove on."

John hesitated. His instincts as a man were to follow the SS. And Margo. His instincts as an officer were to make sure Mussolini was not executed out of hand.

"You in there," Valerio shouted. "Come out with your hands up. You cannot escape. You must surrender." He waited for a few moments, then fired a burst from his tommy-gun.

"Wait," a voice shouted. "We will surrender. Where will you take us?"

"I will take you back to Milan," Valerio said.

Another brief hiatus, then the farmhouse door opened, and Mussolini came out. Clara Petacci followed him, a short, slight

young woman with curly dark hair; her face was too distorted
with fear to be attractive.

"How are the mighty fallen!" Valerio remarked, and levelled
his tommy-gun.

"Wait," Mussolini cried. "You promised—"

"To take you to Milan," Valerio said. "That is what I am
going to do."

"Hold on!" John shouted, as he realised what Valerio
intended.

Valerio ignored him. Clara Petacci also realised what was
going to happen. She gave a shriek and threw herself in front
of her lover. But Valerio was already firing. The bullets sliced
into the woman's body, hurling her backwards into Mussolini.
Then they were slicing into his body as well. He went down
without another word.

The partisans uttered a great shout of triumph.

"That was murder," John told Valerio. "And you gave him
your word—"

"It was an execution," Valerio said. "Were we then to take
him to Milan for a show trial, with hundreds of lawyers all
putting their point of view? Why . . ." he grinned. "He might
even have been acquitted. As to my word, I will keep it, and
take him to Milan. I did not say it would be alive."

And after all, John thought, would I not have shot him down,
just like that, had Renaldo not betrayed me? "What will you do
with him in Milan?" he asked.

"I will expose him, so that our people, all the world, will
know that he is dead."

"And the woman?"

"Her too."

John swallowed, then turned away. "We have work still to
do," he told the two women. "Father?"

"I will come with you," Pasquale said.

They got back into the car and drove north. "That was barbaric,"
Aileen said.

"War is barbaric," John reminded her.

They topped a rise and looked down into the next valley. Halfway across, on the road, there was a truck. "They have left a barrier," Bianca said.

"No," John said. "They have run out of petrol." He braked, used his binoculars to look to either side of the road, then further along the road itself . . . "There!"

Three people, two in uniform, the third in a skirt. He engaged gear, drove down the road, swerved past the exhausted truck. The people on the road heard the engine, stopped to look back. John could imagine the relief they must be feeling as they identified a German vehicle. One of the men waved his arms.

"Be prepared," John said, and braked to a halt.

The officer ran forward. "Thank God," he said. "We need help."

He paused, staring at John. They had never seen each other before. But Bianca had recognised the man. "Heinrich!" His head jerked, and he reached for his pistol. Bianca shot him through the chest.

The orderly promptly raised his arms. Margo hurled herself into the bushes at the side of the road, drawing her pistol as she did so. John thrust Aileen to one side as he jumped down from the car. Bianca came out with him, and was struck by Margo's bullet, which half turned her and sent her down to the road. John hesitated, torn between the necessity of settling with Margo and the equal necessity to tend to Bianca, and was himself struck by the next bullet. He flew over backwards, aware of pain, of the dazzling blue of the sky. And of Margo's face, as she left the bushes to stand above him. "Are you armed?" she asked Pasquale.

"Only with my faith, murderess," the priest said.

Margo snorted. "You amuse me, Father. Get down. I need your car. Well, Johnnie my lad, this is the end. It's been a long time coming." She levelled the pistol. "But it was fun, from time to time." Then she frowned, as Aileen slowly crawled out of the ditch into which John had hurled her. "Well, well," she said. "My little friend. Would you like to come with me, my dear? Or go with him? With him, I think."

She levelled her pistol, and stared in horror as Aileen shot first, drawing the pistol from her waistband and holding it in both hands, her fingers wrapped around the butt and the trigger. Margo gave a shriek as the bullet slashed into her chest. Then she dropped to the road, and lay still.

Aileen knelt beside John. "You're making this a habit."

"The last one," he said. "Bianca—"

Aileen laid him down and stooped over the Italian woman. "She's dead."

"Damnation," he said.

Pasquale was kneeling beside him and binding him up. "But you will live, and soon fight again, Don Giovanni. This is no more than a flesh wound."

"Never again, Father, I hope and pray."

Aileen was still kneeling beside the dead woman. John dragged himself across to be beside her.

She looked up. "Did you love her, Johnnie?"

My wife, he thought. Who has proved herself as good as anyone. And Bianca. He looked at the calm features, beautiful even in death.

"Yes," he said. "I loved her. But I love you too. Can you understand that?"

"I don't know." Aileen looked down at the pistol she still held in her hand. "But after all this, I'm certainly going to try."